The Forbidden Powers

The Gallant
Conqueror

R. Kane Maurer

HELLBENDER BOOKS

an imprint of Sunbury Press, Inc.
Mechanicsburg, PA USA

an imprint of Sunbury Press, Inc.
Mechanicsburg, PA USA

For information about special discounts for bulk purchases, please contact Sunbury Press Orders Dept. at (855) 338-8359 or orders@sunburypress.com.

To request one of our authors for speaking engagements or book signings, please contact Sunbury Press Publicity Dept. at publicity@sunburypress.com.

FIRST HELLBENDER BOOKS EDITION: June 2024

Set in Adobe Garamond Pro | Interior design by Crystal Devine | Cover design by Lawrence Knorr | Edited by Sarah Peachey.

Publisher's Cataloging-in-Publication Data
Names: Maurer, R. Kane, author.
Title: The gallant conqueror / R. Kane Maurer.
Description: First trade paperback edition. | Mechanicsburg, PA : Hellbender Books, 2024.
Summary: Seven years have passed since the Cup of Power's destruction and the defeat of Darvor. Now, in search of old friends and new adventure, Jonny returns to the land beyond the cave to find darkness haunts the edge of the realm and hints at the rise of new evil. When King Swarlar is hesitant to act, Jonny must gather friends and allies to stop the next great threat before it becomes the last great threat.
Identifiers: ISBN 979-8-88819-241-2 (softcover).
Subjects: FICTION / Fantasy / Epic | FICTION / Fantasy / Action & Adventure | YOUNG ADULT FICTION / Fantasy / Epic.

Designed in the USA
0 1 1 2 3 5 8 13 21 34 55

For the Love of Books!

To Rosemary. All my best stories start and end with you.

For all your days be prepared, and meet them ever alike.
When you are the anvil, bear—when you are the hammer, strike.

—EDWIN MARKHAM

Legend

◇ Capital
• City
✕ Ruins

Shrouded Island

The Land of the Trolls

The East River

Crags of Bone

Swamps of Nehum

Guard Tower Island

The Ruined City

Plains of Lydie

Mowka

The Great Forest

The North Branch

The Middle Branch

The South Branch

Slink

City of the Forest Folk

The Small Lake

Gluton

The Lost Lands

Mountainstream

The Great Lake

Lanak

Burma

Bayman

The Great Bay

Jawe Island

TABLE OF CONTENTS

Prologue

It had been twenty winters since the Watcher had heard another man's voice. He no longer counted the days—there had been too many. Now the only thing that marked the passing of time was the changing seasons. In winter, the snows that covered the surrounding mountains descended, invading the small vale until everything but the lake was covered in a foot of snow. In the summer, the trees spread their leaves so thick and dense that the warm sun could barely touch the valley's floor. Every season brought renewed splendor to the valley, but it was autumn the Watcher loved most.

As he sat on the shore of the small lake, he smiled at all the splendid colors. The sky above was blue. The mountains gleamed in purest white. The trees were a mosaic of fiery reds and oranges, vibrant yellows and golds, and rich greens and browns. This was not a penance, the man thought, this was heaven.

He had not always felt that way. At first, he had been lonely, so lonely that he would scream and shout at the Creator, but the only answer came from his own echoes bouncing off the towering peaks. For a time, he had pleaded with the Creator for a message that his penance was over. But as always, if any higher power could even see into this forgotten valley, they kept silent. And so it was not long before the sadness filled his heart. He had no appetite and no will to continue living. Some days, he would not even get out of bed in the small cabin he had built. But then, one by one, the leaves of the trees began to change colors. It was the beauty of autumn that saved the Watcher and reinvigorated him with new life.

That was so long ago he could scarcely remember, and he remembered even less of his life before he arrived in the valley. The one thing he could remember clearly was his brother. Every day, part of him wondered if his brother was still alive . . . if he was happy. But somewhere in his heart, the Watcher knew his brother was well. He could feel it.

But today, there was something more. Something different. He sat on a rock beside the turquoise waters of the small lake with his legs crossed and his walking staff lying across his lap. His eyes were closed in meditation. He did this often, but today he was not trying to clear his mind and dwell in the magic of this sacred vale as he did every other day. Instead, he was focused with dogged determination, letting his mind silently probe for what was different on this day. And then, finally, he heard it.

He knew his home better than his own eyelids. The trickle of streams that flowed from the high mountain passes, the chitter-chatter of birds hiding unseen in the boughs of the trees, the whistle of the cool breeze as it chased the dying leaves off their branches. Those noises and a thousand others were as they always were. But he could hear a far softer sound today, carried down from the mountains on the coming winter winds. It was a sound he had not heard in his twenty years in the valley, but he knew it at once. He snapped his eyes open. Someone was coming.

Walking stick in hand, he sprang from the rock and darted into action. As he left behind the shore of the peaceful lake, he grabbed his hunting bow, slinging it over his shoulder. He only had a dozen arrows— he had to make them all himself, and he had learned years ago that good arrows were no easy thing to craft. He raced between the trees. Over the years, he had come to know every tree in the vale like an old friend. He could run through this forest with his eyes closed if he needed to, dodging every tree and hurdling every twisted root with nothing more than memory to guide him.

As he reached the edge of the tiny valley, the ground rose steeply. The mountains protecting the hidden valley closed in like a wall on every side. There was only one way in or out of the vale, a narrow, treacherous path that wound high into the snowy peaks on the north side of the valley. That was where they were coming from, and that was the way the Watcher headed.

He could not tell who, but from the faint noises blown down from the mountains, he knew there were many of them. Anyone coming into the valley was more likely to be foe than friend; this valley was forbidden to all but the Watcher. The invaders would be forced to take the lone path that led into the valley; they could not possibly find a different way. But in twenty years, the Watcher had learned other secret paths. He left the trail that snaked into the mountains and picked his way up the slopes by ways only he knew. Higher he climbed, skipping across ledges and crevasses as familiar to him as all the trees in his valley. The terrain grew icy and snowy, and he had to be careful not to lose his footing. After all, he was the only guardian of the vale.

He left the trees and grass behind as he climbed higher and, soon too, the bushes and shrubs. Eventually, even the lichen and mountain flowers fell away, and still he climbed, scrambling over the shale and ice.

He did not grow tired. Years in the thin mountain air had grown his lungs large and legs strong. And on this day, the valley itself seemed to lend him energy, offering up its strength to him in return for protection. The vale did not want visitors.

He scrambled up a final rock face and dipped into a crouch. As lithe as a cat, he inched to the edge of a looming cliff until the mountain trail came into view below. The narrow trail was the only way into the valley. It snaked through treacherous passes as it wound for several days through the mountains. Here the trail pierced through two soaring cliffs, each two hundred feet tall, before diving down the mountain's slope into the valley.

His lungs heaved, stealing what thin air they could from the wind. In between breaths, he listened. He strained to hear the rhythmic patter of marching boots, counting. Two, four, six . . . There were too many. He slipped his bow from his back and fit an arrow to the string. Then he waited.

The intruders came into view as they wound around a bend in the trail. He had known them to be trolls even before he could see them. Their footsteps were heavier and more oafish than that of men, and even in silence, their breath gargled out in grunts and snorts. In the cold, their putrid green faces were hidden behind thick black scarves, but their bullish bodies and hunched shoulders identified them nonetheless. He counted forty trolls marching in pairs.

Their commander was the last to emerge from around the bend. His feathered helmet gave him away and made for an easy target. There would be no armor just below the chinstrap. The Watcher drew back on his bow. In a heartbeat, he knew twenty years of peace in the valley would be shattered. He closed his eyes and breathed deeply, allowing himself to sink into the melody of the wind. Then, in the instant when the air went still, he released.

The arrow fell without a sound. The troll commander was not as quiet.

With a shriek, he fell to the ground, clutching at the feathered arrow tail protruding from just above his sternum. The other trolls froze, staring in shock at their fallen leader. When the second troll fell with the butt of an arrow in the back of his head, the others snapped into action.

Already the Watcher was on the move. They had not seen him, but they had realized where the attack was coming from. Several trolls had already nocked arrows and stood with their bows pointing toward his perch. Others had set about scaling the rocky embankments around the cliff. A few minutes later, another troll slumped to the ground with an arrow in the small of his back. There were shouts of panic and frustration as the trolls turned again toward the spot from which the arrow had been fired.

The fourth arrow came from yet another new location and caught an unsuspecting troll through the knee. But this time the Watcher was spotted. He rolled behind an ice floe as a flurry of arrows narrowly missed him. He reached for another arrow but was stopped by a bellowing roar from behind him. He spun in time to see two trolls charging at him with their weapons held high. They had found their way up the treacherous slopes faster than he had expected. The Watcher dropped his bow and snatched up his staff as they bore down on him. Sidestepping, he drove the first creature off the narrow ledge with a blow from his staff. The beast bounced twice as it fell, its lifeless body landing far below.

The Watcher parried the second troll's attack and jammed the butt of his staff into the creature's belly. With a grunt the beast stumbled backward and careened into the ice floe. The wall of ice shattered, and the troll was swallowed in the torrent of snow and shale that slid down the mountainside.

The victory was short-lived. The Watcher spun in search of his bow, and a searing pain ripped through his shoulder. An arrow had torn through his shoulder muscle, and blood was already soaking his sleeve. Another arrow whistled by his head, and the Watcher darted for cover.

Clutching his wounded shoulder, he wound through the mountaintops. His mind raced as he coursed down secret paths toward the valley. There were too many trolls for him to defeat. With growing despair, he realized the vale had fallen. But he knew his orders. If he could not defend the vale, he had to get word out that he had failed. Carrier pigeons would not fly over the soaring mountain peaks, so he had only one option.

When he reached the valley floor, dusk was settling over the autumn leaves. Blood had soaked the whole of his sleeve, and it ran down his injured arm, dripping hot and thick off his fingertips. He could hear the trolls behind him as he hurried toward the lake. The enemy had reached the valley floor and the birds cried out in terror at their arrival. When he reached his cabin, he heard the invaders shouting to each other. Their voices were rough and bestial, but he understood their intent: "Spread out and search the vale".

The horse penned next to his cabin whinnied in fear as the Watcher emerged from the thick shadows now enveloping the valley. He shushed the animal and ran a blood-soaked hand over its mane to calm it. The horse had been a young pony when he had ridden into the valley those years ago. Now the once spry creature was aged and wearied. But all the same, the old stallion sensed urgency as the Watcher leaned in and whispered. Though the animal did not know the words, it stomped a hoof in determination.

One final ride.

The Watcher stuffed a carrot for the horse in his pocket and wrapped his thickest cloak over his shoulders. The last of the day's light had fled the valley, and darkness surrounded them. The trolls were closer now, crunching through the forest. He gritted his teeth as he swung himself onto the horse. The move sent fiery pain racing down his arm. With a deep breath, he drove his heels into the horse, and they launched forward.

He wound through the trees, racing around the lake toward the trail out of the valley. Somewhere off to his right, a troll shouted. He had been spotted. The shout was echoed by three dozen trolls scattered around the valley as they converged toward him. The horse galloped forward, winding between the trees with expert precision. The valley floor sloped up as they approached the mountain's base. The trail was close; they had almost made it.

And then, where the soft grass of the valley parted to the sharp stone of the mountain trail, the man gasped, the breath ripped from his chest. The arrow buried itself in his upper back be-neath his shoulder blade. It was followed by another that tore through his leg above the knee. The horse carried them on faithfully, sprinting up into the mountains. Blood bubbled up his throat, and when he coughed, it sprayed back into his face. He did not even feel the fourth arrow that found its mark in his ankle. Struggling to breathe, he bent forward and wrapped his arms around the old stallion's neck. Fading in and out of darkness, he left the valley behind. For the first time in twenty years, he would not watch the sun rise over the valley.

The Vale of Joy had fallen.

GOING BACK

Two hundred ninety-eight . . . two hundred ninety-nine . . . three hundred. Jonny stopped and turned around. Three hundred telephone poles. Five miles.

He ran a hand through his sweat-slick hair, pushing it out of his eyes. It was a hot day, even for late summer. It was going to be a strenuous trip home. He took a deep breath and started running again.

Even on cooler days, Jonny never went beyond the three-hundredth telephone pole. It marked the corner between the Johnson's cornfields and the Zeller's cow fields. It also marked five miles, which meant a ten-mile round trip. He did not run more than ten miles anymore. That was when the noise would start.

He started running over six years ago when he first realized how much it calmed him. For months after he came home, he could not sleep. But on days when he ran, the nights were not filled with dreams. And the longer he ran, the better he slept. *But never more than ten miles.*

The noise always started with a distant rumble, but it would grow. He could usually push it from his mind for a while, but eventually it would increase until it threatened to drown out reality. There were battle cries and the roars of giants, the distinctive clash of steel and the piercing shrieks of *grevices*. But worst of all were the screams. The screams of dying men and widowed women. They rattled around in his head until it was enough to make him sick.

Jonny shook the thoughts from his mind and focused on the road ahead of him. The old farm road stretched out before him for almost two miles before it turned onto the county road. From there, it was three miles to home, and from home, another four miles into town. Out here it was always quiet. He would pass the yellow farmhouse with the noisy donkey, but otherwise, the only sound was the ceaseless rhythm of his shoes on the asphalt. Sometimes he would finish the whole ten-mile run without passing a car.

It was a sunny day—all blue skies and not a cloud on the horizon. Green fields and rolling hills stretched out in every direction. It was hot but not without a breeze. A perfect day for running. Jonny smiled.

He had made up his mind even before reaching the three-hundredth telephone pole. Tomorrow was the day. He leaned forward and sped toward home.

By the time he reached his neighborhood, his shirt was dripping and his legs, were burning. He slowed as he rounded onto his driveway, fighting to catch his breath.

"Perfect timing," Jonny's mother shouted from the garage, stepping out of her car. "Give me a hand with the groceries."

Jonny laughed and grabbed a bag from the open trunk. "Didn't you just go to the store yesterday?"

His mother made a face. "It's not like I want to all the time. You and your brothers give me no choice, clearing out the fridge every other day."

"We're growing boys, Ma. Growing boys gotta eat."

She sighed and reached into the trunk, pulling out milk and eggs. "One more week, then we have one less mouth to feed."

Jonny nodded as he followed his mom into the kitchen. "Gonna be quieter around here . . ."

She set the milk and eggs on the counter and turned to take the bag from Jonny's arms. "Speaking of that, have you done any more packing? Your dad and I want to be on the road early Saturday morning, so you need to be finished packing by then, not starting."

"Yeah, yeah, I'll be done." Jonny crossed to the cupboard and reached for a glass. "Did you get me the sheets for the bed? I think the dorm beds are a different size or something."

"Not yet—you never told me what color you want."

"Blue." Jonny poured a glass from the sink and hopped onto one of the bar stools that lined the far side of the kitchen counter. He watched his mother as she began putting the groceries away. Everything had its proper place: the chips in the "snack drawer," the eggs in the fridge, the cans in the pantry.

"How was your run today?"

Jonny took a sip of water. "Fine."

"Fine?"

"Yeah."

"Just fine?" she pressed.

"Yeah."

His mother slid across the kitchen to drop the apples in the fruit bowl. "Okay, what's the matter?"

"Nothing."

"Jonny, a mother always knows." She looked over her shoulder at him. "Are you getting nervous?"

"No."

"Everyone gets nervous about going to college."

"Not me," Jonny said with a shrug.

His mother turned and fixed him with a look of caring empathy he knew only a mom could make.

"It's nothing." Jonny looked down at his water.

When he looked up, his mother was leaning forward, resting her elbows on the granite counter, patiently waiting.

He sighed. "I'm going back." A weight lifted off his heart as he spoke the words.

His mother made a confused face. "Back where?"

"Back," Jonny replied, knowing she would get his meaning.

After a moment, his mother's expression shifted. "No, you're not." She turned back to the groceries, dismissing the idea altogether.

"I *have* to."

"Are you kidding me?" She put her hands on her hips as she turned back to face him. "Are you doing drugs? Is that what this is?"

"What? No," Jonny sputtered. "I've been thinking about this for a while. I have to go back."

"You most certainly do not! I thought we put all this stuff behind us. All those years of therapy, a dozen psychiatrists, three schools. It has to stop."

"I'm trying to make it stop." Jonny clenched his teeth. "I can't move on and go to college and get a job and start a family and live a normal life like everyone else. I can't do any of that, knowing he's still out there! That he's still plotting, scheming, and waiting for his time to strike. He'll destroy everything!"

"Listen to yourself! You're eighteen years old."

Jonny set his glass down with more force than he had intended. "Don't you think I know that? I remember it all from those first few years. The panic attacks, the nightmares every single night . . . you never understood."

He saw the light glint in his mother's eyes and realized she was fighting back tears. "I held you every night when you screamed in your sleep. Don't ever say I don't understand."

Jonny was struck by a pang of guilt and dropped his gaze to his lap. "I—"

"Stop. Go shower and then try to make a little progress on packing."

Jonny slumped from the kitchen and trudged upstairs. Once showered and changed, he began parsing through clothes and other belongings, sorting them into their designated boxes. Neither his heart nor his mind were much focused on the task.

To some extent, his mother had a point. Monsters and magic had no role in his life at college. They had no role in his life here at all. But as he had tried to tell her a dozen times before, it was not so simple to walk away from it all. A door had been opened in his mind—one he could not shut. He knew in his heart that he had to go back, regardless of what his parents said. And there was no better chance than the present. He would soon be leaving for college and could not bear the thought of going on while being torn between two existences. *First, I go back, then I move on.*

Tossing a sweatshirt into one of the cardboard boxes, he looked out the window. The afternoon sun was setting, and it would be dinner soon. Despite his mother's protests, he had already made up his mind to make his move tonight while the house slept. He would act like everything was normal until then.

But everything was not normal. It had not been normal since he had first entered the cave years ago as a young boy. He had returned different. Different than when he entered, different than anyone else in this world. Of course, he had kept the extent of his difference a deep secret.

Checking the door was locked, he took a seat on his bed and cupped his hands. He closed his eyes and took a deep breath. He focused his mind inward and searched for the swirling, warm energy within himself. Like he had practiced a thousand times in solitude, he drew the strength from within, directing it through his lungs and toward his shoulders. The gentle heat coursed down his arms and radiated from his hands. A mellow orb of fire took shape between his palms. He folded the energy in on itself, and the flame grew more intense as he rolled it between his fingers like a baseball. The fireball was weightless and yielded no smoke. *Magic.* No matter how many times he used his powers, they felt new and exciting.

As he held the fire, staring into its dancing light, he felt the slight drain of the spell. It pulled from his strength with a constant thirst. When Swarlar had first taught him the essence of controlling his gifts, lighting a candle had been a taxing endeavor and a spell such as the current one left him exhausted, collapsed on the floor, fighting for his breath. But with time and practice, his endurance had grown. Like any other physical exertion, the more he worked at it, the greater his ability. Years of secret practice had strengthened him. The spell in his palm was now only a slight trickle from his strength, like hiking on level ground.

He relaxed his focus and the flame blinked out with a soft poof. He knew how important it was—not only for his safety, but the safety of his whole family—that his powers stay a secret. Looking at a stack of comic books on his desk, he needed no reminder of why. *No superhero is ever better off when their identity is revealed.*

He had diligently practiced at home for years and had grown adept at hiding any evidence of it. Where, once, his bedroom or his family's basement had been suitable training spaces, a few accidents that had nearly burned down the house forced him to practice elsewhere. In the wild forests outside his hometown, he had found the solitude he needed. There, in the deep woods, away from prying eyes, he could unleash his powers. In the early days, his spells had sometimes been chaotic and haphazard. Twice, he had nearly started wildfires before learning that the best times to practice were after deep rains. But there in the wilderness, his control over the fire increased and, with it, his stamina. With great care, he had avoided detection as the years passed and his strength had grown considerably. But whether it would be enough for what he feared would come, he did not know.

He opened his eyes. The sun was lower still and cast orange rays across his bed and lap. Downstairs, he heard his mother calling for dinner. He looked at the half-filled boxes on his floor. "I guess that's enough packing for today."

After dinner, he returned to his room and flipped through some old adventure novel until night had settled. The sound of a sports broadcast drifted up from the television downstairs. On another night, he might have enjoyed watching the game, but it seemed unimportant now. At last, the television winked off after a home team win. Footsteps on the stairs. His parents knocked.

"Come in," Jonny called from his bed.

The door swung open, and his parents' heads appeared through the crack, his father's rising above his mother's.

"Get any packing done?" his father chimed. An honest man with a kind face. Jonny got many of his features from his father.

"Some." Jonny gestured to the boxes on the floor.

"You better get more done tomorrow." His mother smiled, pushing a strand of hair from her face. Her ruddy brown hair and warm smile were the two features Jonny had not gotten from his mother.

"Yeah," he said. "I'll do more tomorrow."

"Good night!"

"Good night," he echoed.

A moment later, the hallway light blinked out. Jonny flopped back on his bed and turned out the lamp beside him. He fixed his eyes on the ceiling, where moonbeams painted silvery streaks across the paint. *Now we wait . . .*

Under other circumstances, he might have fallen asleep, but a nervous energy held him awake and his eyes never drifted. Over an hour passed. The crickets outside chirped their tireless soliloquy, and the hoots of a distant barn owl carried from the trees. Feeling adequate time had passed and his siblings and parents were sure to be asleep, Jonny slipped from his bed.

He pressed his ear to the door. Silence. He slowly opened it and peered outside. The hallway was dark, and no light slipped from his parents' room. With careful steps, he slid across the hall and down the stairs. The keys were on the counter by the side door, right where he knew they would be. He paused with his hand on the door. The golden dragon pendant was cool against his neck. *What if it doesn't work?* He would be grounded for sure. But scarier than that, he would be helpless. *Helpless to stop him.*

With a deep breath, he slipped out the door and hopped into the car. He was a mile down the road before his parents would have had a chance to rub the sleep from their eyes.

He had to drive fast—in case his parents were behind him in the other car—but not too fast. *The last thing I need is the cops on my tail.* He rolled through the stoplight at the edge of town and pulled onto the expressway ramp. His family had moved almost thirty miles from the cave in the years since his adventure. The further they were from the cave, the closer they thought to normalcy. At first his siblings weren't happy to move, but eventually everyone adjusted. *Everyone but me.*

Jonny glanced in his rearview mirror as he eased off the road—no headlights in sight. The gravel crunched under his tires as he guided the car down the old access road. Eventually, he reached a rusted chain stretched across the road and switched the engine off.

He produced a flashlight from the glovebox, grabbed his backpack, and set off into the woods. He was not that far from town, but the towering trees blocked out any light and pressed the darkness in on him. He tried to calm himself, but the twisted shadows cast by his flashlight caused his heart to race. *Maybe I should have done this during the daylight.* He flipped up his hood to block out the breeze and pressed onward.

The forest was thick, and it took Jonny twice as long as he expected to work his way through the brush, but eventually he heard the babbling water of a small stream and knew he was getting close. By the time he reached his destination, the silver sliver of moon had traced a long arc through the sky.

The cave had changed. Thick vines crisscrossed its yawning mouth and thorn bushes threatened to choke out the cave entirely. A crude circle of stones had been fashioned into a fire pit in the clearing in front of the cave, and a few makeshift benches had been made from old timber. Dry leaves half-covered a graffiti-stained warning sign. No one had been here in years.

Jonny crossed the clearing and squinted at the cave. A wire mesh fence had been affixed across the cave's entrance to ward off reckless teenagers. The boy sighed and slipped off his backpack. Rummaging through its contents, he produced a pair of wire cutters and attacked the fence. Once he cut an opening, he squeezed sideways and disappeared inside.

He flashed the light around and found the cave much as he remembered it. Some crude paintings were splashed on the walls, and more rusted beer cans littered the ground than before, but the fearsome stalactites and ancient musty air were unchanged.

He touched his necklace; it was still cool with the night air, but perhaps some spark of warmth had stirred within the pendant. Suddenly, his heart was pounding in his chest. The whole night had been like a dream. He had thought about this moment for so long that when it had finally come, he went through the motions like some jaded actor, too familiar with the script to bleed any passion into the act. The drive, the venture through the forest—even cutting through the fence—had all felt like little more than steps in a process.

But now the reality came crashing down on him. He stood on the cusp of uncertainty. He was older and better prepared, but he had no way of knowing what he was walking into. Perhaps it would be the same world that had filled him with so much fear and joy and wonder and awe . . . or perhaps it would be something else entirely. The weight of the moment left him breathless.

A voice came from behind him. "Jonny?!"

He spun only to be blinded by a beaming light in his eyes. He held up his free hand to shield the light and squinted against the brilliance. "Mom . . . Dad . . . ?"

"Jonny, what the—" his dad started.

"Get out here now!" his mom shouted.

They both started toward him, keeping their twin lights pinned on him.

"I'm sorry. I *have* to." And with a quick breath, Jonny turned and plunged deeper into the cave.

A New Familiar

Jonny awoke on his back with his stomach in a knot. He kept his eyes closed and waited for the spinning to pass. *It wasn't this bad last time.* He opened his eyes and was greeted with a familiar scene. The small hollow was the same as all those years before. Thick trees loomed overhead; their immense roots twisted together and supported the roof of a small dugout in the hillside.

Jonny climbed to his feet, stooping to avoid hitting his head. He had stood before in the same spot without hitting his head, but the years had added inches to his stature. And last time, he had not fully appreciated how fresh the air was. He filled his lungs with the crispness and in two quick steps, climbed out of the hollow and stood in the sunlight filtering through the leaves above.

The air was warm, stirred by a gentle breeze that swirled through the trees. High above, the leaves were still green and an army of birds hiding among them sang a beautiful melody. The sunlight sparkled through the foliage, dotting the forest floor in golden light. The soil beneath his feet, the air around him, the music in the air—it all buzzed with a magical glow.

Jonny grinned. *I'm back.*

After allowing himself a long moment to soak in the ancient wonder of this place, he brought his thoughts back to his present situation.

It was still morning, so he had plenty of daylight to travel. Gluton was his destination; that is where the king would be. *That's the best place to start.* Last time, he had flown on a dragon to reach Gluton. This time, it seemed he must walk. With a sigh, he started off.

With good luck, he could reach Gluton in only two days. He was confident he knew the general direction, and once he got close, there would be farms and villages where he could stop to ask for further directions. That still left him with two problems. He could solve one by drinking from streams and creeks and stealing food from any farmers' fields he passed. But his clothes might prove a more challenging fix. His current clothes were not proper attire for this world, and he still remembered how people had reacted to his modern clothes on his last visit.

By late afternoon, he came across his first farm, a small hamlet surrounded by fields overgrown with every manner of produce. Nestled among the green, rolling hills of Lydie, the quaint farmhouses were something out of a postcard.

Jonny could not see anyone among the overgrown wheat, but he heard the singing voices in the field and knew it was time for his plan. With a deep breath, he slipped out of his clothes and tucked them into the hollow of an old tree. He grabbed a fistful of leaves and twigs to cover himself and conjured up his most embarrassed look.

He plunged into the wheat fields, trying to balance being out of breath without seeming too panicked. He staggered out of the field on the far side and almost collided with an old lady tying up a sheaf of wheat. The lady shrieked and scampered away, mumbling something he couldn't understand.

Just as he expected, the old lady's startled cry drew the attention of the other singing harvesters. The melody died in their throats as they turned to face him. The harvesters were an odd collection—three gray-haired women and one old bald man binding up bunches of wheat, four thin women wielding scythes, two children playing in the piles of shorn hay, and a man with no legs sitting on a wagon loaded with bound sheaves.

At the sight of the naked stranger, the old ladies mumbled hasty prayers and three of the women turned their backs to avert their eyes. The nearest of the women, a sinewy farmer with gray-flecked hair, hoisted her scythe and marched toward Jonny.

Jonny reminded himself to remain calm and look embarrassed. He had not expected so many people.

"I'm sorry," he sputtered. "I'm so sorry . . ." He retreated into the wheat and feigned his best to keep himself covered with the billowy straw.

"What's going on?" The lady kept stern eyes fixed on Jonny, unperturbed by his lack of clothes.

"My nakedness . . . may the Creator strike me down." Jonny raised a hand toward heaven but quickly dropped it, acting as though he forgot it exposed him. Behind the lady, the two children laughed as one of the other women shepherded them away.

The lady squinted. "I imagine you came into the world as naked as you are now. Hardly seems a reason for the Creator to take you out of it."

"My apologies, let me explain—"

"You better," the woman snorted, tightening her grip on the scythe.

Jonny gulped; he had expected someone friendlier. "I was off yonder taking a swim in the stream, you see. And I took off all m'clothes to keep'em dry. And then, while I was washin' off in the water, a couple of shepherd boys stole m'clothes."

"Carhsen's boys?"

"I didn't get a look at their faces."

"I'll bet it was them. They're always causing problems," she said with an eye roll.

"I'm worried I'll catch a chill tonight without clothes if I don't make it back home."

"Where are you from?"

Jonny froze. He was not prepared for more questions. "Um . . . Fiddler's Ford," he said with all the confidence he could muster. He had once heard of a Fiddler's Ford in the countryside near Gluton, but knew nothing else of the place.

"You're a long way from home." She eyed him, raising the scythe onto her shoulder.

"I was traveling to see a girl I fancy," he blurted in response.

"I hope you still had your clothes when you visited her." Her demeanor shifted and her stern face broke into a wide smile. "Come, let's find you some clothes." She dropped the scythe.

Jonny felt the eyes of the old man on the wagon as he scampered after the woman. "Carhsen's boys stole his clothes," she shouted as they passed. The man laughed. "It's gonna make for a good story at the harvest fair."

An hour later, a clothed Jonny waved goodbye to the woman and started down the wagon-wheel road in the direction of Gluton. Some part of him felt guilty for taking advantage of the farmers. He vowed to return the clothes the first chance he got, plus interest. *And besides, I gave them a good story to tell.*

He whistled an airy tune as he continued down the country lane until the hamlet was well behind. Passing fields ripe for the autumn harvest, he soon encountered other farms and quaint villages. He waved to children playing in the meadows and bent-back peasants threshing summer wheat. A pair of lean sheepdogs followed him for half a mile before losing interest, and a dull cow tried to block the bridge over a lazy babbling creek. But the sun was shining, and he was in no great hurry, so the miles fell away beneath his feet.

In the end, it took him much longer to reach Gluton than he expected. When the towering granite walls came into view, he was tired, hungry, and cursing himself for a series of wrong turns that had cost him a half day of walking. But the familiar sight of the city breathed new life into him, and he quickened his pace.

He crossed the wide fields surrounding the city and fell into line between a caravan of textile merchants and a wagon loaded with radishes. As they neared the gates, Jonny listened to the wagon drivers.

". . . we made good time up the King's Road. Little bit o' mud by Hough-barrow . . ."

He hoped for information on the realm's current state. *Is Swarlar still the king? Have the trolls attacked again? Has the south rebuilt?* Seven years had passed in Jonny's life, but he had no guarantee that time moved at the same speed here. *A hundred years could have gone by for all I know . . .*

". . . can't wait to get me a pint of ale from the Burnt Pub. Been missing that since the last visit . . ." The wagon drivers were not saying anything of substance.

Jonny sighed and hurried past them. The looming gates drew near, and he was pleased to note they were swung wide open. Carts rumbled in and out as people squeezed through the places in between. Four soldiers were stationed near the gate, inspecting the wagons with all the interest of underpaid laborers nearing the end of their shift. They would give Jonny no trouble.

Jonny slipped through the gates and was greeted by the bustling streets of Gluton. From the liveliness of the narrow avenues, it seemed the realm must be prospering. Merchants lined the streets and shouted bargains on offer, traders hauled goods and produce over the cobblestones, smiths hammered metal in their shops, and children chased each other through the spaces in between. Jonny wove through the crowds, reveling in the sights and sounds. *The smells, however, I could do without . . .*

Gluton sprawled over five hills, each crowned in its own way. The nearest hill was topped with the palace, and as Jonny neared it, the cramped streets opened into the expansive King's Square. He smiled. *Not the grand entrance I made the last time I came to this world,* he thought, recalling landing in the middle of the square on dragonback.

The palace was unchanged in form, a grand structure built from whitest marble and polished slate, but it looked smaller than Jonny remembered and less imposing.

Reaching the curtain wall that surrounded the palace and the gate to the courtyard, Jonny encountered a pair of royal guards. Erect as carved stone, they stood, surveying the crowds that swirled in the square. The purple half-cloak pinned to one shoulder gave them a regal appearance fitting their duties.

Jonny knew they would not let him pass freely. His beggarly clothes identified him as the sort of person the guards were charged with keeping away. But he had rehearsed such a moment a hundred times and strode toward them undaunted.

"Halt!" the two guards said in unison, lowering their gleaming halberds to obstruct the gate.

"Is King Swarlar present?"

"Who's asking?" the taller guard said.

They didn't react, Jonny noted. If Swarlar was no longer the king, he might have expected confusion or laughter from the guards. *He must still be king.*

"Jonny Cupbreaker. I would like to speak with him."

At that, the guards exchanged uncertain glances. "Run along, my good man. Only those with official business may pass."

"Let him know Jonny Cupbreaker is here and he'll welcome me."

The taller guard laughed and swatted at Jonny with the butt of his weapon. "His Majesty doesn't need someone breaking his glassware. Get out of here!"

Jonny smirked. He was ready for this reaction. "I said, let him know I'm here." He closed his eyes and searched inside his soul for a familiar spark. The heat swelled from some deep place within, where old secrets were forgotten and true love slumbered in wait. It rose from his heart to swirl around his ribs before racing down the bones of his arms. The flames flitted out from his fingertips to coalesce in his palms. He opened his eyes to meet the guards' shocked faces. "He'll want to know."

Jonny let the flames die in his hands and stifled a cocky grin. The guards glanced at each other but said nothing. The shorter guard nodded to his comrade and disappeared through the gate.

Jonny waited patiently with the remaining and visibly shaken guard. He understood the guards' astonishment; they had never seen magic. He looked down at his hands. Years of secretive practice and still he was awed that he could summon the fiery energy.

The gates to the palace courtyard swung wide to reveal King Swarlar in snowy robes. His white beard hung below his belt and a thin circlet of gold balanced lightly on his head. Surprisingly, he looked younger than he had on Jonny's first visit. A web of wrinkles crossed his face and he looked older than anyone's grandparents, but there was more color in his cheeks, and his blue eyes, ever a marker of the king's quiet vitality, beamed with life.

A smile spread across the king's face from ear to ear and he opened his arms wide. "Jonny Cupbreaker, long the years have been."

Jonny returned the smile and strode forward. As he neared, he dropped to one knee in a deep bow. "Your Majesty."

"Nonsense—up, my boy," the king beckoned Jonny forward. "Welcome back, let us talk!"

Jonny rose as the king spun to cross the courtyard. The palace gates slowly swung closed behind them, leaving two confused royal guards. Jonny raced to catch up to the king's long strides.

"I must say, Jonny, I am happy to see you. You have come at a most wonderful time. Summer is rapidly fading, and the harvest is in full swing. The dragonflowers in the garden have just turned a most spectacular shade of ruby."

"I'm happy to be back, sir. It feels like some part of me never left."

The king glanced sideways at Jonny with a mischievous twinkle in his eyes. "You call yourself Jonny Cupbreaker now?"

Jonny blushed. "I had to get your attention."

The king laughed. "And you've grown so much—you're almost a man grown."

Jonny followed the king into the palace. "You don't look like you've aged a day."

"Oh, you are too kind," the king said, grinning. "My bones ache more with each passing day. What I wouldn't give for a younger man's knees. But, yes, the nights are not so long as they once were."

They crossed the great hall and snaked through the palace's inner passageways. "You have to tell me everything I missed," Jonny said.

"I don't have to do anything—I'm the king," Swarlar chided. "It's a perk of the position." He gave his beard a playful tug. "You have missed less than you imagined. Seven years of mild winters, bountiful harvests, and a surprising win by Mowka's thitch team in last year's tournament. Their keeper played a remarkable game . . . historic, some would say—"

"What about the trolls?"

Swarlar stopped at the door of his study. "What of them?"

"Have they attacked again? Any signs of Darvor? What's his next plan?"

He offered Jonny a sad smile, and for a moment, the blue light flickered in his eyes. He showed Jonny inside the quiet study. "Seven years and not a single troll has crossed into our realm. Their strength was exhausted in the grim year of your prior visit. The threat of our time has passed."

"And Darvor?"

The king sank into the large chair by the fireplace. The sunlight from the open window filtered through the dust hanging in the air and made the king's rich robes shine. "I hope you have not spent your youth worrying about his return."

"Every day."

The king grimaced and motioned for Jonny to take a seat opposite him. "No sign of him. And believe me, I have searched. It seems he walked away from you on Guard Tower Island and off the map." He crossed his hands in his lap. "The board was cleared that day, and he has not returned to reset the pieces."

"Rumors? Shadows?" The boy leaned forward.

"Nothing."

Jonny slumped back.

"I hope that is not why you have returned to us." The king raised an eyebrow.

"That's exactly why I'm back. To stop him . . . before it's too late."

A silence fell over them as heavy as a wet blanket. The king stood. "Wine?"

Jonny looked up. "I'm not—" He stopped. *There is no drinking age here.* "Just a little."

The king crossed the study and poured two glasses. "Tell me, what did you expect to find here?" He returned, handing Jonny a silver chalice filled with blood-red wine.

"Last time, I stepped into a world teetering on ruin. I guess . . ." He trailed off, unsure where the sentence should end.

"Adventure." Swarlar held up his glass and inspected the contents. "Honor, glory, all the things that call to young men."

Jonny glared. "*Him.* I thought I'd find him. And some evil plot to swallow the world."

Swarlar took a sip from his chalice and made a soured face. "Oh, that's no good." He stood and took Jonny's cup. "A poor vintage. Almost vinegar."

Jonny smiled despite himself.

"I'll tell you what, my dear boy," he said, setting the wine aside and returning to his chair. "I imagine you are not ready to return home so soon after you arrived, and I think there is a friend who would very much like to see you. Tomorrow morning, you'll pay a visit to Cazar."

CHAPTER
3

OLD FRIENDS

Jonny found the son of Aazar on his farm, two days' ride northwest of Gluton. He might have made it in much less time, but he had wasted several hours failing at navigating through the countryside. It was nearing sunset when he first sighted the farmhouse under a gold-orange sky. The house was partially shaded by a small stand of trees and surrounded by rolling pastures and bristled hedges. It was modest in size, stoutly built of cut stone and oak. The roof was a mix of slate shingles and thatch, while the chimney was well set and stood straight.

Dismounting, Jonny tethered his horse to a tree and approached the house. The shutters were thrown wide in the mild air, and the warm smell of gingerbread greeted Jonny from afar. He stepped around two chickens and reached the door. Singing came from within, soft and sweet as pressed lavender. *I have heard that voice before,* he mused.

A thick iron knocker, fashioned as a snarling dragon, was affixed to the door. He beat the metal on the wooden door and the melody died. "Coming," came the woman's voice.

The door swung open, and a familiar face greeted him. She was as pretty as he remembered, with eyes that glowed like honey in the sun and lips that hinted at beautiful secrets. When she squinted at Jonny, subtle lines appeared at the corners of her eyes and mouth—the only mark she had aged even a day since Jonny had last met her.

"Can I help you?" she asked, a fleck of guarding in her voice.

"Lady Delena, you are as stunning as ever," Jonny said with a bow.

If she was flattered, she gave no hint of it. Her eyes searched him, trying to place his features among her past. At last, the familiarity spread across her face like a sunrise. "Jonny, son of John?!"

"The same," he said with a smile.

She threw her arms around him and pulled him tight. "It's so good to see you! Cazar always said we would see you again. Come on, he's working out back."

She showed him around the house to a small patio in the back. Paving stones had been set in the ground with great care, sheltered on two sides by the house. On the far side of the patio, the green hillside sloped away, offering a grand view of verdant meadows, tumbling vineyards, and, in another few hours, a painted sunset.

Cazar sat on a low stool, bent over a boot he was mending. Scattered grays hid among his shaggy black hair.

"If you can't fix the boot, we could amputate his foot instead," Delena quipped as they drew near.

"He's got two left feet so it would be an easy decision which to take," Cazar said without looking up.

"If you are referring to his dancing ability, I assure you, he takes after his father." At this, they both laughed.

Cazar's broad shoulders unfolded, and he rose to his feet. The child's boot he held looked comically small in the man's large, weathered hands. "An old friend is here to see you," Delena buzzed.

The warrior's steely eyes fell on Jonny, and the hint of a smile played at the corners of his lips. "Careful with our cups around this one." Jonny allowed a stupid grin.

Delena gave Jonny a playful push toward Cazar. "Go ahead," she said, "you two catch up—I'll finish fixing dinner."

Cazar put aside the boot and showed Jonny to a set of chairs. "My, you've grown . . ." he marveled. "But perhaps someone could show you how to shave."

Jonny blushed and rubbed his cheek. The scattered whiskers sprouting on his chin were no excuse for a beard, and at home he kept it diligently trimmed, but he had not bothered with that since going through the cave.

"I see you found your happy ending." Jonny gestured at their surroundings.

"Aye," the warrior nodded. "After my duty to the Guards was completed, I set off at once to find Delena. I'll spare you the details of that adventure, but in the end, we were married at Lord Delanor's chapel. My family has owned this land for a few generations, though I never spent much time here growing up." He looked down at his hands, rubbing the calluses in his palms. "The life of a farmer is a good one. The soil here is rich. The winters are mild, and we have plenty of rain.

"And you have a child." Jonny pointed at the small boot near Cazar's foot.

A smile spread across the man's face. "A son, coming up on his third winter. He's really something, Jonny. Bold in courage, mild in manner. He is loving, thoughtful—"

"And then there is the matter of his appetite," Delena said, appearing in the doorway behind them. At her feet, a small child clutched sheepishly at the hem of her dress. "I swear he eats more than all the pigs in our sty combined." She bent and nudged the child. "Go to your father."

The child wobbled forward on rubber legs, arms outstretched toward Cazar. "I assume you named him after me?" Jonny quipped.

Cazar scooped up his son and bounced the child on his lap. He shook his head, laughing. "The thought did cross our mind, but no. Perhaps if Delena gives me another."

"Let me guess . . . Dazar."

Cazar blinked, surprised at Jonny's guess. "Yes, did Swarlar tell you?"

"No, lucky guess, I suppose." *Dazar, son of Cazar, son of Aazar.*

Delena returned from the house and began setting a table. By the time the sun kissed the distant hills, they were deep in their plates, lost in conversation. The intervening years melted away as they talked. Cazar's term of service with the Guards of Gluton completed, he had retired with highest honors. He split his time between the quiet farm and training future Guards at the Academy. Delena had reconciled with her family and kept the farm running while Cazar was away.

"Make no mistake," Delena announced. "It's no easy work keeping this place afloat. That's why Cazar runs off to the Academy every couple of weeks to teach."

Cazar looked down at his feet.

"I joke." She took another bite. "We're a team, and a darn good one too. But it is always amusing to play at his guilt."

As they continued to regale each other, Jonny settled into a warm ease. Coming back to this world had been more natural and smoother than he had feared. He had dreamed of his return for years, always unsure what he might find. A hundred turbulent fantasies he had conjured, but rather than falling into a cold and stormy sea, his return had been like wading into a calm pool.

Cazar started a fire, and they settled into a warm night surrounded by the sound of autumn crickets. Dazar wavered on the brink of sleep, fighting to keep his eyes on Jonny, secure in his mother's arms. Delena rested her chin on the child's black hair.

Jonny leaned back and patted his belly. "That was delicious, Delena. The stew was as close to perfect as anything I've had."

She smiled. "An ancient family recipe. As old as House Delanor itself." Her eyes drifted shut and she gave Dazar a gentle squeeze.

Cazar kicked at one of the burning logs and a shower of sparks raced toward the stars. "Jonny, why are you here?"

Jonny looked up. "What do you mean? Swarlar told me I should come visit, and I wanted to see you."

"Not here—I know why you came to our farm. Why did you come back to this land?"

Jonny blinked. He had done his best to avoid the question all night, but now he was trapped. *What do I tell him?* Years of anxiety, nightmares, and therapy. That would not do. He remembered how Swarlar had looked at him; he did not want that sort of pity. *Cazar found his happy ending; I can't trouble him with that.*

"I missed you . . . and this place. The magic and beauty of it." It was the truth. Not the whole truth. Not half of it. But it was the pretty side of the truth, and most of the time, that is all anyone needed.

Delena yawned, cutting through the silence that had settled. "I think the magic and beauty of sleep is calling Dazar and myself." She climbed to her feet, gently rocking the boy in her arms. "Jonny, I'll fix you a place to sleep on the floor inside by the fire. Stay out here as long as you like. I'll see you both in the morning!" She crossed and gave Cazar a quick kiss before disappearing inside.

Cazar made no move to follow. "Do you miss the adventure?"

"Some."

"Jonny Cupbreaker has a nice ring to it." Cazar rested his eyes heavily on the boy.

"You, Swarlar, Turion, Delena, Lord Groy—you're the only ones who know what that name really means." Jonny shrugged. "My name isn't famous throughout the realm like yours."

Cazar leaned forward and the lines of his face deepened in the firelight. "If it's not adventures and it's not fame, why are you really back?"

Jonny pursed his lips. There would be no escaping it. "Darvor's still out there. We delayed him; we did not defeat him."

"Cannot your role in the grand saga of that dark lord be over?"

"I—" Jonny started. Cazar's steel eyes pierced him, and he faltered. "Someone has to stop him."

"But why does it have to be you?"

"Go ahead and ridicule me." Jonny's tone was sharper than he intended. "No one understands. Swarlar just dismissed me and sent me off to you."

Cazar's expression softened. "I am not dismissing you. I am merely trying to understand."

He's right, Jonny breathed. There was no point in lashing out. "When I first went home, I thought that was the end of the story. My happy ending. But there's always been this . . . darkness." A fullness rose in his throat, and he pushed it away. *I'm too old to cry.* "I close my eyes and see bodies stacked like firewood. A warm afternoon swim, and I feel the *tentali* grabbing at my ankles. A squeaking hinge is a *grevice*'s cry." He closed his eyes. "I hear his voice on the wind—whispers reminding me . . . mocking me."

Jonny looked back to Cazar and was greeted with a gentle smile. For a moment, the old tiredness had returned to the warrior's eyes. "It never goes away. I won't lie to you about that. It's always there. Even here, on my perfect farm with my beautiful wife and sweet son, even here there are screams that echo in my head." He chewed on his lip. "It never goes away . . . but you do learn to live with it."

Jonny's eyes welled. "How?"

"Practice."

THE WOUNDED GUEST

Jonny's horse meandered through the green meadows. A cool breeze kissed his nose even as the sun warmed his cheeks. He was no different than he had been a few days before, but an ease had settled in him. The days he spent at the farm had balanced him, and Cazar's words had beat true against his soul. He had expected to find a world in need of saving—to be swept up into another grand adventure. But what he found was a world at peace. *As Swarlar had said: Seven years of bountiful harvest, mild winters . . .* And that was no bad thing. Cazar was happy, Gluton was bustling; perhaps it was time to devote himself to putting the darkness behind him.

He trotted past a field where an old woman was inspecting some pumpkins and offered a friendly wave. The road back to Gluton was easy and the weather lifted his spirits as much as Cazar's nightly campfire talks. There would be no grand adventure this time. The threat of Darvor was not gone, but perhaps Jonny's part in the "grand saga" had passed. Still, he had stirred his parents' wrath to return to this world and was in no great rush to face them. He would first go to Gluton and, from there, south toward Lanak and the hospitality of his old companion, Lord Groy. *Groynof, as I knew him.*

Time in his home would wait. *It did last time . . .* Once he had his fill of traveling and minor adventures, he could go home to reappear at the exact moment he left. He touched the golden necklace under his shirt. A soft power simmered beneath the dragon's scales. There might not be enough magic left in the charm to ever bring him back to this world. *This might be my last trip.*

His horse snorted, annoyed with the slow pace Jonny had set. The boy laughed. "Right, off we go. Let's see what else this world has to offer." The horse kicked into a gallop, and they raced through the rolling fields toward Gluton looming ageless in the distance.

At the royal manor, the same purple-cloaked guards stood sentry. They recognized Jonny and ushered him through. As he crossed the courtyard's weathered cobblestones, a cold breeze slithered down his neck and left him unsettled. Something felt off.

Jonny climbed the stairs to the keep and paused to look around. The sun was shining, and birds chirped in the eaves above while the bustle of King's Square drifted over the palace walls. He could not identify anything wrong, but the unease persisted. He shivered and scampered into the keep.

Inside, his eyes adjusted to the dim light. The smell of strange herbs and rotten flowers overwhelmed him. The great hall was abandoned, but a commotion echoed from down the hall. *Something's not right . . .*

Two men, marked as healers by their gray and red robes, emerged from a side door carrying rolls of cloth and jars of poultices. They crossed the great hall and raced out a side passage as fast as their heavy robes would allow.

His curiosity piqued, Jonny followed. At the hall's end, he found a high-vaulted chamber crowded with men in gray and red robes. Curtains shrouded the tall windows, but the sunlight pierced the thin cloth and bathed the occupants in a dull warmth. Dust and smoky fragrances wafted high above the commotion. The healers were massed around a table in the middle of the room, working and talking in quiet tones. Between their hurried movements, Jonny caught glimpses of a bloodied body.

To Jonny's relief, the patient was not Swarlar. The king stood at a distance with his back to the boy, overseeing the excitement. His white robes burned bright among the crimson-gray sea, and his stillness cut a sharp contrast to the frenzy before him. He stood as he often did when deep in thought, with his arms crossed behind his back.

Jonny approached cautiously. He was a welcomed guest in the palace, but he knew that did not give him a free license to roam, and there were affairs among King Swarlar's chambers that were not wise to intrude upon. "What's . . . uh, what's going on?"

The king did not take his eyes off the healers. "Jonny, welcome back. How was your visit?" His casual tone seemed out of place among the somber healers.

"Fine." Jonny found a place next to the king. "Who's this?"

Swarlar's eyes were gray, and his brow furrowed. "Someone I have not seen in many years."

One of the healers pulled at something and the wounded man's leg jumped on the table. The healer turned to one of his acolytes and passed off a bloody arrowhead before bending back to his work.

"He is a druid," the king said. "One of the last."

Jonny craned on his tiptoes, trying to steal a peek between the gray robes. "What's a druid?"

"A member of an ancient order, all but gone from the world. They protected and studied Old Magic." One of the healers held up a flask to the light, swirling and inspecting the green fluid.

"What happened to him?" Jonny asked.

A sudden loud boom caused one of the robed men to drop a jar of pink powder on the ground. The healers turned to look down the hall, past Swarlar and the boy, toward the source of the noise. More booms followed and the men looked to the king for answers. Swarlar was unfazed and remained still and silent.

But panicked shouts soon erupted from the palace's throne room, echoing down the hall. The healers stopped again, looking at Swarlar with uncertain expressions. Still the king was unperturbed. He offered a small nod as reassurance, but the healers grew more confused and more afraid with each noise that carried down the hall. Two of the acolytes backed away, retreating toward the corners of the room.

It sounds like a fight, Jonny thought. *What's going on?*

There were more crashes and shouts until only Swarlar retained any poise.

At last, the king spun on his heel and started toward the commotion. "Come, let's see what damage has been done before someone gets hurt." The king's calmness was enough to make Jonny laugh.

Leaving the healers, they started toward the great hall. The cries and clash of steel grew louder. With it, the sound of splintering wood tumbled toward them, followed by a bestial roar. *I've heard that roar before,* Jonny realized. His heart quickened. There was only one man who sounded like that . . . *and he died years ago.*

They arrived at a chaotic scene. The looming great hall was destroyed as if by a tornado. Chairs lay scattered and splintered, tapestries hung torn and burnt, and the thick oaken table was flipped and split asunder. The braziers were bent and flipped, spewing their hot coals on the floor, while the titanic doors had been smashed and hung from broken hinges.

A handful of guards lay in various degrees of injury, wrapped in mangled armor and dust. In the middle of the anarchy, a wide ring of purple-cloaked soldiers encircled a hulking, bloodied man whose immense size left no doubt to Jonny of his identity. Rard.

Swarlar surveyed the scene and clicked his tongue. He did not yell, but his voice resonated with an unnatural boom and split the room into silence. "Enough."

The guards fidgeted, their weapons still raised and bodies tensed. Rard's giant chest heaved. His eyes burned. Old, gnarled scars gleamed from holes in his tattered shirt.

Jonny's stunned mind conjured old memories. He had last seen the colossal man a lifetime ago, being devoured by *grevices* in a desolate corner of wilderness. The outlaw had thrown himself into the beasts to save Jonny's meager fellowship. Fleeting glimpses of the martyr still burned in his mind. *He survived?! How?*

"Where is he?!" Rard boomed. "Where is my brother?!"

"He is right this way. Wounded but still alive," the king replied.

Jonny's thoughts raced to keep up.

"Men, put down your weapons," the king ordered. "This man is no enemy." The soldiers begrudgingly lowered their spears.

"Where is he? Take me to him now!" Rard barked.

"He is just down this hall—"

Rard did not wait for a guide; he charged forward, and Jonny jumped aside to avoid being trampled by the barreling hulk. The man blew past them and disappeared. A moment later, dismayed shouts echoed from the passage. A swarm of startled healers scampered from the hallway, spilling their potions as they went.

Swarlar sighed. "The healers salivate at gory wounds and seeping pustules that would make most queasy, but a single large and grizzled farmer from a forgotten corner of the map causes them to run in terror. Funny the things that frighten us." He bobbed his head in amusement. "Walk with me, Jonny."

To the boy's surprise, the king did not start after Rard and his wounded brother. Instead, measured strides took them out the de-hinged doors of the great hall and toward the royal gardens.

A thousand questions swirled in Jonny, but before he could form one into words, Swarlar began.

"Our wounded guest is named Gerald. As I said earlier, he is one of the last druids, and for many years he has lived in a long-forgotten corner of the world—"

"Sorry to interrupt, but shouldn't we go back to check on them?"

"No, no, let them have their privacy. I do not well know this brother, but if he is anything like Gerald, he would not like to be seen crying."

Jonny recalled Rard's gruff manner and had to agree.

"Gerald arrived only hours after you left to visit Cazar," the king continued. "He was teetering on death, plucked full of arrow wounds, carried by a horse drowning in exhaustion."

"What happened to him?"

The king produced a tattered, blood-stained parchment from the folds of his robes. "Before he lapsed into a coma, he managed to write down enough. A band of trolls wandered into the valley in which he lived. He tried to fight them off, but they were too many."

They rounded into the garden and ventured into the thick maze of hedges.

"Will he survive?" Jonny asked.

"No," he said bluntly. "He is fading."

"And the healers can't help him?" The answer, he knew, was evident

"His wounds are too great for them. But they will toil as is their nature."

"Why can't you heal him with magic—like you did for me when Darvor attacked?"

The king grimaced. "That was something different . . ."

"How did Rard know he was here?"

"I sent word to him." The king paused in front of a marble bench and allowed himself a seat. "I thought it only fair that he come to be with his brother at the end."

Jonny slid into place next to him. A cool breeze snuck through the hedges, sending the verdant leaves spinning on their branches. "And how did you know he was still alive? The last time I saw him, he was being torn apart by *grevices*."

The king offered a sly grin. "I'm the king; it's my job to know."

Jonny had grown accustomed to Swarlar's cryptic ribbing. Often, it was frustrating and only raised more questions. *Why won't he give me a straight answer?*

Swarlar looked toward the sky. The pillowy clouds above echoed a thousand times in the blue pools of his eyes. "Have you noticed the days are getting shorter? As winter creeps closer, the nights grow longer. And the winds change . . ."

As if on cue, a cold gust swirled through the garden, stirring the fallen leaves into a frenzy and crawling between the layers of Jonny's tunic.

"This is the first time the trolls have ventured beyond their border in seven years," the king continued. "It was a good peace while it lasted." His tone was wistful, wet with warm memories long gone.

Jonny pulled his cloak around him while grasping at what to ask next.

"Do you care for another adventure, young man?" Swarlar turned to Jonny.

The boy leaned forward. "What do you have in mind?

"I believe these trolls that attacked Gerald are a renegade detachment wandering in search of pillage and plunder. They invaded a small, long-forgotten valley high and deep in the Great Mountains. Thankfully, Gerald was the only one in the valley. But they will likely not stop there. Left to their own devices, they will eventually find their way across the mountains and begin attacking the mountain villages in the lands of House Hillan. We should stop them, or more precisely, you should stop them."

"Me?" Jonny sputtered. "By myself?"

"Don't be ridiculous. I'll give you men."

Jonny fought to contain a smile. "How many?"

"There were maybe two or three dozen—"

"No, how many men?"

Swarlar gave his beard a thoughtful tug. "I think two hundred should do."

Jonny's jaw dropped. *Two hundred? I'm gonna command an army!*

The king pressed on, ignoring Jonny's surprise. "They'll be good men, seasoned soldiers from the royal army. You'll have good maps and a guide that knows how to read them. Once you find the valley, find the trolls. Any questions?"

"Only one," Jonny said, rising to his feet. "When do we leave?"

CHAPTER
5

A SCREAM IN THE NIGHT

The column of men snaked over the rolling hills. *Two hundred and change.* True to Swarlar's word, they were good men—seasoned warriors and disciplined soldiers. Many were veterans of the War of the Three Armies and had manned the walls during the siege of Gluton. They brought more than a dozen wagons and three times as many horses and mules laden with supplies, food, weaponry, and armor. An army of squires and orphan boys bolstered the ranks, the former seeking training and glory, the latter food and shelter.

Jonny paused his horse on the ridge and looked back at the line of men. His heart swelled with pride. *My own army . . .* He allowed himself a tired smile. It had taken three days to muster the men, and Jonny had spent most of that time organizing and planning. There had been far more work to prepare than Jonny had imagined.

First, he had met his lieutenants, then he'd spent a full day studying maps and charting tactics. Organizing and packing supplies alone had cost a day and a half. Each man required enough rations for a month: bread, cheese, dried fruit, salted meat, pickled onions—foods that wouldn't spoil on the road. It all had to be loaded onto wagons, along with tents, arrows, and casks of watered ale and wine. While the soldiers would carry their own bedrolls, waterskins, and weapons, heaps of other supplies were needed too, and Jonny would have known none of it without his lieutenants' help. Bandages, spare boots, horseshoes, medical poultices, cookware . . . it had been enough to make Jonny's head spin.

Whenever possible, he had stolen away to an abandoned room in the palace to practice his magic. Swarlar had shown him to the empty room and given him the key with a knowing wink. There, he would hide away where none might see him and, after locking the door and drawing the curtains, conjure fiery spells and blazon enchantments. The fire he summoned drew its strength from him, sucking away his life force with every tongue of flame he cast. Late into the night, he poured himself into the practice, trying to bolster his strength and sharpen his skills. And all the while, in the back of his mind loomed the shadow of Darvor . . . *waiting*.

What awaited his small army in the distant mountains was not Darvor, Swarlar had assured him, but a renegade detachment of trolls hungry for blood and glory. Still, Jonny knew, his powers could prove indispensable in defeating them, even if his men outnumbered the rabble of trolls. And so, at the end of each day or whenever a break presented itself, Jonny had slipped away to practice his magic and keep his endurance sharp.

The routine left him drained and exhausted. He barely slept and had to be reminded to eat and drink. When the time came to depart Gluton, Jonny decided to conserve his strength whenever possible. And so, for the last week, he had not conjured a spell.

Jonny turned in the saddle as one of his companions galloped up beside him. The young man tossed Jonny an apple. "We can make another league before sunset, I reckon."

Jonny nodded, thanking him for the apple. "We've made good pace so far."

Jonny was introduced to the young man by Swarlar in the hours that followed Rard's return. "I should think a keen set of eyes and a strong bow arm should serve you well," the king had said. The young man's name was Alyk and he was the same age as Jonny. Once a fisherman's son on the shores of Lanak, he had lost his family when the trolls attacked seven years ago. He had shown great skill with a bow and, through a series of fortunate happenstances, had ended up as a ward of the king. He was marked with fiery green eyes and a handsome smile. Busy hands kept a tangle of brown hair swept behind his ears, and a finely wrought bow was ever strung in the quiver behind his back.

Jonny had taken an instant liking to Alyk's relaxed demeanor and biting wit, and the archer had become his unofficial second-in-command. "You didn't see any signs of trouble ahead when you were out scouting?"

"Just that this army is led by a real half-wit," Alyk quipped.

Jonny rolled his eyes as he sunk his teeth into the apple.

"There will be a frost tonight," Alyk said, stretching his arms behind him.

"Pretty soon we'll reach the mountains. Then we'll have worse than frosts to worry about. Swarlar says there will be lots of snow in the high passes this time of year." Jonny's eyes fixed on the distant white-capped peaks. From the green plains of Lydie, the Great Mountains looked a world away, but Jonny knew from his past adventures how biting the cold could be among those towering giants.

"Why now?" Alyk asked. "Seven years and the trolls haven't stirred within thirty miles of the East River. Now they cross half of Lydie and head into the mountains. It makes no sense."

The same thought had crossed Jonny's mind. The first human to encounter trolls in seven years was a lone druid guarding a forgotten valley deep in the mountains. It was too great a coincidence to dismiss.

Jonny shrugged. "Like King Swarlar said, they are searching for pillage and plunder."

Unconvinced, Alyk fixed him with a sideways look.

Jonny took another bite of the apple. "Maybe they thought the Emerald Peak was really made of emeralds," he remarked, referencing one of the shimmering mountains in the distance.

"Or maybe they thought the newly appointed Commander of the King's Expeditionary Force was too much of a blockhead to stop them," Alyk chided.

Jonny laughed and threw his apple core at the archer. "That's enough out of you."

The days passed quickly as they drew toward the mountains. Jonny recalled his first journey across Lydie—a dull and arduous affair. But between Alyk's companionship and the business of leading his host of men, the journey now was far less boring.

He tried to learn the names of as many of his men as he could, though by the time they had reached the mountains' foothills, he had learned less than half. There were his four lieutenants Thom, Davinnof, Lyam, and Sedrin; the healer Josten, son of Josta; the camp's cooks Hjaren and Lharen; at least eight men named Marten; and a singular bullish man who insisted the others call him the Hammer of Dorndale. By the time they had climbed high enough in the foothills to feel the first crunch of snow under their boots, Jonny had resigned himself to the knowledge that, try as he might, he would never learn all the men's names.

Their guide was a wizened former trapper named Gjarn. A few winters past his prime, he hid his face beneath a thick gray beard with barely a nose visible beneath the whiskers. His flinty eyes spent all day scouring the horizon, and he spent the better part of most nights scuttling spittle juice. Equal parts rugged outdoorsman and wandering madman, Gjarn would in one moment show them a hidden path around a treacherous ravine and the next spend a few minutes licking a tree to get a sense of "whether any of the birds who landed in the tree foresaw any danger in the hills ahead."

Jonny had been leery of the man's guidance at first, but in the days since they left Gluton, they had not met any serious trouble and, aside from a broken wagon wheel, had made good speed. He cautiously found himself acknowledging Swarlar's wisdom in choosing Gjarn. "He knows where he's going," Jonny found himself often assuring his lieutenants.

But he did not let that stop him from sharing jokes on the subject with Alyk. "What do you get when you cross a drunk goat with an almanac? . . . Gjarn."

"That's a good one," his friend laughed. "How about this: What's the difference between a bear and Gjarn? The bear takes a bath more than once a year."

The jokes faded once they left the ease of Lydie for the looming slopes of the mountains. Gjarn skillfully guided the column of soldiers higher into the mountain passes until even the shale and moss were replaced by ice and snow. Cold winds howled down from spires above and up from ravines below. Forced to leave their wagons and many of the horses behind as the air grew thinner and the path rougher, they advanced on foot.

One night, huddled around one of the camp's fires, Gjarn slipped up next to Jonny with a grunt. The mountain man's ripe odor greeted Jonny even before he spoke. "Commander Jonny, we are almost there." He pulled out a crinkled parchment folded against itself. His yellow fingernails worked to unfold the leaves until a faded map emerged. "Two days ago, we passed here—Crocket's Ravine." He gestured to an indistinct squiggle on the map. "Now we here." He tapped a large black spot.

"There's nothing there," he said.

"Yes, people don't come here. Maps—they don't know."

Jonny had learned this much from Swarlar. Cartographers had put pen to paper and mapped most places in the realm, but they had not mapped every corner of the land. In the most distant moors or the highest mountains, mapmakers had either left the unknown blank or filled in with their imagination.

"Tomorrow, we reach where Swarlar told me take you." Gjarn's thick accent highlighted his broken grammar and sounded like he was rolling a marble on the back of his tongue.

"Good," Jonny said, brushing off the snowflakes that had accumulated on his shoulder. "I'd rather be out of this cold before a snowstorm buries these trails."

"No, Commander. Soon we see high mountain, narrow path . . . that is where king say trolls go. But it is not good place. I no go there, no one go there."

Jonny shrugged off the shiver that ran down his spine. "Gerald the Druid lived there for years. We'll be fine." Even if there was something to fear in Gerald's valley besides the trolls, with two hundred men and Jonny's magic, it should not pose a threat.

"It is not good place." Gjarn's dark eyes pleaded beneath thick silver eyebrows. "We see no signs of trolls anywhere. They gone now. We can leave."

Jonny wanted to dismiss Gjarn's concerns; he was surrounded by hundreds of battle-hardened soldiers and hardly felt unsafe. But the earnest glint in the guide's eyes shook him. He glanced away, looking to the next fire over, where Alyk was locked in an arm-wrestling match with the Hammer of Dorndale. A cheer erupted from the onlooking soldiers when Alyk slapped down his opponent's arm. Jonny swallowed hard. "We won't linger. We'll scour the valley for any signs of trolls. If they aren't there, we return to Gluton."

Gjarn nodded his thanks and retreated from the light of the fire.

The following day, true to Gjarn's word, they sighted the narrow path to their destination. The constrained trail stretched their column long, and the men often had to pause to catch their breaths in the wispy air. As they neared the trail's summit, Jonny often heard eerie noises echoing down from the crags above. Whether it was monsters or ice splitting, he was never sure. With every step closer, Gjarn's words echoed in his mind: *It not good place.*

By midday, Jonny crested the summit and paused at the view.

Behind him, Josten, the healer, gasped his pleasure. "Now that's fit for a song . . ."

The narrow path snaked down the mountain in front of them, ending in a quiet valley squeezed between towering mountains. A thick sheen of ivory snow blanketed the valley floor and wrapped the trees in fluffy beauty. From Jonny's elevation, the towering pines lining the valley were blades of grass peeking through a spring snow. A silver lake sliced through the valley's heart like polished glass, reflecting the snowy mountains and icy glaciers.

Jonny's anxiety melted away at the sight of the tranquil vale. *It's beautiful.*

The Vale of Joy, it was called, though no one seemed to know why. Indeed, in talking to Alyk and the lieutenants, no one had ever heard of it. Only Gjarn had any knowledge of it, and his expertise only went as far as knowing it was a place best avoided. As always, whatever Swarlar knew of the place, the only information he deemed to impart on Jonny was that it was where the druid Gerald lived when the trolls attacked and that any search for the trolls should start in the valley.

"What's the plan, Commander?" Davinnof, a young lordling lieutenant, inquired.

Jonny scanned the valley. He spied no disturbances in the snow, but at such a distance that meant little. There were no smoke plumes to suggest campfires. "As far as I can tell, no signs of trolls."

"Is this the only way in?" Alyk chirped.

Gjarn pulled at his beard and grunted.

"Each lieutenant takes their fifty men and we split up. Search the valley floor. Meet at the far end of the lake. We'll shelter there for the night, and we'll put this valley behind us in the morning."

Jonny and Alyk traveled with Davinnof and his troops along the north shore of the small lake. Thom took his men to the south side while Sedrin and Lyam each broke away to patrol the valley's perimeter.

Jonny's cohort reached the far edge of the lake first. The thick snow padded their footsteps and swallowed the men's hushed whispers.

"This place is quiet . . ." Alyk muttered, ducking under the bough of a great pine bent low with snow.

"Aye," Jonny agreed. He had long ago learned there was more to fear in the quiet places than anywhere else. *That's where secrets set down their roots.*

"Jonny!" Davinnof's gruff voice cut the frozen air. "Have a look here."

Jonny and a dozen of the nearest troops converged on Davinnof's voice. The lordling stood before a mound of ash and blackened wood—a yawning chasm of darkness among the white wilderness. Jonny paused to absorb the burnt ruins. Gjarn's words echoed again in his mind—*not good place.*

Davinnof approached the charred remains and squatted to inspect the ashes. He ran his hand through the dust and pulled up a scrap of metal, black and twisted by the heat. "It seems it was a house. There are some pots there, and some of these ashes look like they were once clothing."

"Gerald's cabin," Jonny exhaled. "There's his horse's pen." He pointed to another ring of ashes half buried by the drifts.

"There's no footprints here," Alyk remarked. "If the trolls did this, they left before the last snow."

"Davinnof! Commander!" From the excited accents, Jonny identified the shouting as either Hjaren or Lharen, the cooks.

There was no fear in their voices, but Jonny ran all the same. He outdistanced Alyk and the others, arriving at the cooks' location first. They stood, wrapped in their thick furs, a distance from their discovery.

Rising from the rolling snow banks at the lake's shore, an elegant stone gazebo loomed beneath a stand of birch trees. Jonny stepped around Hjaren for a better view. The structure was old and weathered, cut from graystone now leeched by the elements. A tangle of spidery vines climbed the slender columns and disappeared beneath the snow perched on the pavilion's top.

Jonny crunched up the snowclad steps and under the arbor's roof. On a dais at the platform's center rose a fountain. A stone bowl rested on the carved column of rock. *It looks like a baptismal font.* Jonny recalled similar fountains in the churches of his home world.

Alyk arrived at the head of the other soldiers. "What is it?" he asked, climbing the stone stairs.

"I have no idea," Jonny whispered. A breeze tickled the back of his neck. Between the Caves of Sliok and the Crags of Bane, Jonny had been around enough Old Magic to recognize the feel of it rising from the stones around them. The air was thick with it. He inspected the fountain. The bowl was empty. He ran his finger through the bowl's cavity. Bone dry.

He turned to Alyk. "I don't think the trolls arrived here by chance."

Lyam and Thom's detachments converged on the pavilion. "We circled the far sides of the valley and the lake shore," they reported. "Found this, but no other signs of trolls." Lyam held aloft a handful of broken arrows, some clearly made by the hands of trolls.

"The druid's house is back that way, just through the trees." Davinnof shoved a thumb over his shoulder. "Burnt to the ground."

Sedrin's men emerged from a grove to their left. "Nothing," the gruff lieutenant puffed, tightening his hood tight around his head.

Alyk twirled an arrow between his fingers. "They aren't here. The valley isn't big enough to hide them. And there are no tracks. They *were* here, but they're long gone."

Jonny surveyed the land around them. They had come to the far side of the valley, opposite the trail over the mountains. It would soon be night; shadows were already swallowing the valley. The impassable walls of the Vale of Joy loomed high behind them, and the slender lake guarded their front. The snow was piled high, the mountains blocked most of the wind, and the thick trees ate up the rest. *A good place to camp for the night.*

"Get some fires started," Jonny announced. "Hjaren, Lharen, start up a stew! Davinnof, make sure the area is secure. I want double the watch tonight." His eyes fell on Gjarn, standing at the lake shore in the shadow of the stone fountain. At a distance from the other men, the guide was still as ice, eyes fixed on the lake's placid waters. Gjarn's trance-like stance unsettled him. "And no one goes near the lake! Not within a hundred paces . . . all night," he added. "Alyk, get Gjarn away from the waters. I don't like it."

By the time the first stars winked into view in the night sky, two dozen fires dotted the thin strip of land between the mountains and the lake shore. Occasional bursts of color erupted from the fires as the soldiers swirled their spittle juice, and competing songs bounced back and forth among the circles of men, beating back the night air's chill.

Standing by one of the fires, Jonny stretched his hands toward the heat. A thousand questions swirled in his head, and half of them were given voice by the officers huddled around the fire with him.

"What's the deal with the fountain?" Davinnof pondered.

"I imagine it has something to do with why the druid lived here," Josten suggested.

"I can't believe the trolls stumbled on this place," marveled Thom.

"And that lake, there's something odd about it . . ."

"It's not frozen." Alyk's words were hollow and rattled the cold air. The others turned to face him. "Not even around the edges." He tugged at the edges of his cloak and stared into the fire. "It's bloody cold . . . why isn't it frozen?"

"I haven't seen a single ripple on the surface," another whispered.

"The Vale of Joy," Jonny mused. "Maybe it's prettier in the spring."

As the fires turned to embers and the nightly ration of spittle juice dried up, the songs faded. One by one, the men retreated to sleep, leaving the sentries to patrol in silence.

Jonny slipped into his tent and pulled his blankets close. Despite the chill in the air, his eyes were heavy, and sleep washed over him.

The scream awoke Jonny with a start. It pierced the night air and echoed off the walls of the Vale. He sat up in bed and craned his head to listen. As fast as it had come, the cry was gone, and silence hung in the air. A nervous energy caused flames to swirl around Jonny's fingertips.

A second scream erupted, and Jonny sprung from his bed. Snatching his cloak from the tent post, he raced toward the noise. The second shriek had not died like the first. It rose and fell, sputtering like a candle in the wind. The screams came from the lake. With Alyk and the lieutenants close behind, Jonny raced toward the waters.

Shouts went up from the sentries, and other men stirred to their feet, grabbing their weapons, and pulling on boots. In a blur, Jonny passed Gjarn huddled beside a dying fire, rocking and crying hysterically.

An ambush? Jonny thought. *Maybe the trolls had never left the valley.* It could not be; the screams were coming from the lake.

He leaped over a soldier still untangling himself from his blankets. Ahead, the silver moon was reflected in the black waters. As he neared the shore, the screaming grew louder. In the shallows, the water splashed and tossed. Jonny slowed as he drew near. Three soldiers were already at the water's edge ahead of him and more were arriving every second.

"Don't go near the water," one of them said. "Don't let it touch you."

Jonny held up his hands to stop those coming behind him. His eyes adjusted to the dim moonlight.

The screaming came from the form thrashing in the shallow waters near the lake's edge. Further out, a still form floated on the water's smooth surface. Jonny blinked. The lifeless body was one of his soldiers. The second form, thrashing like a wounded animal, was another soldier. His eyes were wide with panic, and he looked to be drowning. But the waters he flailed in were up to his knees.

"Why doesn't he just stand up?" Alyk whispered.

"Some poor sap wandered down here and slipped in the lake," the soldier in front of them started. His wide eyes were locked on the man splashing in the water, and his words tumbled out in a sobbing deluge. Though a rough-looking man, in that moment, he was reduced to something small and quivering. "He let out a squeal like a stuck pig. Marten was the first of us to get here; he ran down to save him . . . as soon as he touched the water, he screamed all the same. Marten grew up at the farm over from mine—he's the best swimmer of the lot of us."

As he watched the man flopping in the water with a look of terror, Jonny's mind went blank. Like the soldiers at the water's edge, he was paralyzed with indecision. *My magic!* But he could not think how he might use it. He could not hope to burn away all the water in the lake.

"A rope!" Alyk shouted, "Someone get a rope."

One of the soldiers appeared with a coiled rope, and with a single strong throw, they snared Marten. The men joined together and dragged the thrashing man from the water. Once safe on dry land, the assembled men formed a wide circle around him. As the water ran off him, his screams faded and he grew still, twitching and mumbling like a man possessed.

Josten shoved his way through the ring of men. "Let me through! Let me through!" He knelt beside the man.

"Should you touch him?" Lyam's voice was strained.

"I swore an oath to heal." Josten's face was determined. He cautiously laid his hands on the soldier's chest. When nothing happened, he set about inspecting him. "No burns, no injuries. He just looks . . . wet."

"Wet? He looks like a poor sot coming off from ten years hard torture," Alyk quipped.

The man's eyes were locked wide and focused on the stars above. His skin looked inhumanly pale, and his mouth bobbed like a fish stripped of water.

"What in Darvor's name?" mumbled the Hammer of Dorndale, giving voice to all the men's thoughts.

Jonny pulled his eyes away, looking out at the lake and the dead soldier's body bobbing idly on the placid surface. "No one goes near the lake under any circumstance. We leave this place at first light." There was not a word of disagreement.

CHAPTER 6

BLOOD IN THE SNOW

Before the sun had chased the shadows from the valley, the men were working their way up the narrow winding path leading out of the Vale. A somber air had settled over the column. The men marched slow as cold molasses with thick hoods pulled tight against the chill. Behind they left two cairns—simple piles of stone erected for their fallen comrades. Marten passed away during the night. The other soldier's body was never recovered.

Jonny trudged forward with a sunken head, kicking at the shale and ice underfoot. Swarlar had trusted him, and he failed. No sightings of the trolls and two dead men to show for it. *I froze,* Jonny sulked. When Marten had been flailing in the waters, he had done nothing. He could not think, and when the soldiers needed his leadership most, he panicked.

"How're you holding up?" Alyk asked, falling into step beside Jonny.

Jonny shook his head. "Those men died because of me."

"Those men died because they touched the water."

"This isn't what I expected at all."

"What did you expect?" Alyk countered. "That we would find a band of trolls, defeat them without losing a man, and return to Gluton to the cheers of crowds?"

"I don't know what I thought . . . just something different."

Alyk nodded. "I don't know you as well as I might, but the last couple days, I've seen this much is true: You care. And that's a good thing." He reached behind his back and pulled one of the arrows from his quiver. "But you can't hold on to all the hurt. Like stones in your pocket, it'll start to weigh you down. You'll stop moving forward." He spun the arrow between his fingertips. "Hold on to some of the pain. Only enough. And let the rest run off your shoulders like a summer rain."

"It's not that easy." Jonny sighed and his breath swirled in the frost.

"No. No, it's not. Never is." Alyk raised the arrow in his hand and inspected the tip. His eyes glazed with distant memories. "When the trolls attacked Lanak, I was just a boy. I remember the city burning. Screams. Panic. The troll—I still remember what he looked like—he cut down my mother right there on the doorstep of our house. The air was so thick with smoke I could hardly breathe. I grabbed my father's old hunting bow off the wall. I'd never even held the thing before. It was the bow of a man grown. On any other day, I couldn't have even drawn back on it." He blinked away the past. "There was so much bad in that moment I could have drowned. But I let it wash over me, through me. I held on to a little—just enough—and let the rest go. In that moment, there was just me, my bow, and that troll. Only two of those things left that house that night."

The archer lowered the arrow. "Hold on to just enough and let the rest go. That's why I never miss."

Jonny raised an eyebrow. "Never?"

"Never." Alyk returned a wink. "Not when it matters most."

Let the rest go. He knew he could not, at least not that easily. *But maybe with time . . .* He nodded.

Alyk thumped his back. "I don't know about you, but I think the first thing I'm doing when we get back to Gluton is dragging Gjarn to a bathhouse. Don't think he has ever been to one."

And despite himself, Jonny laughed.

The sun rose in the sky and soon slid toward the horizon, casting the mountain passes into long shadows. The column of men stretched as the rugged land slowed their progress. At the head of the line, in his unique fashion, Gjarn led them forward.

Jonny worked his way through the ranks, listening to the discussions. There was talk of the hot meals and warm women they hoped to find in Gluton upon their return. Others whispered about the horrors of the night before and the mysteries of the Vale of Joy. Jonny's thoughts echoed their own. In equal parts, he wanted a good, cooked meal and some answers for what he had seen in the Vale.

He raised his gaze, inspecting the soaring peaks surrounding them. The frozen spires cut toward the clouds, ripping the wind from the sky and focusing it into the passes. Jonny shook his head. *These ravines Gjarn leads us through are wind tunnels.* He blew on his hands, warming his chilled fingers.

With the next gust, the air whistled, and a shout erupted from up the line. Confused cries filled the air. *What now?* Jonny wondered, straightening to glimpse the cause of excitement.

Fifty yards ahead, his trusted lieutenant, Sedrin, staggered to one knee. From his neck, an arrow shaft emerged.

A scream erupted from behind Jonny, and he spun to greet it. The soldier behind him in line collapsed with an arrow erupting through his thigh. Around them, men spun in panic as a wave of confusion washed over the column. Disorder reigned as men scrambled for shelter, dropping bags and weapons. Among the mayhem, Jonny spied Alyk, bow in hand, spinning in search of their assailants.

Jonny swallowed back the fear that seized him. Every moment of inaction would be more of his men lost under the volley of arrows. He had his magic; it was always with him—in him. Without bidding, the familiar warmth rose, surging from the depths of his chest. He raised his hands, directing the force skyward. Just as he had practiced in solitude countless times, the fire arced high in the air. Higher still it rose, like a geyser of light, until at Jonny's bidding, it split outward. It raced across the sky, bathing the men in orange light, and fell back to the earth, swallowing the small army in a dome of fire.

A hushed silence settled over the cowering men. One by one, they looked up with stunned expressions. Alyk was the first to climb to his feet, shock and fear etched in his eyes as he met Jonny's gaze.

"It's all right," Jonny shouted over the roar of the fire. "I control it! It's magic—don't worry, you're safe!"

To envelope all the men, the magic dome was larger than any shield Jonny had conjured: far larger than his first shield in the Swamps of Mohan, larger even than his family's house or his school's basketball court. Beneath its weight, his strength ebbed like water draining from a bathtub. The arrows launched by their unseen foes vanished in the fires of the shield, but each blow landed like a punch to Jonny's gut, and he grimaced under the onslaught.

"I can't hold the magic forever!" Jonny cried.

"It's the trolls," Alyk replied. "They ambushed us! They're scattered on the mountain slopes on both sides of us."

"I spied one peeking out from behind a rock up there," Jonny said, flicking his head in the direction.

"And there were a few on that ridge." Alyk pointed.

"To your feet! To your feet!" Jonny shouted to the soldiers. "Looks like we found what fight we were looking for. Davinnof, your men take the north face, and Lyam, your men take the south. The rest of you, form up around me, shelter the wounded. I'll drop the shield on one . . . two . . . three!"

With a gasp, Jonny let the spell go. The fires swirled out of existence. With a thunderous cry, the battle began. Trolls raced down the slopes, emerging from their hiding places in crevasses and behind rocks. They filled the air with their vile battle cries. The soldiers charged forth to meet them with equal zeal. From their lips burst shouts of bravado, honor, and fearlessness.

Jonny spun, hurling fireballs at whatever exposed trolls he spotted. Beside him, Alyk launched quarrel after quarrel, each felling its troll target. Clashing steel and bestial shouts filled the air. The din of battle echoed off the crags, consuming the silence of the mountains. Among the chaos, Jonny spied the Hammer of Dorndale throwing himself at a pair of troll spearmen. On the other side of the battle, Hjaren, or maybe Lharen, bludgeoned a troll with a frying pan. Arrows flew and blades sang. But as brutal as it was, the outcome was already decided.

The trolls only numbered a few dozen and were quickly overwhelmed by the men. The battle ended as swiftly as it began.

"That was fun!" burst the Hammer of Dorndale as the last sounds of battle died in the wind. The oafish man beat his chest and glowed with bloodlust.

Jonny surveyed the scene. The survivors wandered the ravine, catching their breath and tending to the wounded. Blood stained the snow, both the bright crimson of the men and the dark bile of the trolls. A quick count tallied sixteen dead and twice as many trolls. Among the fallen, Jonny eyed Sedrin, the cooks Hjaren and Lharen, and at least two of the remaining Martens. He sighed. His magic had saved many lives, but if they had not walked into an ambush, he knew he could have saved more. A more experienced commander could have avoided the ambush. Again, he felt as though he failed his men, and the victory was soured.

Alyk approached, twirling an arrow between his fingers. His relaxed stance and easy smile impressed Jonny. "So just what was that?"

"An ambush," Jonny replied.

"No." Alyk pointed the arrow at him. "What you did with the fire."

"Magic." Jonny scratched the back of his head. "I can control fire. And summon it."

"Yeah." Alyk laughed. "I figured that. Just a little surprised."

"So are they." Jonny pointed to the soldiers around them, many of whom eyed him suspiciously and whispered among themselves.

"It's been a while since we left Gluton, and I just thought at some point it would have come up. Maybe a 'Hey, Alyk. Want to see something?' or a 'Don't trouble yourself with starting that campfire, I'll do it with the snap of a finger.'"

Jonny offered a sheepish grin. "I . . . uh . . ."

"Stories and legends, friend. That's where you see magic like that. I feel like I'm in one of those old tales I heard as a child about wizards and giants and lost treasure."

"What about you?" Jonny fired back. "With that bow! You were amazing—what did you do, fire ten shots and kill ten?"

"Eight shots, eight kills."

Jonny shook his head in astonishment. "Like you said, you never miss. That's fit for being in a song with legends like Glu Voramandier and Tomm o' the Hills. I've even fought beside Turion, and let me tell you, you might even be a better shot than he is."

Alyk's green eyes flashed. "I'm sure I am. But I've got no skill with a sword or spear. All I've got is the bow . . . and my charm with the ladies."

"My good men," Josten interrupted. "I'll help the wounded all that I can. But what would you have us do with the dead?"

The question brought Jonny's mind back to the grim reality of the battle. *What would Cazar do?* After a moment's thought, he answered. "Stack the trolls over there; I'll burn them. As for the men, take anything of value to return to their families. We cannot carry them back to Gluton, and the frozen ground is too hard here to bury them. We'll pile stones on them and make a burial mound." His words sounded callous as they left his mouth. "It is the best we can do."

A Pint and a Plot

Jonny stormed up the stairs of the palace, annoyance smoldering like a furnace. There had been little fanfare upon their return to Gluton. The people of the city were jaded by frequent comings and goings; the king's troops frequented the area for some military matter or another, and the arrival of two hundred soldiers did not arouse much interest. But Swarlar . . . *He should have greeted us.* The king's absence was arrogant, he thought, and worse, it was disrespectful to his men.

Jonny was alone in this view; Alyk and the others had neither minded nor been surprised. Apart from Alyk, none of the others had even met the king. They parted with Jonny to return to Gluton's barracks for a warm meal, hot bath, and well-deserved coin. They were soldiers who had merely done their job. They did not expect a royal greeting, but to Jonny, they deserved it. Swarlar's absence stung.

Jonny entered the throne hall, noting, despite his ire, that someone had mended the great gilded doors and set them back on their hinges.

"Where is he?" Jonny inquired of a passing servant.

The servant scanned him and, after reflecting on his countenance, reconsidered any protestation. "In his study. But he is in a closed council with some lords from the hinterlands. You'll have to wait."

Jonny nodded and started off toward the study with no intention of patience. *He may be the king,* Jonny thought, *but I saved the realm.* He threw wide the door to the study and was greeted with a familiar sight.

The study was a modest room lined with dusty bookshelves. The low autumn sun filtered through the window, falling on the table and chairs by the fire. In the relative shadow at the room's other end, a thick desk hid under a layer of scrolls and yellowed parchment. The room had changed little in the years since Jonny had first arrived.

At the desk sat three men, draped in elegant garments, and across from them, Swarlar in his usual whites. At the interruption, the men spun to face Jonny. Their faces soured at the sight of his dirtied travel clothes.

"One moment, Jonny," the king said warmly.

"We need to talk."

"I said one moment." The warmth vanished from the king's tone.

"No, we need to talk," Jonny pressed.

"Your Majesty—" one of the lords said. Jonny recognized him as Godrin Voramandier, the uniquely pompous high lord of Gluton.

The king's eyes narrowed at Jonny, but his displeasure did not reach the rest of his face. "Would my lords be so kind as to table this discussion for another day?"

Godrin's companions hastily rose and bowed deeply. "We live to serve, Your Majesty," they echoed.

After a moment, Godrin stood with a hiss. "Tomorrow, Your Majesty."

The king returned an appreciative nod and the lords filed from the room. Jonny closed the door behind them.

"That was rude of you to interrupt, Jonny." His tone made Jonny shiver.

"It was rude of you not to meet us on our return."

"I did not know of your coming."

"Lies," Jonny spat. "You always know everything."

"Many things. Not everything." He pointed to the fire crackling in the hearth. "I know that without more wood, that fire will burn out. And without the fire, this room will grow cold. I know without wood, the fire will be gone by morning. But I do not know the exact moment the last spark will wither. Just the same, I knew you would return. I did not know when."

A wave of embarrassment came over Jonny, but he was too far in the hole to show it. With a puff of annoyance, he sank into one of the chairs opposite the king. "And did you know what I would find in the Vale of Joy?"

"I had theories. Many and more." Swarlar leaned back in his chair. "Why would you barge in here without permission? You know I always make time for you."

Another pang of guilt, but Jonny pressed on. "Don't dodge my questions."

"I am not; I answered your question. You dodged mine. You interrupted my meeting without permission. Do you know how many lords there are in the realm?"

Jonny knew there were eight great houses, but each had many vassal lords. *A hundred? More?* He shrugged.

"Keeping this realm from tearing itself apart is a time-consuming matter. As I said, I will always make time for you. But I ask that, in the future, you remember that you are one piece of this puzzle. An important piece, but *one* piece."

Jonny's eyes fell to the floor.

"Did you find the trolls?"

Jonny nodded. "They ambushed us in the mountains. We defeated them handedly."

"How many men did you lose?"

"Sixteen to the trolls."

Swarlar sighed. "Make sure you get me a list of their names." He turned his gaze to the window. "I'll see to it their families are provided for."

"What worries me more is the two I lost to the Vale of Joy."

Swarlar's eyes flicked back to Jonny. "They entered the lake?"

"You knew? And you didn't tell me?!" Jonny struggled not to shout.

"I did not think it would kill." A mournful tone echoed in his words.

Jonny jumped to his feet, sending his chair toppling back. "And just what *did* you think we would find?!"

The king did not flinch at Jonny's tone. "A lake . . . and next to it a stone fountain filled with water. And had you stuck your hand in that fountain, you would have been happy—the happiest you have ever dreamed. And had someone touched the water of the lake, they would have been sad, so very consumed with sorrow that they would have cried out in despair. They would not have wanted to go in any deeper."

Jonny scowled and turned to pace the room. "I saw the fountain. What the hell are you talking about?"

"The druids, as you know, are guardians of Old Magic. Gerald, Rard's brother, was one of the last, and his oath was to watch the Vale of Joy and the magic woven into its essence."

"I figured that much out myself, thank you very much," Jonny snapped.

"A long time ago, some wizard," Swarlar started, "bound the magic of the Vale to the fountain." Jonny recalled the thickness of the air around the stone structure. "The water in the fountain would suck away all one's unhappiness," the king continued, "leaving behind only joy and merriment. But all that grief and suffering needed a place to go. And so, with the same spell, the lake turned into a reservoir of sorrow."

Fixed on Swarlar's story, Jonny stopped pacing. "Is that possible?" he asked, though he knew the answer.

"From across the realm, the poor and destitute flooded to the Vale of Joy. Heartbroken lovers, grieving mothers, slighted brothers . . . they all came and plunged their hands into the fountain. Their pain and sadness lifted, leaving them to return home with light hearts. And all the while, the lake swallowed their sadness whole."

"How come not a single one of my men had ever heard of it?"

"The journey was too far for many to make, and local lords taxed the mountain roads to the valley. Still, it was always there, an oasis of elation for the pained. But then came the fall of the Keepers of the Cup and the black years of Darvor the Elder. When the Cup was finally sealed away within Sliok, the ancients sought to bury all knowledge of Old Magic. Only with Old Magic could someone enter the caves and find the Cup. And they were determined not to let that happen. So the druids went into hiding and the leaders of men swept Old Magic from the histories. They brushed it into the corners of the realm, into nameless crypts and blank places on the map. Old Magic retreated into legends, and with it, the Vale of Joy faded from memory."

"So when those men went into the lake . . ." Jonny mumbled with a growing sense of horror.

Swarlar nodded. "Had they slipped only their toe in to test the water, they would have grown despondent and cried. But they would have been unharmed after a few moments. If they went in too deep, too quickly . . ." A pained expression washed across the king's face. "All that pain and rage and agony would have flooded them."

Jonny clapped a hand over his gaping mouth. His knees grew weak.

"Had they touched the water in the fountain in time . . . maybe."

"Except, the fountain was empty," Jonny said.

Swarlar leaned forward and narrowed his eyes. "Impossible."

Jonny shook his head.

"It couldn't be empty. That was part of the spell. There are records of bandits and good-for-nothings who tried to steal a cup of water from the fountain. By the time they reached the steps, their cups were empty and the water back in the fountain. The fountain always had water."

"Then the spell was undone," Jonny snorted, his anger returning.

"That's not possible."

"I saw it with my eyes! The fountain was dry. And two men are dead because you didn't tell me what was really in the Vale of Joy!" Jonny turned and stormed from the room, slamming the door hard enough to cause a decorative shield to clatter off the wall and bounce down the hall.

He was out the palace gates and halfway across King's Square before he had processed everything Swarlar had said. His stomach churned when he thought about the last moments of the two men who had gone into the lake, thrown into a bottomless pit of despair. He could think of no worse fate. He clenched his fists and swallowed back the thought. Despite his best efforts, he knew some part of the ordeal would stay with him. He could hold onto the memory and the disdain for his indecisiveness, but the regret and anger would do him no good. *Let the rest go,* he reminded himself.

Leaving the large square behind, he started down one of the broad avenues that linked the five hills of the city. Ahead, looming on the adjacent hill, was the formidable barracks of the Guards of Gluton, and sprawling around it were the quarters for enlisted troops in the king's army. Unlike the spacious and polished rooms of the Guards, the common troops were given cramped, simple rooms in long dormitories. Lining the lower limits of the military hilltop were pubs and comfort houses where idle soldiers squandered their earnings.

Jonny turned down one of the winding side alleys and pressed his way through the bustle of people. The air was filled with the din of smith's hammers, the squeals of butchers' victims, and the ballads of drunken soldiers, but Jonny's mind pushed back the noise in favor of the earliest hatchings of a bold plan.

He found Alyk exactly where he expected—in a dim tavern at the end of a narrow alley. It was no coincidence; Alyk had often boasted of that particular tavern's mead on their journey, saying it was always the first place he went upon returning to Gluton. Still, Jonny was relieved the search had been as easy.

The archer sat at a small table, nestled in a smoky corner of the noisy room, surrounded by three pretty girls and two who wished they were. His green eyes ate up the room's firelight as he spoke, and from his animated gestures, Jonny knew whatever story he told was embellished. The girls leaned forward, sighing and cooing with each turn of the tale.

". . . they wasted no time coming for us. Ten . . . twenty . . . thirty . . ." His eyes met Jonny. "Jonny, my good man—come!" He gently shooed back one of the pretty girls and offered her seat to Jonny. Motioning for the bartender to bring another round, Alyk pulled Jonny into the open seat. "Ladies, here's the fire-spinner himself."

Jonny flashed his friend an angry look. *He's telling everyone.*

The girls laughed. "I thought he'd be taller," one said.

Blood rose in Jonny's cheeks. He turned to Alyk. "Can we talk . . . in private?"

A hint of confusion blinked across Alyk's face, but he turned to the girls with an easy smile. "Ladies, if you would be so kind . . . perhaps another time."

He waved away their protests and returned his focus to Jonny. "That was quick. I thought you'd be at the palace all day. I only just got my first pint." He lifted a wooden mug and inhaled deeply.

"You shouldn't be telling everyone," Jonny said in a hushed tone.

"Two hundred men saw your magic. They'll be spending the night in pubs and pillow houses across the city. By this time tomorrow, the whole city will have heard about Jonny the fire-wielder. And I'll bet almost a quarter of them believe it."

"I know. Doesn't mean you have to help it spread," he replied.

The bartender dropped a mug of mead in front of Jonny and held out a hand. Jonny produced the appropriate coin and the bartender departed. "You know, I've never actually had this stuff." He eyed the chestnut brown liquid.

"No?"

"Where I come from, I'm not allowed. I'm not old enough." He took a sip and sputtered as it burned his throat.

"I guess it's not for everyone," Alyk said with a shrug. "Did you talk to the king?"

"Yeah." Jonny set down the mug. "That's what we need to talk about."

Alyk reached across and claimed Jonny's mug. "Well, I've got two full pints here. I say you start talking, and I start drinking," he said with a wink.

After a moment to gather his thoughts, Jonny began. The words tumbled freely, and Alyk was a receptive audience. The archer nodded with understanding, only talking to clarify some minor detail. Jonny wove the story from its beginning, speaking about the Cup and its destruction, Sliok's depths, Darvor's ire, and his dragon necklace. He turned the tale to the Vale of Joy and Gerald's return, and finally, as Alyk finished off the second pint, Jonny repeated the magic of the fountain.

Alyk chased a drop of mead from his chin with the back of his hand. "So that's why you're called Cupbreaker?"

"Why'd you think I was called that?"

Alyk shook his head. "Clumsy hands, I suppose."

Jonny laughed. "No, not that simple." He looked around the tavern. Guests were starting to fill in the empty tables as nightfall settled over the city. "This fountain has me worried."

"Because it ran dry?"

"Yes and no." Jonny scratched at the fuzz on his chin. "Swarlar didn't know the fountain was empty. Gerald would have told him if it was. So, I think it was emptied after Gerald fled the Vale. And there is the matter of the spell that wouldn't let it run dry. No, I think Darvor is behind this. He didn't die during the War of the Three Armies—he just retreated to wherever it is he goes. This has his name written all over it. Think about it: The first time that trolls venture beyond their borders in seven years and they coincidentally attack a forgotten valley in the mountains containing one of the last remnants of Old Magic? No . . . I don't believe it. He's up to something. And this time, we don't have the magic in this necklace to save us if we lose." He tapped the pendant at his neck, recalling how the magic stored within had saved Guard Tower Island from the troll attack.

Alyk looked away. "A month ago, if you walked in here talking about magic and cursed fountains and evil lords, I would've thought you had a taste of bad spittle juice. But I felt the air in the valley, I saw the look in Marten's eyes when we pulled him from that lake . . . I was convinced before I ever saw your magic." He grimaced. "What do you want to do?"

"I'm not sure yet." Jonny drummed his fingers on the table. "If we sit back and do nothing, Darvor will spin his webs. We have to disrupt his plans . . . we have to take the fight to him."

"You said Darvor was too strong."

"He was last time, but I'm stronger now. So much stronger. I spent the last seven years training. I can do so much with my magic. I can stop him if I get the chance."

Alyk chewed on Jonny's words for a moment. "Then we should talk to Swarlar. See what his plan is."

Jonny sighed and slumped back in the chair. "I know what his thoughts will be. He'll think it's foolish—that it can't be done. He won't believe in me. Even if he agrees that Darvor is behind this, he won't want to act. Not until we know what Darvor's plan is."

"But by then it could be too late."

"Exactly," Jonny agreed.

A silence fell over them.

"We could do it without Swarlar."

"What do you mean?" Alyk asked.

"Even if I can't defeat Darvor, we just have to disrupt his plans. And if we can get some help, we might be able to do that without the king's aid . . . or permission."

Alyk leaned forward. "Go on."

"How loyal do you think those men we took to the Vale of Joy are?"

"After they saw you conjure that fire, they think you're a hero stepped right out of legend. They'll follow you anywhere."

"Then we call them back," Jonny continued. "We call them to arms again and we head east, to the land of the trolls. They'll outnumber us, but if we play our cards right and stay out of a fair fight, we can disrupt whatever Darvor is planning."

Alyk grinned. "I have a better idea. Do you know where that soldier called the Hammer of Dorndale is from?"

"Dorndale?" Jonny eyed his friend.

"And where is Dorndale? I've got no idea. And I know every town from here to Lanak. And Davinnof—his father is the lord of a small tract of land in the westerlands. Josten is from the highlands by Tommdale Castle, and each one of the men named Marten is from a different village around Gluton. My point is, all the men Swarlar put under your command came from different corners of the realm. They all saw what I saw . . . they believe. Send them back to their homes to recruit others. If each one of them comes back with a few friends, we'll have ourselves a thousand men." Alyk's excitement grew with each word. "While they're recruiting, you and I can do the same. With any luck, we'll have ourselves a whole army!" He threw his hands wide. "For hundreds of years, we've defended our lands from the trolls. It's time we take the fight to them. It's time they fear *us*!"

Jonny wanted to applaud. The plan was good. Alyk's charismatic pitch had added to the appeal, but even on its own legs, the scheme rang solid. "Tomorrow morning, I'll talk to King Swarlar. If he wants us to do nothing, like I expect, then we go with our idea. If he has a better strategy, we'll listen."

Alyk clapped his hands together and motioned for the bartender. "Well, Jonny . . . we're gonna change the world."

PERMISSION OR FORGIVENESS

Under a grim morning sky, two hundred riders rode from the gates of Gluton. Most were men who had served under Jonny's command, but some were new—trusted friends and comrades. To the four corners of the realm they rode, scattered by the winds of change. They carried with them letters for their local lords and supplies for long journeys. What they did not have was the permission of the king.

Jonny had tried, as he told Alyk he would, but the king was of a different mind than the young men. Three days earlier, after hashing out the details of their plan, Jonny had departed to speak with King Swarlar. He found the king in the royal study, bent over a mound of scrolls.

"Darvor is behind this. I can feel it," Jonny had said.

"It's possible," the king replied. "In fact, I think it's quite likely."

"What are you gonna do about it?" Jonny asked.

"Gather more information," the king said, gesturing at the yellowed parchment before him. "Lord Corben Larthan, the third so named, was a brilliant record keeper. During his eighty-four long years, he amassed a most valuable account of the eastern reaches of the Hillan lands, including the Vale of Joy."

"Have you found anything?" Jonny pressed.

"Not as of yet," Swarlar answered. "Perhaps with time. But until we have more understanding, we cannot act."

Just as I suspected . . .

The king straightened and fixed his gaze on Jonny. "He is like the wild wind. Until we know from which way he will blow, we cannot set our sail against him. Of itself, the water in the fountain is harmless, but if he unbound an ancient spell, it is for a reason." His eyes traveled to the window and settled on the distant horizon. "For seven years, the pieces on the gameboard have sat idle, gathering dust. Now one moves. We must know to what end."

"Why wait to see what his next move is?" Jonny asked, careful not to overstep his bounds. "We can take the fight to him, disrupt whatever plans he has."

Swarlar offered Jonny a tired smile. "We know too little. We are not even certain he is behind this. Why condemn hundreds or thousands to die based on nothing more than the shadows of a shadow? And there is, of course, the possibility that any move against him now would be just as he wishes."

"That's your plan, then?" Jonny was stone-faced.

"Aye, we wait . . . and we learn." The king drove a bony finger into the stack of scrolls.

Jonny had not wished to press the issue any further—it would be both useless and risk endangering his own plans—and so he left the king to his scrolls.

In the back room of a blacksmith's shop, he gathered his surviving lieutenants, along with Alyk, Josten, and a few other close confidantes. There, they scripted their stratagems. The soldiers under Jonny's command and a few trusted others brought into the fold would depart for their own farms, halls, and villages to recruit what volunteers they could muster. Those who answered the call would meet near Gluton after the first planting of the spring. By the solstice, they would march on the lands of the trolls.

Jonny penned letters to local lords, great and small, to be carried by the soldiers-turned-messengers. Although he expected most of the levees to come from commoners and peasant volunteers in search of glory, the support of whatever noble house could be had would prove an immense help. The nobility, he knew, could force their serfs and subjects to enlist, and could provide needed weapons and food. *Help us end the scourge of trolls upon this realm,* he wrote again and again.

Though not illegal in any formal definition, Jonny knew that such a plan would not stand if it rose to the ears of the king or the reigning house of Gluton, the Voramandiers. The possibility of several thousand armed men descending on the lands around Gluton would terrify the Voramandiers; if the army were to go awry, havoc would eat through the countryside. And Swarlar had already dismissed any action.

Once beyond the city walls, Jonny hoped the call to arms would spread like a spark through a dry wheat field. At that point, he told the others, it would be too late for Godrin Voramandier or the king to stop the movement. And so, while the plot remained a vulnerable hatchling in the backroom of a blacksmith's shop, Jonny had urged secrecy of his co-conspirators. "It is better to ask forgiveness than permission with something like this," he beseeched them.

Their secrecy held, and in the cold hours of an autumn morning, the riders filed from the city unhindered. To the westerlands rode Davinnof and a dozen others to rally their countrymen and muster the vaunted cavalry of the western marks. Toward the mountains of House Hillan rode Josten and other highlanders. Lyam went south to Mountainstream's fields, Thom east to Guard Tower and the island above which it loomed. To Tommdale Castle, Dorndale, Estermont, Britshall, Miller's Ford, and the Islands of the Teeth men went. And to a hundred other places great and small, the men scattered, and with them went a single message: The end of the trolls is nigh—we march at the summer's solstice.

Wishing to ensure his messengers were sent off without issue, Jonny was the last to leave, lingering beneath the gates. With him waited Alyk. The two planned to venture south together until they reached the borders of the Great Forest. From there, Alyk would continue to Lanak; he had known Lord Groy in the years before he came to Gluton and could help bring the Lanaki to their cause. Jonny, meanwhile, would turn east, into the Forest. Few of his men hailed from the Forest, and recruiting the Forest Folk would be daunting. The Forest lords were infamously reserved about matters beyond their trees. If Jonny hoped to marshal their aid, it would take a personal touch.

"So far, so good," Jonny mumbled, watching the last cluster of riders leave. The pair started off, passing the farmers and merchants driving their carts into Gluton before the markets stirred. Jonny looked to the east, where the rising sun struggled against the thick clouds. "I hope we make it south of the mountains before the winter snows really start."

"Aye, we'll take the road by the shores of the Great Bay—it'll be mild enough," Alyk replied.

"Jonny?" An unexpected voice halted the pair in their tracks.

Jonny twisted in his saddle to look back at the hooded rider they just passed. "Cazar?" he stammered.

Dropping his hood, Cazar returned a warm, albeit confused, smile. "I thought that was your voice I heard." The Guard urged his palfrey toward Jonny, and the two shook hands. "And who do we have here?" He offered a hand to Alyk.

"This is Alyk, son of Alyn," Jonny said. "Alyk, this is Cazar, son of Aazar, brother of Bazar, captain of the Guards of Gluton—"

"Former captain," Cazar corrected. "Retired now."

"What are you doing here so early?" Jonny asked. "The sun is barely up."

"I'm making my way to the Guard's barracks to spend a few days drilling the newest Guards. They too often think their training ends when they graduate from the Academy. And the harvest was good this year, so Delena and the farm can spare me for a fortnight or two." His steely eyes narrowed. "I can ask the same of you?"

Jonny knew the question was coming, but it gave him pause all the same. A lie would not stand, he knew. And so, with a breath, he recounted the recent developments. Alyk looked to the ground but kept silent.

Cazar's face darkened as the boy spoke. When Jonny finished, the Guard ran a hand through his hair as though he hoped to find the right words among the black locks. At last, he replied, "Well, I can't say I like the plan. In fact, I think it's altogether a horrible idea. But the bridge is burnt, and the ashes scattered; there's no going back now."

"You're not going to try to stop us?" Jonny asked, suppressing his surprise.

"I would that I could. But my efforts would be useless now. Your messengers have already scattered. Were we to try to stop them now, people would still arrive at Gluton in search of a war. There would be problems all the same. You've dug your grave; all I can do is make sure it's deep enough." He looked over his shoulder at Gluton's looming walls. "Go ahead, rally what men you can. I'll go to His Majesty and do what I can to smooth this out. I'll use the winter months to set matters ready."

Alyk looked up with a grin. "You are too kind."

Cazar scowled. "I'd wager you haven't spent half the time it takes to empty your bladder planning for what comes after the realm answers your call. There will be much work to do before spring. But if you are to do it, I must see it done right." He leaned in the saddle to rest a hand on Jonny's shoulder and locked the boy's eyes in his own. "Promise me, Jonny. If too few men answer your call, you'll abandon this folly. Anything less than victory could spell our doom."

Jonny returned a solemn nod. "I promise. I'll see you when the first flowers bloom."

With the winter winds at their back, Jonny and Alyk pressed south. They traveled by way of the king's road through the fertile lands south of Gluton and along the shores of the Great Bay, steering well clear of the Lost Lands. The road was not paved, and except for segments that ran through small towns or villages, most of the "road" was little more than cart tracks carved into the mud. But it was the safest and easiest route of travel between the north and south of the realm, and as such, regular traffic kept the road clear and smooth.

They never came within a league of the Lost Lands, but Jonny found himself recalling his prior adventures in those craggy wastelands. Among the shale and thistle of that wilderness, he had met Delena and the man-giant Rard. Many years had lapsed since, but the memories returned, fresh and vivid.

So many things were different than that first journey. Before, he had been a child in every sense of the word, filled with all the fear and wonder of youth. He had been treated like a baby, a burden, and a bore. But the years had done what only time could. Layered in experiences, he was stronger, wiser, and more confident. Where once he had been tepid and afraid, now he was calling forth an army. *I wonder if the "old me" would even recognize me now.*

But as much as things had changed, much was still timeless. The long hours on horseback still drained him, leaving him sore and chafed. Sleeping under the stars remained both unsettling and exhilarating. And, despite his best efforts, his mind still often returned to thoughts of home.

Though only gone for a few weeks, his heart ached at the absence of his family. His last look at his parents, their faces etched in fear and confusion as he slipped into the cave, burned in his mind. Time, he hoped, would remain frozen in his home world like last time. *But what if I never return?* He had set himself down a dangerous path, for at the end would lie Darvor. And although he boasted to Alyk that he could defeat the Oathbreaker's son, some part of him knew that was far from certain. He hoped that before he finally came to face Darvor, Swarlar would come to his side. *Darvor can't stand against the both of us.*

As the pair moved further south, they left the shores of the Great Bay behind and entered the southern marches near Mountainstream. The days were filled with riding, the nights with easy conversation and campfires. Alyk spoke often of his past. Like any good Lanaki, he had learned to swim at an early age, and by the time he was six, he could pull an oar and cast a net. After the death of his family, he found employ in the service of House Groy and distinguished himself with a bow. Whether the adventure was hunting rabid *grevices* in the borderlands or courting the maids of Lanak, he made the story live and left Jonny laughing in fits every night.

Jonny returned Alyk's tales with exploits of his own, recounting his many adventures during his previous quests. But he left the rest of his life vague and skirted away from questions about his home. Alyk had embraced his magic and the existence of Darvor, but Jonny feared his reaction to talk of other worlds. *There is only so much a person can believe.*

In between stories, Jonny would entertain them with shows of magic. Their campfires would dance at his bidding and take on the shape of fantastic beasts and monstrous creatures. Though he did not pretend to understand the powers, he had grown adept at controlling them. Whereas the talents had first bubbled up from the depth of his heart in moments of great need, he could now summon and control them with the ease of calling words from his tongue.

They passed several towns and farms as they neared Mountainstream, and although they entertained the idea of recruiting as they went, the pair decided against it. As Alyk stated, "Imagine a stranger riding into your town or knocking on your door and asking you to abandon your farm, crops, animals, and family to travel half a world away to fight, bleed, and potentially die in the name of some young man with magical abilities. You'd be lucky if you didn't get the door slammed in your face." Instead, Alyk would go to Lanak to petition Lord Groy and engage his contacts there. Meanwhile, Jonny would go straight to the lords of the Forest and win them over with shows of magic.

The dragons, they discussed one night, would have been a welcome addition to their cause. But Jonny knew that any effort to bring them to help would only be wasted. Ancient and mysterious as they were, the dragons were aloof to much that transpired in the human realms. Though they had sided with mankind during Jonny's previous adventure in the world, their alliance was tenuous at best. They had only ever helped to defend humans from trolls, and only when their elders felt generous, or their nesting grounds were threatened. *No, we do this alone.*

The miles fell away in a blur, and south of Mountainstream, the pair arrived at a fork in the road. Among green meadows and freshly bound sheaves of wheat, the country lane split, diving to the south or snaking to the east and the distant forests.

"This is where we part ways, Cupbreaker," Alyk said. He stretched a finger toward the horizon. "This trail will lead you to the Lake Road and, from there, through the woods to the shores of the Small Lake. With any luck, you won't have much trouble chartering a vessel to take you downstream to Arborton and the City of the Forest Folk."

"It's been a pleasure sharing the road with you," Jonny replied.

Alyk smirked. "Don't get sappy with me. I'll see you in the spring, marching up the road at the head of a great Lanaki host. I'll deliver your men. Make sure you do the same."

"I will." Jonny nodded, though he knew it was far from a certainty. The one awaiting him in the Great Forest, he knew, would be the hardest of hearts to turn to his cause. Still, he donned a grin and added, "I'll wager you a pint of highland sweet ale that I get more men than you."

Alyk recoiled in surprised amusement. "You know the lakelands have five to one more people than the Forest Folk?"

Jonny laughed. "I did not."

"I'd be a fool not to take your bet," Alyk said, spurring his horse down the road. As Jonny turned his own horse toward the forest, the archer stopped. Without turning, he spoke. "It's a funny thing, a fork in the road. You must always choose one path and leave the other. You can't have both, and you can't ever really know where it's going to lead you. There was a moment, back at the tavern in Gluton, where we were at a fork in the road. We chose a path and set ourselves on it." He glanced over his shoulder at Jonny. "I wonder what will be left of us when all this is over."

Without another word, he rode into the distance.

A Call to Arms

Jonny sat on the edge of the crowded town square, perched on the gnarled roots of an immense oak tree. With little event, he had traversed the western reaches of the Great Forest by way of the Lake Road. In the small fishing village at the terminus of the Lake Road, he had tried to win some swords to his cause before securing passage on a broad-hulled barge headed downstream to Arborton. Despite a rousing speech and impressive displays of fire magic, the lord of the village, Lord Greanlay, had refused to pledge him any men. A few ruffians from the village tavern agreed to join his cause, but Jonny doubted whether they would be present in Gluton the following spring. Two other fishing villages the barge had called on had not yielded better harvests. The string of failures had soured Jonny's mood. He had thought it would be easier to recruit an army. Hopefully, Alyk and the others were having more luck.

He readjusted his seat, trying unsuccessfully to find a comfortable position on the twisted roots. The night before, he had arrived in Arborton, where the truest test would lie. A bustling town nestled at the outlet of the Small Lake, it had long been the seat of House Arimor, an upjumped vassal of House Arthrin. And, as Jonny knew, whether he could garner the support of the Forest Folk rested entirely on how Arborton responded.

The Arthrin family ruled as high lords of the Forest Folk, and all other nobles were pledged to them. House Arthrin officially ruled from their palatial home of Willow-water in the City of the Forest Folk, but as Jonny had been forewarned, much had changed since his last journey to these lands. Lord Lendon Arthrin had died young under mysterious circumstances, leaving the lordship to fall to his only son, Brenton. As Brenton was only a child, Lord Lendon's wife, Lady Arthrin, assumed the regency to rule the forest lands until young Brenton assumed his maturity. Rumors ran rampant that Lady Arthrin had been behind Lord Arthrin's untimely demise. Poison, men had whispered as Lady Arthrin moved her household back to her father's home in Arborton. *I have no trouble believing that.* Jonny recalled the cold welcome and attempted imprisonment he and his former companions had suffered at Lady Arthrin's hands.

Despite the rumors, Lady Arthrin held the key to the Forest lords, so Jonny wasted no time seeking her out. The barge had arrived at Arborton's port late, but as soon as the sun had risen, Jonny presented himself to Longleef, the home of House Arimor, in search of an audience with the Lady-regent.

The castle was built from carved white stone, lined and loomed in thick oaks. Set on a low hill that commanded a view of the whole town, the keep's great hall was hemmed by two polished towers, gleaming in the morning sun. *White as bone,* Jonny had mused, marveling at the twin spires. *Not a good sign . . .*

He was turned away at the gate after being told by the guards that the lady would hold court after the midday meal. Although he considered flashing his magic to gain an earlier meeting, he knew that would do him no good. After fending off his hunger with a loaf of butterbread from a nearby bakery, he settled into the roots of a massive oak tree overlooking the town's square to wait.

His entertainment was provided by the preacher, who had filled the square with an audience. A wide, grassy plot, the square was lined with looming trees. And between the encircling trees, several hundred had crowded. Most were the poor and destitute, Jonny surmised. Street children and beggars, drawn by the preacher's promise of divine blessing. But others had gathered too: Merchants, fishermen, hunters, and shopkeeps jammed into the plaza, craning for a better view.

Jonny's perch atop the tangled roots afforded him a chosen view, close enough to hear the whole sermon. At first intrigued, Jonny quickly came to understand why so many had gathered. The Forest Folk followed a different religion than the rest of the realm, worshipping the countless gods of nature over the one Creator. But the preacher represented the faith of the one god.

Here, in the depths of the Great Forest, few people had any interaction with outsiders, and so they gathered more out of idle curiosity than any religious fervor. But the traveling priest did not let that slow him. ". . . and just as the Seven Scrolls say," the man shouted over the murmur of the crowd, "only the pure of heart can hope to see the richness of the Eternal Fields."

Jonny tore off another bite from his butterbread. *How long until Lady Arthrin's soldiers come to chase off this missionary?* Although the preacher's sermon was not strictly illegal, he had no doubt the commotion was undesirable for the local leaders.

"But I come to you this day, not to speak to you on the words of dusty books and old men," the preacher continued. "Whether it is your shamans of the forest or the priests of the Creator spouting lofty words from their gilded chapels, anyone who tries to keep the divine world wrapped in mystery does so for their own benefit and glory. Not for *yours*!"

He pointed into the crowd. "Allow me then to make plain the powers of man as the Seven Scrolls do say. In the dawn age, when the Creator called forth man from the mud of the earth and the wind of the air and the salt of the sea, He gifted . . . and bound us . . . with certain powers."

"That's not how people were made," someone shouted from the back of the square. "We grew from the branches of the great spirit-tree!"

The preacher continued undaunted. "There is, of course, the first power, that power which we cannot do without, without which we are not alive, and without which we cease to exist. Love." He lingered on the word. "Not a soul walking this earth is free of this power. It may be buried so deep that even he or she knows not its existence. But this power alone, the Creator bound to the soul of all mankind . . . It is our greatest gift or our greatest burden. Whether we will it or not."

The preacher's charisma was winning over the crowd, and the heckling yielded to attentive silence.

"He then imparted on us countless powers, both good and ill. The power to sing, laugh, and dance. Climb mountains and swim rivers. The power to cook tasty food . . . brew strong ale . . ." Several men let out hoots of agreement. "Even woo pretty girls." He pointed at a throng of young men in the front and gave a playful wink. Jonny joined the crowd in a laugh.

"And then there are those powers he offered us, but with guidance to never use. The ability to hurt each other. To steal, insult, lie . . . to murder." His eyes grew dark. "We have the power to make each other cry and scream. But to not use these powers is our test. It is how we will be judged at the end of times."

The priest lowered his voice and the crowd leaned forward. "But there are other powers too. For on the other side of the river of our being, the Creator set the Forbidden Powers . . . those wondrous powers that belong to the Almighty only. Immortality and Resurrection. No prayer or spell will ever grant us these. Not even the fabled Cup of Power could do that."

The once-existent Cup of Power. Jonny stifled a grin. Few knew the Cup had been destroyed, and most people believed the ancient artifact was still lost to the depths of Sliok.

"Why, you ask? Why out of all that we can do . . . why these? Wiser men than I have spent their lives arguing it, so I cannot promise you the truest answer. But I can offer you my opinion, the humble opinion of a poor believer in His divine wonders." The preacher looked to the heavens. "We are afraid. Afraid to die, afraid to lose those we love. Afraid to be so small a part in something so big. Were it up to us, we would seek these powers more than anything. More than life, more than love. And we would lose sight of all else. The Creator has made a wondrous place for us beyond this life, and when it is our time, we must answer the call with faith, not cling to this life desperately like a castaway to the remains of his ship. And when our loved ones must pass beyond the veil of life, we should celebrate them, not bend ourselves to bringing them back."

Jonny scanned the crowd and marveled at their rapt attention. *He can turn an audience. I need some of his oratorical skills.* At the corner of the square, he noticed a commotion. A dozen guardsman were filing in, pushing their way through the crowd.

"Consider for a moment," the preacher pressed on despite the growing clamor. "What if the Forbidden Powers were not actually forbidden so much as lost?"

The soldiers reached the preacher. The old, frail man yielded without protest and was dragged from the square. Without the flow of the sermon, the audience snapped from their entrancement and slowly scattered.

Jonny, too, stretched and reminded himself why he had come. Throwing the last of his bread to the squirrels, he looked to the sky.

"Noon already?" he sputtered, surprised at the sun's high stance.

Leaving the square behind, he scurried through the narrow streets up the hill to Longleef. The castle gates were open, and a small crowd filed across the yard and into the hold. Jonny fell into line and was swept into the great hall.

Impressively arrayed, the hall reflected the might of the Arimor family. Two hundred people gathered in the chamber, but twice as many could fit with ease. Gilded tapestries and polished statues lined the walls while crystalline hangings scattered the sunlight that filtered through stained windows. But most impressive of all was the ceiling. At first, he mistook the room for having no ceiling but realized with wonder that it was an ornate illusion. The thick oaken columns that supported the roof were carved to look like tree trunks, and the ceiling was fashioned into a canopy of tangled branches and fawning leaves. The elegant artwork was indistinguishable from the forest pressing on the edges of the town.

Sitting in the smooth ebony chair at the far end of the room was Lady Arthrin. Years before, Lord Lendon Arthrin had named her a crone when talking with Jonny and his companions, but her appearance was nothing of the sort. She was tall and slender and beautiful as black ice. Her regal posture ate the room's sunlight and spat it back on those gathered before her. But even when her gaze shifted, Jonny could see the light never touched her eyes.

The boy slid into the corner to watch the proceedings from the shadows. He had rehearsed it in his mind; when the last of the crowd had spoken and the lady was preparing to adjourn court for the day, he would step forward. His stomach churned at the thought. Although he was not in any physical danger—his magic could protect him—if he did not bring the Arthrin and Arimor families to his cause, the Forest would be lost to him. The Forest Folk were among the most revered warriors in the kingdom, and without their support, his army might not have the necessary strength.

As he watched, the crowd came forward to present themselves to the Lady-regent. The lords of the realm presided over their tracts of land in different manners, but all held court in some fashion. During such times, the lords' subjects could come and present their grievances and receive judgment. Lesser nobles' days were filled with settling the disputes of their commoners and peasants. As the Arthrins were the high lords of the Forest, they also presided over the disputes of their vassals and lesser lords. In turn, if the Arthrins took issue with another high lord, the matter would fall to King Swarlar to settle.

Although a handful of lesser lords and lordlings were present, most of those gathered were townspeople of Arborton. The nobility went first, squabbling over a new tax on turnips or the ownership of a sacred grove of birch trees. Once Lady Arthrin had heard her fill, she passed down her rulings and the nobles scampered to the periphery.

A dozen commoners took their turns next. Some petitioned for brewing permits, others for the right to hunt a region of forest. There were disputes over dowries, stolen chickens, and soured wine. One man argued his wife be set aside for infidelity, another that he be allowed to marry twins "because they're truly the same person." A thief was sentenced to lose his fingers for stealing bread, and a drunkard's son was awarded to a childless miller and his wife.

Less than half the crowd had brought forth their affairs when a gaggle of guards emerged from a side door. They led a frail man with wizened hair, bound in chains. Jonny recognized him at once as the preacher from the square.

"My lady," the attendant announced, "this man stands accused of heresy." The preacher grew small under Lady Arthrin's piercing blue eyes. He held his chin high as the charges were read against him, but even from afar, Jonny spied the man's lip quivering.

"How do you plead?" the lady asked.

"The only judgment that concerns me is that of the Most High," the preacher spat, though his shaking hands belied his defiance.

"Then the only question is your punishment." She ran a finger through her golden hair.

Jonny straightened. From the glint in her eye, he knew what the punishment would be. He recalled how fiercely she had espoused the faith of her many gods when they met on his last quest. The timing was all wrong, but he knew he had to act.

"With the gods as my witness, you are sentenced—"

"Let the man go," Jonny shouted, stepping forward.

The hall went quiet and those in front of him stepped aside.

"Excuse me?" the lady replied. One of the guards loosened his sword.

"Under the king's law, heresy is no crime. Everyone is free to worship the faith they choose."

"That is true." The woman's eyes flashed. "The charge of heresy is hereby dropped. He is, however, guilty of gathering a crowd without a permit. My master-at-arms claims more than two hundred people attended this unauthorized sermon."

The preacher gulped. "'Twas but a hundred, m'lady."

"Very well, a hundred. A hundred lashes upon the back." She nodded to the guards, and they approached the man to drag him from the room.

The blood drained from Jonny's face. That many lashes would kill the man. And it would be far worse a death than had his head been taken off by the executioner. *It's my fault,* Jonny realized. *I can't let that happen.* But he was no lawyer, and anything he said might just make matters worse.

The preacher finally broke and let out a frightened cry.

There must be another way. Jonny closed his eyes and sighed. "Wait!" he shouted again.

A hushed whisper stirred the hall and the eyes of the crowd fell on the boy. Lady Arthrin's gaze was the heaviest. "What is this?"

Jonny strode to the center of the room with a searing purpose. "If you are such a god-fearing woman, then let the gods settle this matter. If they bless the sword of your strongest champion to strike me down, this man is guilty of all the charges leveled against him and worst ones still. But if the gods do not permit your champion to strike me down, this man goes free and unharmed."

Lady Arthrin leaned back in her chair and pinched her chin. "As you stand before us now . . . against my champion. No tricks?"

Jonny spread his arms wide and slowly turned a circle for all to see. "As I am. Here and now." He carried no weapons and knew that his physique was not in the least fearsome.

The woman looked to her lords-attendant, and they returned uncertain expressions. With a cool shrug, she waved her approval. An excited murmur ran through the crowd like wildfire.

As space was cleared in front of the dais, Jonny approached the preacher and fixed him with a reassuring wink.

"I'm not so sure about this," the preacher mumbled. "You couldn't have at least asked for a knife?"

Jonny laughed and bent to tighten his boots.

The man Lady Arthrin chose was an imposing warrior, six and half feet tall with a shaved head and polished black-steel armor. The man's only eye surveyed Jonny for a long moment before he donned his feathered helmet.

As the man slowly unsheathed his broadsword, Jonny rolled his shoulders around and shook out his fingers. *Old me would have fainted at the thought,* he mused.

Lady Arthrin let the nervous mumblings of the crowd build to a frenzied roar. "Begin." Her voice split the tension like cracked ice.

With a shout, the man charged like a bull. Jonny raised a hand and breathed in deep. Like a bow being drawn, he pulled in his energy. The man had closed half the distance, bearing down with his sword raised. Jonny loosed the spell from his palm and fire snapped through the air.

The warrior's momentum carried him forward even as the flames wrapped white-hot around his blade. By the time the sword slashed down on Jonny, it was nothing but a hilt. A trail of red, boiling lumps of liquid steel traced the man's charge. Jonny stepped aside to avoid his opponent, who tumbled through the air and fell to the ground with a crash.

The crowd was silent. Somewhere in the back, a woman collapsed. Lady Arthrin did not flinch; her gaze remained locked on her champion, her reaction veiled. The man slowly sat up and flipped off his helmet. His one eye stared at the nub of his ruined blade, still glowing red. His expression was equal parts confusion and disbelief.

"Darvor's blood," the preacher mumbled. "His sword . . . it melted."

The Lady-regent finally broke the silence with a slow, haunting clap. "Well done . . . well done."

Jonny turned to the Lady-regent, unsure whether to bow or run.

"The god-man goes free," she hissed. "But now I think we all must know, who are you?"

"Jonny Cupbreaker. And I am come to herald the dawn of a new era." He raised his hands. "The age of the trolls draws to a close, and I come to know, will you join me?"

"Lofty words for a petty magician."

"It's no illusion," Jonny replied. He flicked a fireball into his hand and hurtled it toward one of the unlit torches lining the wall. The torch burst into flames. "It's real magic. Old Magic." He turned to address the crowd. "Seven years ago, when the trolls descended on the south and your late Lord Lendon Arthrin and Lord Groy beat them back, I was at Guard Tower Island and turned the tide of battle. I return to you now to finish what was started. Join me and we will end the threat of the trolls forever!"

"I've heard the stories of the battle at Guard Tower Island," Lady Arthrin said. "A dagger-wielding fool brought down the Black Beast. The son of Aazar felled the troll leader. Some boy, who I can only assume was you, was seen casting fire tricks among the fray. But it was Turion, the singer's say, who turned the tide."

Her words brought Jonny's blood to a boil. *Eibbor was no fool . . . and Turion was a traitor! Are those really the stories that survived from that day?*

He clenched his fists. "Don't you believe me?"

"I'm not sure that I do, but you've certainly got my attention." She sat stone-faced for a long moment, lost in thought. As an uneasy chatter crept through the crowd, she finally allowed the hint of a smile. "Walk with me. I wish to speak with you."

With an elegant sweep of her hand, Lady Arthrin motioned that the court was dismissed. She descended from her chair while the crowd dispersed, carrying what they had witnessed to the whole of Arborton and beyond. Jonny followed the woman toward a side door, pausing next to the preacher as the guards unlocked the man's manacles.

Resting a hand on the old man's shoulder, he said, "You are brave to preach in a land where you are not welcome. I hope you don't stop."

"I'm doing what I believe I must," the preacher replied.

"I know the feeling," Jonny said. "I must stop the trolls, even if it means my life."

"There are heavier costs than your own life. You should be sure you are ready." The man rubbed at where the chains had chafed his wrists. "I'd say I owe you my life, but it belongs to the Creator. Name something else, and it is yours if I can give it. I owe you that much, at least."

"Tell the world. In every town and village you give your sermons, preach that the time has come to end the trolls. Tell them we meet below the walls of Gluton in the spring. Tell them we march at the solstice."

The preacher offered a warm smile. "May He smile on you and your cause."

Jonny turned and found Lady Arthrin at the door. Together, they left the hall and arrived in a small courtyard speckled with crimson dragon-flowers and shadowed by the swaying wisps of a golden willow tree.

"Quite the spectacle back there," the woman purred.

"I had to get your attention somehow." Jonny smirked.

"You're a cocky one, aren't you?" She eyed him.

Jonny grinned but said nothing.

"I remember you, son of John," she said, her tone slicing. "I said if I ever saw you or your companions again, I'd have your heads."

Jonny laughed despite her frigid stare. "You said if you ever saw us *in your city* again. We're not in the City of the Forest Folk, are we?"

"I think now is the part where you tell me why I should help you." She stroked the petals of the nearest flower.

"Don't you want to end the tyranny of the trolls? Do you forget that only seven years ago they nearly destroyed your lands? They burned thousands of your trees, killed hundreds of your people. Lord Groy and your late husband only barely drove them off."

She snatched a petal and rolled it in her fingers. "I remember. I also remember my history, and in the thousand years since Darvor summoned the trolls, they have invaded our forests fewer than a dozen times. The trees always protect us. Why join you when we can let others fight this war for us? And besides, we already send dozens of our good boys north to serve in the king's army at his decree, and most of those poor boys never come home. They are left to rot in unmarked graves on the Plains of Lydie, with no trees to cradle them in their roots."

Jonny ran a hand through the waves of his hair. "I'll tell you why: I'm gonna do this with or without you. And if the realm comes together to fight and the Forest Folk do not march with us, it will look . . . poorly. Your son, Brenton, will be scorned by all the lords beyond your borders and many within. Brenton the Coward, they will call him."

Lady Arthrin cracked into laughter and pressed a hand to her mouth. "So that's how you will play this—guilt me into it?" She led Jonny to the base of the sprawling willow and an elegant bench carved into the tangled roots.

"Should I threaten you instead?" Jonny summoned a flame in his palm.

The woman shook her head and motioned for him to sit next to her. "Goodness, no, don't be silly. If you want the Folk at your side, you must do something in return." She ran her hand over the polished roots. "The Forest Folk were once a separate people, a proud people. We were a kingdom of our own. But King Wilyem Arthrin, the fool that he was, bent the knee to King Gideon the Good to join us to the rest of the realm so we could stand united against the trolls. In doing so, he enslaved us to that foreign throne King Swarlar calls his 'for so long as trolls shall threaten the realm.'"

She glanced around to make sure they were alone. "My son is destined for great things. Truly great things—I can feel it. When I look upon him, I can see there is something so . . . *kingly*."

Jonny read her eyes at once. *She wants to declare her son King of the Forest Folk.* It was suddenly evident. *If the trolls are no more, the ties between the Forest Folk and the rest of the realm can be severed. The realm of the Forest Folk would be an independent kingdom again. This is the opportunity she has been dreaming of.*

"But first my son must learn," she continued. "He must learn how to fight, to command men, lead armies. He must learn what it is to be a ruler."

"And you want him to come with me to learn these things?"

"Those are my terms. Take him with you, keep him close, keep him safe. Make him seen by his men and others so that someday, the singers will remember that Lord Brenton helped bring down the trolls. Do all this, and you have the full strength of the Forest Folk at your command."

"He's only a child, too young to even be a proper squire," Jonny replied.

"Then he can be your cupbearer. He can help you don your armor, clean your tent, feed your horse. I care not. But he is the cost of my armies."

Jonny studied the dragonflowers at his feet for a moment. It was not such a steep price. "I'd be honored to have him," he said, meeting the woman's gaze again.

"But know this: If anything should happen to him, a thousand times worse will come to you." Her tone was haunting, and her words sent a shiver down Jonny's spine. "Even with all your magic, there will be nowhere you can hide."

THE CALL ANSWERED

As the last of the winter winds fled north, Jonny neared Gluton at the head of a small retinue of men. He had spent the winter months rallying support from the lords of the Forest before traveling to Mowka and the lands of House Hillan. There, in the city of the highlanders, he was delayed by more than a month when the snows set in. Lord Hillan had been as welcoming as Jonny's last visit to the city at the base of the mountains, and Jonny spent the dark months in the warmth of Stonehearth, swapping games of battleboard with the aging lord's young heir and nephew. Though neither Lord Hillan nor his nephew would join Jonny's crusade, he succeeded in securing the support of the highlanders under the command of Lord Hillan's brother, Arvin.

When the snows melted, Jonny went west toward the Great Lake before bending north to Gluton. The miles were far, and farther still on the cold days when the wind snapped at his hood and bit at his nose, but Jonny enjoyed the journey. The freedom of the open roads and the sense of adventure breathed life into his cold bones. He smiled often and rarely thought of home.

Throughout his travels, the young Lord Brenton was ever-present. He had proved an enthusiastic traveler, if not a particularly capable one. Though small for his age, he was healthy and well-spoken, asking infrequent but thoughtful questions. As a lord of one of the realm's great houses, it had been deemed inappropriate that he travel without a full retinue of men. A cook, a tutor, two healers, three serving boys, and two dozen guardsmen joined them when they left Arborton.

The large group traveled slowly, but Jonny didn't complain. The cook ensured they always had something good to eat, and the guards allowed Jonny to sleep, confident in their safety. The serving boys were useful too, distracting Brenton and playing with the young lord as friends. The presence of a high lord, even if the lord was still a child, meant they feasted and received fine rooms and warm beds in every town, village, and castle they passed. But the best part, Jonny found, was the effect on recruiting. Armed with the pledged support of the High Lord of the Forest, lesser lords and commoners alike flocked to the cause.

A frost still hung in the early spring air, but the sun was shining bright and golden when Jonny at last sighted Gluton. Against the blue sky and green fields, the great city looked like a painting.

"That's the king's city?" Lord Brenton asked.

"Yep, and there are the first people to answer the call." Jonny pointed to the flock of tents laid out under the shadow of the city's looming walls.

"How many do you think there are?" The boy's voice was wet with energy.

"Maybe a thousand." He tried to breathe optimism into the words, but in truth, it looked like less than half that number. His heart sank at the sight of the meager tent city, dwarfed by Gluton's towers. He sighed. *I thought there would be more.* "More will come," he reassured the boy.

As if on cue, a horn sounded in the distance and a column of men appeared over the crest of a neighboring hill. Jonny raised a hand to block the sun's glare and squinted at the men rolling over the distant rise. He could see more than a thousand, and more were coming into view every minute. *Alyk!* He smiled at the sight of the archer riding at the head of the line of arriving men.

Jonny turned to Lord Brenton's master-at-arms. "We've arrived. Take the boy into camp. You can find a suitable location to set up the tents and settle in; I'll find you later." He broke away, guiding his horse toward the other arrivals.

"Son of Alyn!" Jonny shouted as his courser galloped across the green hill.

The young man's eyes flashed, and he returned a smile. "Cupbreaker, how did the winter treat you?"

Jonny slowed his horse and fell into pace beside his friend. "I can't complain. Looks like you did well!"

"Certainly, better than you," Alyk laughed. "Is that all you got to join you?" He pointed to the small company Jonny had separated from. "A few dozen?"

"More will come. The Forest Folk, a host of highlanders under Arvin Hillan's command, and many more I won over on the way. They are finishing setting their affairs in order and then they will join us. We still have a few weeks until the solstice—there is time."

Alyk smirked. "Tell yourself what you will, but come the first of summer, I'll have won our bet, and I'll be sipping down a pint of sweet ale. Mmmmm." He rubbed his belly. "I can taste it already."

Jonny rolled his eyes. "We'll see." He twisted in the saddle and looked back at the line of people still rolling over the hilltop. "How many did you bring?"

"Nearly five thousand fighting men. Plus, near as many camp followers—squires, wives, stableboys, cook women, and all the other rabble that wants to be where the action is."

Jonny's lips split with the wideness of his smile. "Wow, that's better than I dreamed."

"Lord Groy was very agreeable. Financed a large part of the supplies himself and encouraged his vassals to do the same. You know how he suffered at the hands of the trolls; he has more disdain for those beasts than most."

They reached the edges of the small camp, and Alyk directed the lords and lieutenants of his legion to oversee the expansion of the camp. With the arrival of Alyk's men, the camp would soon be more than ten times as large. Jonny and Alyk continued toward the camp's center, winding through the patchwork of tents and pavilions.

"Well, well, if it isn't the youthful idiots responsible for all this . . ." Cazar emerged from a tent beside them. He wore his customary black and silver clothes in the fashion of the Guards of Gluton, though now retired, none of his robes bore the brotherhood's insignia. As Jonny and Alyk dismounted, the former Guard took the reins of their horses in hand and passed them to one of the nearby squires.

Still uncertain what reception awaited him, Jonny tried to read his old friend's eyes, but the steely glint was as indiscernible as ever. "How have you been?" Jonny asked, half-fearing the response.

"Busy," Cazar replied. "But for the most part, successful. Come, follow me."

He turned and led them into one of the larger pavilions. Inside, a table and several chairs were arranged. A thin rug had been laid down over the grass, and several braziers provided a smoky warmth. The table was cluttered with charts, maps, and the half-eaten remains of someone's lunch.

"You remember Klorvone?" Cazar gestured to a large man in the corner.

Jonny recognized the man as a guardsman they had met at Mowka on his previous adventure. A tall, imposing man with dark eyes and large muscles, he had been captured by trolls as a child and had his tongue cut away. The man returned Jonny's greeting with a stiff nod. Unable to speak, Klorvone let his dark eyes do most of his talking. He silently bent to sharpen his great poleaxe.

Cazar swept a hand over the pile of papers on the table. "While you two were prancing around the realm spouting promises of glory and adventure, I've been doing the hard work of making sure you idiots don't mess this up." He leaned on the table. "I've been calling in favors to secure food and weapons from several of my friends among the nobility. And I was able to win over several of Gluton's wealthiest merchants to promise financing and supplies. Some were easy to convince; most were not."

"Where is Swarlar?" Jonny asked. He had expected the king to be awaiting his arrival if only to scold or imprison him. "How has he reacted?"

"As you might expect, he was not pleased. I suspect you will hear from him before long. Though the worst opposition came from Lord Voramandier. He flew into a rage when the news of your plan reached his court. He petitioned the king to send forth the royal army to close the roads to Gluton. It took all my goodwill to persuade King Swarlar not to. Worse still, Lord Voramandier sent all the birds in his rookery flying with messages to lords across the realm, bidding them to forbid anyone from joining your cause. I could do nothing to prevent that, and we will not yet know how many may have aligned with that position." The warrior sighed and Jonny felt the fatigue radiating from him.

"I see the lakelands answered Alyk's call," Cazar continued. "And an impressive answer too. How did you fare with the Forest Folk, Jonny?"

Jonny recounted his efforts and travels, adding at the end, "More will come. We have time."

"Aye," Cazar looked uneasy. "We still have a few weeks for men to gather. Except for those Alyk brought from the lakelands—only a handful have come so far, mostly men from the lands close to Gluton. I've heard nothing yet of the westerlands or Guard Tower Island."

"More will come," Jonny repeated.

"And if they don't, you will send these people home? You promised you would put this madness to an end if we don't have enough. We need many times more to even stand a chance."

"We have time," Jonny said curtly. "More will come." He turned and left the tent.

More did come. Over the following days, men began to arrive in scattered groups. Three retired soldiers from Well's Point, a dozen young shepherds from the western reaches of the Great Mountains, a score of archers from Gestor. They trickled in at all times of day and night, slowly swelling the growing city of tents beneath Gluton's walls. Most were poor—second sons and peasants from nameless villages—who came because there was nothing for them at home. They arrived with naught but the clothes on their backs, armed with rusted farm equipment or nothing at all. A few were wealthier—lordlings or successful merchants. With them came household guards, polished armaments, and carts of food, furniture, and supplies.

Others came too; those with no intention of fighting. Singers and minstrels flocked to the camp, as did smiths, bakers, fortune tellers, comfort women, and many others, hoping to find a profit among the crowds. They turned the rabble of tents into a patchwork city, complete with streets and markets, smoke and noise.

Jonny's days were spent trying to bend the collection into something resembling an army. Like a blacksmith, he toiled from sun-up to sundown, hammering out some dispute here and smoothing out another there. He tried to polish the training of the newest recruits and rework the weaknesses where he found them. And like a smith, the work left him tired, sore, and dirty. This "army" was more crude iron than fine steel, and at any moment, he feared the whole thing might shatter.

He was grateful for the help he had. Alyk, though young, had won fame throughout the realm as a skilled archer. With his natural charisma, he quickly turned that fame into respect as he organized and trained the army's archery cohorts. Similarly, Cazar used his widely respected reputation and years of experience to organize and train the infantry. Even Klorvone, tongueless and silent, trained battalions of spearmen with his great poleaxe.

Those men who had not arrived under the command of a lord or lordling were assigned to levies under the command of various nobles or respected lieutenants. As more arrived every day, new units were created and organized. And so, with time and tireless work, the chaotic host slowly took the form of an actual army.

But as the fields greened and the air warmed, Jonny found himself growing glum. Despite the slow arrival of new recruits, there was no denying they had too few fighting men. When Jonny and Alyk dreamt up their plan in the dank tavern months prior, they had pondered all they could accomplish with a thousand men. But the reality, they had come to realize, was sobering.

By Cazar's estimate, no army of less than ten thousand could hope to make a meaningful invasion of the troll lands. Although the troll legions had been utterly quashed years ago in the War of the Three Armies, it was believed Darvor could still muster several thousand trolls. And while Jonny and Alyk had first envisioned their mission to be to harass and disrupt the trolls, they now agreed the only meaningful goal was a total conquest of the troll lands. Jonny's magic would help, but it was not enough. They needed more soldiers.

With the first scents of summer in the air, Jonny's hope wore thin. Privately, he mulled over how to disband the army. He was not sure they would be willing to go home, even if ordered to do so. Most had come hungry for glory, and the collective bloodthirst of the army was palpable. Fortunately, two days before the solstice, the question was put to rest.

First came the arrival of the promised Forest Folk. Jonny had expected their arrival; Lady Arthrin had pledged her support and Lord Brenton was already with them. But still, the delay concerned him. They appeared with the sound of horns on the horizon, two thousand strong. Dressed in the colors of the forest, they came well armed and well supplied, with golden hair gleaming in the sun.

Only hours later, another two thousand Mowkans under the command of Arvin Hillan arrived to join the others who had previously come from the mountain regions. With their thick furs and thicker beards, the highlanders stood apart from their forest neighbors, but they were welcomed into the camp all the same.

And just before sunset, three great levees arrived from the westerlands, including almost a thousand cavalry from the western marks. By nightfall, it was clear the army would march. There would be war.

"The day after tomorrow is the solstice," Cazar told Jonny that night. "I'll admit, the realm has answered your call."

"Yeah," Jonny replied as the two strolled through the camp under the light of the moon. "To be honest, I wasn't sure this would work. I'm still not. But I'd do anything to rid the world of Darvor. I'll die for this cause if need be."

Cazar's features glowed dark in the light of the campfires they passed. "It is an easy thing to lay down your life for a cause, harder still to live for it and bear the cost of it. I hope you are ready for what this may cost you."

Jonny nodded solemnly. "I want to thank you. I couldn't have done any of this without you."

"Nonsense," Cazar said in a warm tone. "You could have done most of it . . . not all. But most."

Jonny laughed.

"I thought my fighting days were done," Cazar continued. "Thought my battles were behind me. I still don't know if this is the right move, but if there is even a small chance I can give my children a world without trolls, I must. One more great campaign—"

"Wait!" Jonny stopped. "Your *children*? As in more than one?"

"Aye, Dazar is to have a brother . . . or a sister. We don't know yet. Delena is expecting again. She's still early, but—"

"That's awesome!" Jonny exclaimed and pulled Cazar into a hug.

Cazar smiled. "I'm quite fortunate. We're both very happy."

"We should celebrate!" Jonny released the old Guard and clapped him on the back. "I can find Alyk, and there are always some minstrels playing over by the creek. Should I find us a flagon of ale?"

"No, thank you. It's already getting late, and I should write Delena another letter. It will be hard to find the time once we are on the march." Cazar looked up, surveying the stars above. "I miss her already. It will be hard being away from her for so long."

Jonny followed Cazar's eyes to the night sky. There were so many more stars here than he ever saw at home. *I miss my home too . . .* He had already been away from home for months, and there was no telling how much longer this campaign would last. "Thank you again. I know what you are sacrificing for this."

Cazar nodded stiffly. "I'll see this to the end. Whatever end that may be. Good night, Jonny."

"Good night."

Cazar disappeared into the night, leaving Jonny alone to ponder a sea of stars and an ocean of uncertainty.

The morning brought more good news. A letter arrived from Guard Tower Island signed by the young Lord Leyne and the Lord-regent Jocum. House Leyne was pledging the full support of their lands to Jonny's cause. As their lands bordered the trolls' realm, they were preparing their levees and would join with Jonny's forces when the army reached the East River. The people of Guard Tower Island had suffered greatly in the War of Three Armies, but the boys who had been too young to fight years before were now young men eager to avenge their fathers' deaths.

Late in the afternoon, a final arrival appeared, sending a stir through the ranks. When the whispers swirling through the camp reached Jonny's ears, he had no doubt about whom they referred. Entering the large command tent, Jonny found Rard hunched in a chair by the table.

The chair looked like a child's stool under Rard's great bulk and creaked and groaned every time the man shifted. "You need stronger chairs," the man-giant barked, pointing to the shattered remains of a weaker chair in the corner.

"We'll see to it," Jonny said, surveying the man. Rard wore a simple tunic and roughspun pants. A grizzled stubble hung to his wide jaw, and his thick arms were folded across his chest.

Rard remained quiet for a moment, and Jonny began to wonder if the man expected him to speak first. The noises of the camp drifted through the tent flaps, but they could not break the silence that stifled the air. At last, Rard cleared his throat. "My brother died a good man," he said. "Loyal to the very end."

After the druid had passed, Jonny knew Rard had left Gluton, despite Swarlar pardoning his crimes, and disappeared back into the Lost Lands.

"They're filth, Jonny. The trolls that killed him. They're all rage and hate."

"Does that mean you are with us?" Jonny had seen Rard tear *grevices* apart with his bare hands. *I wonder what he could do to a battalion of trolls!*

"Aye, I reckon it's what Rald would want of me. Besides, I have nothing left to live for except vengeance."

"We're glad to have you," Jonny replied. "Let's get you settled in." He gestured to the door. Rard followed Jonny out of the tent, leaving behind a very relieved chair.

After seeing that Rard was taken care of, Jonny spent the rest of the afternoon rounding through the camp, ensuring that all was ready for the following day's march. Most of the wagons had already been loaded with food and supplies, but he helped load some of the remaining carts with extra weapons and armor. Later, he oversaw the tearing down and packing up of the larger pavilions. The many horses had been freshly shod earlier in the week, but he double-checked with the master-of-horse that they had packed enough replacement horseshoes for the hundreds of miles ahead. As the sun settled, he called on the lords and lieutenants to ensure their troops were organized and ready. He did not want to waste hours in the morning for the officers to corral disordered soldiers.

By nightfall, the camp buzzed with anticipation and the air was thick with war-hunger. Bawdy drinking songs wafted up from the troops gathered around campfires while laughter and cheers split the night air.

Satisfied with the state of the camp, Jonny returned to the command tent for a quiet meal before bed. As he parted the flaps and entered the tent, the sounds of the camp died away. His supper had been left on the table—a heel of bread and bowl of stew, still steaming. The tent was lit from a dozen candles on the table and darkness clung to the edges of the space.

"Hello, Jonny," a familiar voice emanated from the shadows.

Jonny turned. "I've been waiting for you."

The king stepped forward. His wrinkles were deeper than usual and the light of his eyes dimmer. He stood tall, arms folded behind his back. "So you mean to go through with this?"

Jonny eyed the king. He had rehearsed this conversation a thousand times since he had departed Gluton. "I expected this conversation weeks ago." He strained to keep his voice level.

"Oh?" The king raised a bushy white eyebrow. "And how did you expect it to go?"

"You were going to yell at me for raising an army. Tell me how dumb my plan was. Explain how we needed to wait for Darvor to make the next move, how it was too soon to move against him. I figured you would threaten to imprison me, command that my troops be sent home."

"You're not a child anymore, Jonny." Swarlar drew himself closer with measured strides. His robes swirled silently around him, gathering the light of the dim tent. "It's not my place to shout and spank you on the bottom."

Jonny laughed. "So that's the way you're going to play this?" The edge in his voice was sharper than he intended.

The king cocked his head. "What?"

"Take the high road. Act all mightier-than-thou." Jonny sunk dead-weight into one of the chairs, his eyes never leaving the king.

Swarlar furrowed his brow. "What's going on? Why are you angry with me?" His deep eyes studied Jonny intently, and his face was writ with gentle understanding.

The balanced empathy irked Jonny, who threw up his hands and puffed. "You want to sit in your palace, with your nose in dusty old books, and do nothing! Every moment we sit by and do nothing, he gets stronger! You act like you forgot how close we came to losing everything seven years ago. I haven't forgotten!" He slouched lower in the chair.

Swarlar nodded. "So let me understand . . . you come back to our world expecting to find Darvor menacing the realm again. What you find instead is several trolls who have wandered into a distant valley with a magical fountain. So naturally, you feel that must be a sign of his return. And because of that, you want me to call the kingdom to war. And now, because I do not, you are angry with me."

"You see!" Jonny shouted. "That's just it. You act like I'm still a kid. You're trivializing everything!" The candles jumped at the outburst, but the king didn't flinch.

"Ahh," he replied. "Then let us talk like adults." His voice was still level, but his tone had a hint of iron. He stepped toward the table. "I do not believe now is the time to act against Darvor, so I will not call the kingdom to war for a cause in which I do not believe. I am sorry if that disappoints you." He idly leafed through the papers scattered on the table. "Who else knows about Darvor?"

Jonny reached for the bread on his plate, hoping the food would steady him. "Cazar, Alyk, and Klorvone . . . and he's not going to be telling anyone."

"So the soldiers believe this is just a war against the trolls?"

"It's better if they are fighting something they understand. And Cazar thinks we have a fair shot to destroy the trolls once and for all."

Swarlar lifted one of the letters to the light and casually scanned the contents. "And since the trolls are Darvor's agents, destroying them would cripple him. Believe me, Jonny, I understand the appeal of the plan." He gently set the letter down and brought his gaze back to Jonny. "But at the end of this road is Darvor. And make no mistake, there can be no true victory so long as he remains, no matter how many trolls you kill."

"I know," Jonny replied.

"I do not think you are ready to face him. And if you fail, he will wipe this army away with the flick of his wrist." The wrinkles shifted on his face to intimate his concern.

"So, join me." Jonny pressed his lips into a thin line.

"I have told you before, I cannot move against him. My powers are like a shield, not a sword."

"Then I'll do it myself! I would die for this!"

Swarlar sighed. "I don't doubt you would. But there are costs greater than one's own life. And I hope you are ready for those."

Why do I keep hearing that?! Jonny rolled his eyes. "Then you aren't going to stop me?"

The king stroked his beard. "You want to be treated like an adult . . . so be it. All these people, these soldiers," he gestured at the army sleeping outside the tent, "are here of their own wishes, of their own volition. They can follow you if they choose. If you are an adult, you can make your own decisions. But your decisions will come at a cost. If you can bear that responsibility, do as you feel is right."

Jonny pushed to his feet. "I'll bring you Darvor, dead."

"No need." Swarlar straightened. "As long as you come back alive."

With a swirl of white robes and dancing candlelight, Swarlar turned to the exit.

"Jonny." He paused with one foot out of the tent. "Good luck." The tent flap swung, and he was gone.

The First Test

"Join us, Jonny!" Alyk's friendly voice cut through the laughter. The archer sat beside a crackling campfire with a dozen companions. Klorvone was there, Rard too, and several others Jonny recognized but did not know.

Jonny approached the fire and found a seat beside Rard. Even seated, the man was twice as tall as Jonny.

"What have you been up to?" Alyk asked.

"Just taking a walk through the camp, making sure all is in order."

Alyk passed Jonny a mug of watered wine. "And is it?"

"It is. The scouts are at their posts, the soldiers finishing their suppers."

"Klorvone, here, was just telling us, or rather"—Alyk eyed the axe-man—"gesturing to us." The tongueless man clicked his annoyance, but Alyk carried on. "The Ruined City is less than a day's march from where we are now. Did you know?"

Jonny nodded, recalling seeing it at a distance years earlier.

"I've been there once before," Rard grunted.

"You have not, you liar," Alyk laughed.

"I'm not lying." Rard refilled his mug. "There were no ghosts. Just the bones of a city. Rocks and weeds. Anything of value was looted years ago."

"Spoken like someone who has never been," Alyk quipped.

Several of the men and women around the fire snickered. Even Klorvone let slip a croaking noise that might have been laughter.

"We won't come any closer than we are now," Jonny said. He knew that most people feared the ancient ruins. *Superstitions and ghost stories.* "Our path continues straight east."

"We've made good pace so far," spoke one of the men. He was a mid-level captain, the eldest son of a lesser lord from one of the Islands of the Teeth.

"Yeah." Jonny nodded. "Perhaps in another fortnight, if our pace holds, we will join Lord Leyne's host from Guard Tower Island." In truth, their pace had been slower than Jonny expected. In two weeks, they had only reached as far east as the Ruined City and had much of the Plains of Lydie left to cross. Given its size, the army moved slowly. The limiting factor was not the soldiers' marching but the hundreds of supply wagons accompanying them. All the food, tents, weapons, and armor had to be carried on horseback or hauled on wagons. There were few roads across Lydie, and what meager paths existed were tired, muddy pockmarks riddled with bumps and lumps. The carts broke often, and it seemed every couple of miles some reason or another delayed their column.

"I'm glad you joined us tonight, Jonny," Alyk said. "I've been wanting to introduce you to someone." He wrapped an arm around the waist of the girl next to him and she leaned closer. "This is Siley; she's the one I mentioned to you several nights ago."

She was a pretty girl with ruddy hair and smooth skin. Her frame was slender and her lips narrow. Her only flaw was a faded scar that marred her chin. "Pleasure to meet you, Cupbreaker," she said with bells in her voice. The firelight pooled in her green eyes.

"The honor is all mine," Jonny replied, dipping his head.

"I met her in Lanak," Alyk hummed.

"I was a serving girl to Lord Groy's aunt," Siley added. She gave Alyk a playful shrug. "Somehow I thought coming along for this adventure might be better."

"It was my wicked humor that won her over." Alyk winked. "I'm too funny and too sweet."

Siley gave an exaggerated roll of the eyes. "He's funny," she said, pointing at Rard. "And he's sweet." She pointed at Klorvone. "You're just an ass." She tugged one of his curls, causing him to squeak.

"Jonny," Cazar interrupted. "You must come with me at once." His tone shattered the merriment.

"Is everything all right?" Jonny turned.

Cazar stood, wrapped in shadow at the edge of the firelight. "Follow me."

Jonny fell into step with Cazar as they headed toward the command tent. Alyk, Rard, Klorvone, and Siley hurried at their heels. Cazar's long strides led them to the large round tent at the center of camp. Inside, most of the lords and officers had already assembled.

"My lords," Jonny greeted the gathered men. They were all older than him, and most were seasoned veterans of a dozen campaigns. They had accepted his leadership only grudgingly, and Jonny knew too well it was Cazar for whom they held respect.

Arvin Hillan, the loud, grizzled lordling commander of the Mowkan cohorts, raised a finger to one of the men seated at the end of the table. "I think you'd like to hear what he has to say."

The figure at the end of Arvin's finger was a frail, dirty man hidden behind mangy, unkempt hair and a patchy beard. His clothes were tattered and threadbare, and his boots were held together with frayed leather strips. One arm was missing at the elbow while his remaining hand rested on the hilt of a rusted dagger hanging from his belt.

The man lifted his gaze to meet Jonny, revealing a dozen scars hiding beneath his beard. "Hello, Jonny," the man said in a voice as thin as the first frost.

Jonny's heart leapt. *I know him!* He blinked in disbelief. "Eibbor?"

"Aye," Cazar said. "The dagger-wielding, Black-Beast-slaying hero of Guard Tower Island."

Jonny had met Eibbor years before, but Cazar's colorful friend had not been found after the bloody battle at Guard Tower Island and was declared dead, widowing his pregnant wife. *He survived! But how?*

"You'll have time for answers, boy," Eibbor mumbled. "That time isn't now. I come with news you'll not want to ignore." He raised the stump of his arm to rub his chin. "A troll army is marching to meet you even as we speak. I've come to warn you."

Behind Jonny, Alyk clicked his tongue. "About time. How many?

"We outnumber them more than four to one," Cazar replied. "But we're untested, so do not mistake this for child's play."

"They'll be here by midday tomorrow," Eibbor continued. "They are the first, but they will not be the last. Deep within the troll lands, they are readying themselves. Massive legions are on the move. It will be war."

The lords and officers looked to Cazar for direction. *I'm the one in charge*, Jonny fumed. He stepped forward. "If it is to be a battle, let us get ready."

Arvin Hillan let out a hoot. "No better way to spend my birthday than in battle!"

Jonny spent the next hours drawing up battle plans with Cazar, Alyk, and the lords and officers. The news spread quickly, and soon the camp was abuzz with nervous excitement. By dawn, the army departed the camp, leaving behind a few men to guard the wagons and supplies.

A broad open plain two miles to the east was chosen as the best place to meet the trolls. The ground was solid and could support a charge of heavy cavalry. A gentle hill would allow the commanders and archers a position to survey the battle. Arvin Hillan had begged for command of the vanguard, and being one of the highest-ranking nobles, Jonny was compelled to give him the honor. Alyk's archers would bolster the center, while the horsemen of the western mark would sweep in from the right flank. The young Lord Arthrin assumed "command" of the reserves, where he could be kept safely away from the battle without insulting his rank.

Filled with nervous energy, Jonny surveyed the dramatic scene. The sun's first rays painted the hills in golden hues and bathed the army in warm light. *What a glorious sight.* Ten thousand soldiers and half again as many archers and cavalry stretched across the green field. Hundreds of banners fluttered in the morning breeze, bearing the colorful insignia of dozens of noble houses. Drummers and horn-blowers played rousing melodies as lords in gleaming armor rode their powerful destriers between the columns, shouting orders and words of encouragement. *Like something out of a blockbuster movie!*

A mile to the east, the dark shape of the troll army emerged, rolling over the horizon like a shadow. Their war drums beat a haunting melody as the creatures drew near.

"A hundred times I've fought battles on the Plains of Lydie," Cazar said.

Jonny turned to his old friend.

"And I remember every one. Every detail. Scarred in my memory." Tired lines lurked in the corners of his eyes. "It always looks so impressive.

The shining armor, the rows of spears, the banners blowing in the wind. It's all so beautiful . . . until it's not."

Jonny looked out on the columns of men. He had taken a place in the middle of the vanguard, between the front ranks and the first reserves. There, with Cazar at this side, he was well-positioned to command the army. With them stood several of the high commanders, stewards, and flagmen, whose job it was to communicate the orders by raising colored banners.

"You do remember I fought at Guard Tower Island," Jonny replied. "I know what battles are like."

"That's not what I meant," Cazar said, gazing at the approaching trolls.

"Yeah, sure." Jonny stepped forward and clapped his hands together. Raising his voice, he shouted, "All right, I think they've come close enough. Let's send these bastards back to hell!"

He left Cazar and jogged through the columns of soldiers toward the front. He passed Arvin Hillan in his plumed helm and Klorvone with his towering poleaxe. Jonny pushed through the front row to emerge onto the field. With nothing but open grass between himself and the troll army, he turned around. Facing his own army, he was greeted with a bristling row of spears stretching several hundred yards to either side. He spied familiar faces among the ranks: the Hammer of Dorndale stood in the front row, as did Rard, bare-chested and bare-knuckled, twice taller than any other man.

"Today we mark the dawn of a new era!" Jonny shouted. A wave of cheers erupted. "An era without trolls! Without fear! Without war!"

He turned back to the dark swarm of trolls. The foes were now within a hundred yards, and Jonny could make out the details of their twisted faces and yellowed eyes. He raised his arm and extended his hand toward the snarling creatures. He closed his eyes and took a deep breath. *Here goes nothing!*

He released a torrent of fire. At once, the spell drew on his strength, but he leaned forward and poured himself into it. The fire roared forward, falling on the trolls with voracious hunger. The enemy columns wilted under the maelstrom like wheat under a scythe. The thunder of the flames split the air as first dozens, then hundreds, of trolls melted away under the blaze.

I will win this battle single-handedly, Jonny had decided the night before. When he had heard there were shy of two thousand trolls in the approaching host, he knew at once what course he would take. *I will earn their respect!* All the lords that had looked to Cazar would now see him as the true commander of the army. *And Swarlar will see I am capable.* It would be a large and taxing spell, Jonny knew, but they would not need to lose a single life and could continue to Guard Tower Island without delay.

He bent his will back toward the magic and drove more fire into the troll army. Only then did he realize they were still coming. Although two or three hundred trolls had been scorched under the magic, the rest pressed on. Jonny's knees grew weak, and still more than half of the monsters remained. His eyes grew wide. *I can't hold them!* His magic made him feel invincible, but it had its limits. A panic swelled in his throat.

More . . . more . . . He dug his heels into the ground and leaned forward, calling on the deepest stores of his strength. His vision faded and he fell to one knee. *More . . .* His fires sputtered. *More . . .* but there was nothing else. He collapsed and fell into shadow.

The Next Steps

Jonny awoke on his back with blue skies overhead. The smell of smoke filled his nostrils, and the taste of bile swam in his throat.

"Hey, buddy." Alyk's friendly face appeared above Jonny, blocking out the sun. "How're you feeling?"

An immense hand wrapped around his shoulder and helped him to sit. "That's it, lad," Rard said, releasing his grip.

"There you go; easy does it," Alyk added as Jonny fought to steady himself.

"Alyk was worried you wouldn't wake up," Rard grunted. "I wasn't."

"You weren't worried about him not waking up, or you weren't worried he wouldn't wake up?" Alyk shot the man a sly look.

"What's the difference?" Rard rubbed his chin.

Alyk grinned and looked back to Jonny. "You missed all the fun."

"What fun?" Jonny asked, spitting the sour taste from his mouth. He looked around. They were in the middle of the remains of the battle-field. Puffs of smoke floated past, filling the air with the smell of ash and blood. The grass was trampled to mud and littered with broken bodies and splintered spears. Soldiers meandered through the gore, finishing off wounded trolls. Healers tended to the injured men while priests comforted those beyond saving.

"After you passed out, you left the rest of the trolls for us." Alyk flashed a broad smile. "We won . . . if you can't tell."

Klorvone approached, stepping over the body of a troll. His long poleaxe was slung over his shoulder, and he was bathed in dirt and blood. Tall as the man was, Jonny had to crane his neck to see him.

Klorvone clicked his lips and made a series of quick gestures.

"The tongueless wonder is right," Alyk replied. "Let's get you back to camp. You'll feel better with some food in ya."

Rard wrapped his trunk-like arms under Jonny, and the four of them started back to camp. Along the way, the others filled Jonny in on the details of the battle. His magic had killed many of the trolls—almost half, Alyk claimed—but not all. After Jonny collapsed, he lay exposed in the open space between the two armies. Cazar had ordered a full charge to reach Jonny and shield him from the trolls. The fight had been brutal but short-lived. So outnumbered, the trolls were quickly overwhelmed.

But the victory had come at a cost. Several hundred men had been lost, among them the Hammer of Dorndale and Arvin Hillan, as well as two lords and three lordlings of lesser houses. Cazar had survived, as had Eibbor, who, even one-handed, had rushed into the fray.

Back at the camp, Alyk brought Jonny a bowl of stew before stealing off with Siley. After eating, Jonny washed and donned fresh clothes before finding Cazar, Rard, and Klorvone in the command tent. They were joined by Eibbor and the young Brenton Arthrin, along with the boy lord's steward.

"That was foolish of you," Cazar said, looking up from the table. His thick hair was still matted in dried blood.

"I thought I could kill them," Jonny responded. He wanted to shout: *I killed half of them—where would you be without me?* But thinking better of it, he held his tongue. He knew what the answer would be: *Home with my wife and child.*

"Foolish as it was, it was bloody impressive too." Rard raised a mug in toast. "I heard you could cast fire magic but never imagined something like that."

Klorvone pounded a fist on his knee to echo Rard's sentiment.

Jonny turned to Eibbor. The man's eyes were burning a hole in the ground in front of him. *He's so much quieter than before, like a different man.*

"I think we have seen I cannot win this war alone." Jonny found a seat by the table.

"You don't have to," Rard said. "Do that any time we face those bastards, and we'll handle the rest."

"No." Jonny shook his head. "Cazar's right. I'll have to be more careful. I can't waste my strength at the wrong time. As it is, I can barely stand." He met the old Guard's gaze and saw the thought in his mind. *Darvor.* If the Oathbreaker's son should attack in person, Jonny was the only one who might be able to stop him. "If I use up too much of my strength on spells, it will leave us vulnerable to attack."

"It will be some days before we can march onward." Cazar pushed to his feet. "The wounded must be mended, and the dead buried."

"Yeah," Jonny sighed. "We'll stay here for a few days."

"Rard, Klorvone—with me. There's work to be done." Cazar swept his hand toward the door.

"Come now, I just poured m'self another pint," Rard groaned. "Let a man celebrate!"

Cazar glared.

"Very well." Rard shrugged and downed the mug's contents in a single gulp. With a burp, he stood and followed.

Jonny turned to Lord Arthrin. Seated as the boy was, his legs swung freely off the chair. "You should run along. Go see your Forest Folk soldiers. Make sure they are taken care of—that's your job as lord."

The boy bounced off his seat and bobbed to the door. Stopping short, he turned. "You fought most bravely today, Commander Jonny."

"As did you." Jonny returned a courteous nod. "You commanded the reserves most excellently. Your mother would be proud."

The boy beamed and scurried from the tent, trailed by his faithful steward.

Alone with Eibbor, Jonny allowed silence to settle over the tent as he studied the man. The years had treated him harshly. Once muscled and glowing, the warrior was now frail and grayed. His clothes were tattered, and his face weathered. *What happened to him?*

"You're awfully quiet," Jonny observed.

Eibbor looked up but said nothing.

"The old you never shut up."

Eibbor blinked.

"I thought you were dead."

"I am." His voice was the sound of grating gravel.

"I heard you fought like hell for a dead man." Jonny smiled. "They say you cut down twenty trolls today . . . all that with one arm."

"It's my good arm." The joke brought no light to his eyes.

Jonny leaned forward. "What happened to you?"

"It's been a long time . . ." Eibbor scratched at the wisps of his beard. "I suppose you ought to know." He shifted in his chair. "After we split during the battle at Guard Tower Island, I fought on. But . . . not for long. A troll, a big ol' brute, took my arm off with an axe." He raised the remains of his arm. "But they didn't let me die. They threw a binding around the stump to stop me bleeding to death and dragged me off. A few of them took me away before sunset. Before . . . before whatever it was that happened that night. They took me back to their lands. I don't know how long they held me. I don't remember much; it was all pain and despair. And then one day—I know not how—I escaped. That was years ago."

It was Jonny's turn to be silent. He wore a pained expression.

"Since then, I've been here and there. Doing what good I can in the world."

"Why didn't you go back to E'alith? Or your child?"

Eibbor looked at the ground. "I'm not the man I was . . . I did go back when I escaped—kept at a distance so they didn't see me. I just had to know. E'alith remarried. A blacksmith—good at his trade and kind too. They're happy now. And my son, they're raising him together. He's a strong lad." A rare smile graced his face. "He'll grow to be a blacksmith. I know he'll be a good one."

"I saw what you and E'alith had. There's no way she is happier with anyone else. You should go back to her! When we pass Guard Tower Island, you should meet her again . . . and meet your son too. Really meet him, not spy from the shadows!"

Eibbor grimaced. "Sometimes it's easier to say goodbye to something good than hold on to something broken."

Nightfall brought a strange swirl of moods to the sprawling camp. The sounds of celebration were interspersed with the moans of the dead and dying. There were toasts to victory and tears for the fallen, and no one seemed eager to sleep.

Jonny found his companions around a campfire in a corner of the camp where songs of valor drowned out any tunes of sorrow.

". . . the boy is too modest." Cazar was speaking to Siley. "He did not miss a single shot. Not one."

The girl's comely features glowed in the soft light of the fire. Her face was incredulous. "Probably because he only fired a single shot."

"Far from it." Cazar's mouth stretched into a warm smile. "He ran through all the arrows in his quiver before the battle was done."

Siley turned to Alyk with feigned annoyance. "You said you were an archer, not the best bloody archer in the realm."

Alyk blushed and looked away. "I got lucky. The trolls . . . they moved into the path of my arrows."

Jonny snorted in surprise. *Since when is he bashful?* He pulled up a stool and joined them by the fire.

"Cupbreaker!" Rard hoisted a pint, sending its contents sloshing. From the glazed look in his eyes, it was evident the pint was not his first.

"Jonny!" Alyk exclaimed. "Welcome!"

Cazar rested a hand on Jonny's shoulder. "I did not mean to be too harsh earlier."

"It's fine." He shook the Guard's hand. "Water under the bridge."

"Rard," Alyk pointed. "How many of those does it take to make you drunk?"

The mug looked comically small in the bearish man's hand.

"I could drink more of these when I sprung from the womb than you can handle now," he boomed.

Jonny tapped Klorvone on the knee and slipped the man a wink, pointing at Rard. "I've been meaning to ask you, Rard," Jonny began. "Your brother's name was Gerald, right? But you called him Rald . . ."

The smile fled from Rard's face, and he lowered his mug.

"If Rald is short for Gerald, does that mean . . .?" Jonny fought to contain a smirk.

Rard growled. "I swear . . ."

"Gerard?!" Alyk exclaimed.

"Don't you dare call me that!" Rard roared.

"Your name is Gerard?" Cazar puffed.

"I hate it! Why my mother named me that, I'll never know. I swear if any of you call me that, I'll squeeze your head so hard your brains will come out your bum! And if you tell anyone else—"

"Gerard! Gerard!" Alyk sprung to his feet and danced in a circle, singing it.

"Ahhh!" Rard sloshed the contents of his mug at the boy.

Alyk was too slow and caught the whole splash in the face. Siley fell back in a fit of giggles. Even Eibbor laughed.

Alyk ran his fingers across his dripping brow and then touched them to his lips. "Subtle hints of strawberry . . . amber . . . a whiff of pine . . . I'd venture a guess that was an Arimor ale you just wasted on my pretty face."

Jonny smiled. Surrounded by his friends and the glow of the fire, the troubles ahead seemed a long way off. As the moon yawned high above, the companions spent a warm night in laughter and merriment. With each song and joke, the strength returned to Jonny's shaky legs. *I don't know what's coming . . . but I think we'll be ready.*

With the fire wilting and Rard's words sliding into drunk ramblings, Jonny took his leave. Slipping away from the flickering light, Jonny started toward the edges of the camp. He pulled his cloak tight to ward off the hissing wind that snaked through the tents. Before retiring for the night, Jonny wanted to round on the sentries. They had won a great victory, and it would be easy for the watchmen to grow complacent on such a night. *But that is exactly when we must be most vigilant,* Jonny mused as he left the tents behind.

The camp was a small city, a thousand flickering fires sprawling over the rolling meadow. But beyond the light and warmth, the night was dark. The unending wilderness swirled around them like the sea around a small island, hiding secrets and terrors. Leaving the sounds of the camp behind, Jonny found two sentries patrolling the ridge to the north. Their meager torchlight was a beacon in the night. He shouted as he neared so as not to startle them.

"Cupbreaker." They nodded at his approach. From their fettered ring-mail and grizzled beards, they were clearly Mowkans.

"How's the watch?" Jonny fell into stride as they continued their patrol.

"A mild night when first we started," said the older of the two. One of his eyes had gone silver with blindness but the other scanned the shadows beyond their torchlight. "But a nasty wind has blown in from the mountains. It will be an early winter this year; I feel it in my bones."

Jonny touched the gold dragon at his neck. "Winter is a long way off. Summer has only just begun."

"Aye, then perhaps this wind harkens something more sinister." The man's voice was gruff.

"Sinister?" Jonny smiled. "We won ourselves a great victory today. You should be happy. This will be the first of many."

"With all due respect, Commander," the younger man started. If not for his beard, he would have looked half a child. "True as that may be, out here, away from the camp, we feel a different truth. Let those in the camp enjoy their revelries. Those of us who take watch feel something in the air." The young man glanced at Jonny. "The other sentries know it too. It's a feeling of being watched."

"It's like there are eyes in the hills," the older one added. "And they never blink."

The smile drained from Jonny's face. He knew the feeling. It had plagued him for years after his first adventure. Even now, when he was alone, he felt those unseen eyes.

"Some of the other watchmen say they've seen someone—or something—moving out there." The young man pointed to the wilderness. "A ghost, they say, coming and going, always at night, always at the shadow's edge, just a step ahead. Never more than a glimpse."

"A ghost?" Jonny felt flames dance at his fingertips but did his best to dismiss the fears. These were the ravings of tired men spooked by the night air. *A deer, perhaps, or an owl. At worst, a shy bear.* They were close to the Ruined City, Jonny knew, and even his most stalwart soldiers were spooked by that place. "And what does this ghost look like?"

"On that, no one agrees. Some have seen a flash of gold, others a swirl of shadow. Most have never seen it, but only heard foul whispers in the air."

Jonny shook off the shiver that raced down his spine. From the look on their faces, it was clear—they were tired and superstitious. He smiled. "Well, I see no sign of this ghost tonight. Carry on! And if you report anything that leads to this ghost's capture, you'll both be well rewarded. And tell the other sentries the same is true for them." He made to turn back to camp but paused. "And do not speak of any such ghost with the other soldiers . . . just watch and listen."

The men nodded and left Jonny to continue their patrol.

By the time Jonny returned to the camp, a quiet had befallen the tents. A few fires still burned, and some lonely souls lingered outside their tents, but most of the troops had gone to sleep. Jonny yawned as the night air beckoned him closer to bed. He passed Eibbor huddled beside a fire, frail and gaunt in the flickering light. The one-armed warrior offered Jonny a silent nod before turning back to the lingering flames. Further along, Jonny passed Rard's tent, which, from the sound of the snoring, housed a sleeping bear. By Alyk's tent, he heard Siley's giggles and knew the archer was not alone.

As his tired feet began to drag, Jonny rounded a corner and reached his tent. The unexpected sight before stopped him dead, causing his heart to jump. Sleep fled from his mind. He blinked, doubting his own eyes.

Hanging from the tent post at the door were the charred, blackened remains of some creature. It dangled from one leg by a rusted wire, swaying eerily in the breeze. Most of the flesh had been burned away, leaving little holding the bones together besides flaking leather and twisted sinew. It was the size of a large dog and had short horns on its black skull, but there was little else to identify it. Flies buzzed around the creature's gaping mouth in an angry swarm.

Jonny took a step forward. There was no one around. He cautiously lifted the door flap and peered inside the tent. Nothing inside was disturbed. Turning back to the burnt animal carcass, a lump hardened in his throat. It was intended as a message. *Darvor.*

THE WARNING OF GHOSTS

It was a long and sleepless night for Jonny. The stars paced slowly across the night sky as Jonny stared at the burnt animal carcass, letting his thoughts spin to dark places. Darvor was behind it, and that was all he knew. He rubbed his fist in his palm. Whatever came next, there was only one way this road ended. *I hope I'm ready . . .*

When morning finally came, Jonny found his friends in the command tent. Rard was sipping honey tea, with a face that betrayed a splitting headache. Cazar held his storied sword, Ethwayl, across his knees, carefully dragging a whetstone over the polished blade. Eibbor sat stiff and stone-faced in the corner, watching Alyk and Klorvone play a game of dice. The young Lord Brenton was there, as were a few other lords and officers who had assembled for the morning briefing.

Jonny entered without a word, throwing open the tent flaps and dragging the carcass behind him. The space went quiet. A few lords jumped to their feet while others pinched their noses to ward off the stink.

"Lord Brenton"—Jonny glanced at the child—"please see your fellow noblemen out of the tent. I'll send for you."

Brenton voiced no protest and quickly bounced from the tent. The other lords similarly kept any displeasure to themselves and filed out.

With a grunt, Jonny heaved the charred carcass onto the table, sending Alyk's dice clattering to the shadows.

Klorvone clicked his lips.

"You weren't winning by that much." Alyk waved his finger. "We'll call it a draw."

Klorvone pointed to the blackened remains and clicked.

"He says, 'What the hell is this?'" Alyk translated.

"Looks like a fox . . . or maybe a sheep," Rard grunted.

Cazar set aside his sword and approached. He ran a hand over the bones. "It's a goat." He looked at Jonny. "I don't get it."

Jonny scowled. "This was hanging outside my tent last night."

"What does it mean?" Alyk leaned in for a closer look.

"It's Darvor . . . he's taunting me."

"How do you know?" Eibbor's voice cracked from his seat in the corner.

"Because this is what he did to me the first time we met." The memories still burned hot in his mind.

Rard and Klorvone exchanged confused looks.

"How did he get it here in the camp?" Cazar asked, concern dripping from his voice.

Before Jonny could answer, a voice interrupted them. "Cupbreaker," the soldier stammered from the tent's door.

Jonny nodded and followed the soldier outside, his friends falling into step behind him. "What's this about?" Jonny demanded.

"I'm sorry, Commander. You have a guest." The soldier stepped aside and gestured across the clearing. "He just walked out of the wilderness and asked to speak with you. He claims his name is—"

"Turion?" Jonny's mouth fell open.

The soldier nodded. "The son of the maiden fair."

Beneath a tattered cloak and thick hood, the man's golden hair was unmistakable. He was tall and lean and dressed in tired clothes. His face was haggard and wind-washed, but his eyes were still keen and fearsome. "Jonny Cupbreaker. 'Tis quite a name." He lowered his hood.

Jonny took a step back, remembering how Turion had caused the death of dozens at Guard Tower Island years earlier.

The same misgivings did not plague Cazar, who strode forward and extended a hand. "It's good to see you, brother."

"I'm no brother of yours." Turion eyed Cazar's hand for a long moment before extending his own.

"What are you doing here?" Jonny asked.

"I've come to have a word with you." His tone was cold and sharp.

Jonny looked around. Half a hundred onlookers had gathered. "We can speak in the tent."

"No." He tapped his ear. "Follow me. I know a place we will not be . . . *heard*."

Jonny nodded. *He's worried Darvor will hear us.* "I'll go . . . but not alone."

"So be it." Turion turned to one of the soldiers. "Fetch the Cup-breaker some horses."

"Alyk, Cazar—with me," Jonny said.

"Of course," the pair replied in unison.

"Rard, Klorvone, Eibbor—keep the camp in order."

"Jonny, wait." Eibbor grabbed him by the sleeve. His sunken eyes were wide with worry. "Be careful around this one. He brings trouble. We cannot know where he stands."

Jonny peeled away Eibbor's grip. "I don't trust him, but the three of us can handle him. It will be fine."

A few moments later, the men were armed and saddled. In a steady trot, they followed Turion from the camp. As the sun rose higher, the miles fell away beneath them. Crossing green hills, thistled meadows, and brooding moors, they journeyed on.

"I'm glad to see you're alive and well," Cazar said over the patter of hooves.

"And I, you," Turion said. Outside the camp, his demeanor had relaxed, and his tone was warmer. "We are not brothers, but I count you as a friend. You know I regret that day."

"I have heard nothing from you in years. You rode off into the sunset after the battle at Guard Tower Island, and no one has heard of your whereabouts since."

Turion kept his eyes fixed ahead. "It's better that way. I only bring trouble to people." He allowed silence to settle over the group before chasing it away. "I hear you are pretty good with a bow, archer boy."

Alyk beamed. "I hear you are good with . . . well, every weapon really. You're a living legend."

With no one around to hear, Jonny could speak more freely. "Was it you?"

Turion twisted in the saddle. "Was what?"

"The burnt goat. Did you hang it in my tent?"

"No," Turion replied. "I know nothing of it." There was no deceit in his voice.

"The scouts say they've been seeing a ghost at night," Jonny pressed.

"Not here," Turion said sharply. "Just a little more." He tapped his ears and pressed a finger to his lips.

Alyk suddenly pulled on the reins and stopped his horse. "We're close to the city of the Old Ruins . . . is that where you're taking us? Jonny, he's leading us into a trap."

"Relax, archer." Turion rolled his eyes. "That's not where we're going. And even if it was, there's nothing there but old bones and older stones. Even the ghosts have long ago left that place."

"How do you know?" Alyk squinted at him.

"I've walked those shadowed streets . . . and smelled the death of that place." He spurred his horse forward. "Come, it's just over this hill."

He led them to the opening of a cave that split the rolling countryside like the mouth of some great creature gulping at the earth from below.

"I'm not sure this is any better," Alyk mumbled as they dismounted.

Turion parted the thick vines that hung over the entrance. "Welcome." He snatched two torches from between a pair of stalactites. "Jonny, if you would be so kind."

Jonny flicked the torches alight. "We can talk here?"

"Aye," Turion said, leading them into the shadows. "Hundreds of years ago, some druids lived here. They warded the place against watchful eyes and keen ears. Darvor cannot spy on us here."

They entered a vast chamber thirty feet high, adorned with shimmering spires of rock. "Wow," Alyk marveled. "Beautiful!"

"You live here?" Cazar said, pointing to the corner. A small collection of boxes and barrels of supplies were carefully stacked. Next to it, a pile of old blankets had been fashioned into a modest bed.

"For the most part. I come and go where the wind blows me, but I usually end up back here."

Jonny ran his fingers over the cool stones, remembering the trials he had endured with

Cazar and Turion in Sliok years before. *Cazar, Turion, Swarlar, Rard, Eibbor* . . . So much had happened since that time, but one by one, all the ghosts of that adventure had wandered back into his life. *I can't seem to escape the past.*

"Darvor's blood!" Alyk shouted from the far side of the cave.

In Jonny's revelry, he had not noticed the archer had wandered away. Stammering and pale, Alyk came running. "Heavens! What is that?!"

"What is what?" Jonny and Cazar chimed.

"That damn pit!" Alyk cried, looking to Turion for an answer.

Turion sighed but said nothing.

Followed by Cazar and Alyk, Jonny edged toward the far side of the cave. There, shrouded by unyielding shadows, the cave floor dropped away into a vast chasm thirty or forty feet wide. Jonny inched forward and peered over the edge. The sight brought bile to his mouth, and he recoiled in surprise.

The pit was filled with hundreds, perhaps thousands, of severed troll heads. Some were old—all faded bone and empty eyes. Others were fresh, with drooping tongues and sallow cheeks. Many still wore helmets and cowls; a few stared up at Jonny with hollow eyes. All of them wore the pained faces they had worn in death.

Cazar looked back at Turion. "You killed all of them?"

Turion's eyes were wells of pain. "Aye."

"How many are there?" Alyk asked without pulling his eyes from the pit.

"I stopped counting years ago. There are many more since then." Turion turned away from them and crouched by a small pool of water near his bed. Dipping his hand into the water, he cupped some of the liquid and brought it to his mouth. "Killing is what I was always best at." He took another drink. "I can't undo my mistakes. But I'm trying to make the world a better place."

Cazar pushed a few stray locks from his face. "All these years, I wondered where you went after Guard Tower Island. You were hunting trolls . . . thousands of them."

"Seven years without any troll attacks." Without looking up, Turion waved a hand toward the pit. "This is what seven years of peace looks like."

For a moment, Jonny saw a change in Turion. His shoulders drooped and the shine left his hair. There was deep tiredness in his eyes and loneliness too. And then, just as quick, it was gone—replaced by the usual hunger.

"I didn't bring you here to show you my trophies," he sneered.

"Are you the ghost the scouts have been seeing? The flash of gold?" Jonny asked.

Turion touched his blond hair. "I've been following you since you left Gluton, yes. But I did not hang any goat by your tent, nor am I the only one haunting your steps."

"So it was Darvor?"

"You think you are ready for him—you are not." Turion slumped back against a pillar of rock, pulling his legs up in front of him. "He will pick you apart like a child pulling the legs off a spider. He will have you begging for mercy by the end."

"We'll stop him." Jonny clenched his fists. "Cazar, Alyk, the others . . . they'll get me close. And then I'll find a way."

"You will not," Turion sighed. "You do not know him like I do."

"So join us!" Alyk stepped forward.

"No." Turion shook his head. "I have another part to play."

Jonny scowled. "Is that all the reason you brought us here? To warn us? To cast doubt in our minds?"

"No." Turion again shook his head. He swirled his long finger in the pool of cave water and watched the ripples bounce off one another. "You've caught his attention now. He's watching you. It's why we could not speak in the camp. Even now he is moving against you. An army of trolls, almost four thousand strong, has just moved into Broken Ridge Pass. From there, they will emerge south of the mountains, above Mowka. Within a fortnight, they will have the city under siege."

"Only four thousand?" Jonny almost laughed. "The Mowkans can defeat that number."

"Not now, they can't," Cazar countered. "Eight of every ten of their fighting men marched north with Arvin Hillan to join our army. The city is all but undefended. And what's more, if the trolls take up a place on the cliffs above the city, no southern army could hope to break the siege."

Jonny slumped. He recalled how the city's unique position beneath towering cliffs left them vulnerable to bombardment from above. "He wants me to turn away . . . he's trying to distract us." He chewed his lip in thought. After a moment, he grunted. "We leave the city on its own."

"Abandon them?" Cazar said incredulously.

"They can last the siege. I've heard Stonehearth Keep has enough room in its catacombs and tunnels for everyone in Mowka to have shelter. And Lord Hillan himself has boasted the keep is impregnable."

"Be that as it may," Cazar argued, "thousands of our soldiers are highlanders. Their homes and families are in that city. Not to mention Arvin Hillan, the brother and heir of their high lord, died in yesterday's battle. They are without their leader. If they hear that you are abandoning their homeland, they will revolt. I promise you that."

"What would you have me do?!" Jonny shouted. "We cannot turn the whole army south and traverse Broken Ridge Pass and then turn back. We'll lose too much of the summer. Thousands more will abandon us if the campaign threatens to extend into the fall harvest."

"Who says it has to be the entire army?" Cazar asked. "We can split the men. The cavalry and fastest soldiers can go south, bringing minimal supplies so as not to slow them down. They can break the siege and immediately turn back northeast. The remainder of the army continues marching east at a slower pace. We meet near the East River with Lord Jocum's forces from Guard Tower Island. It would cost us very little time at all."

"I don't like it," Jonny groaned.

"I can't say I do either." Alyk rested a hand on Jonny's shoulder. "But I don't think there is a better way."

"What if Turion is lying?"

Turion gave a wry smile. "Then you know where to find me." He gestured at the cave around them.

Jonny turned to exit the cave. "Come on, we don't have much time."

Alyk and Cazar started after him.

"Jonny . . ." Turion added from his seat by the pool. "I'm sorry."

Jonny looked back.

The warrior's green eyes danced with the reflections of the cave walls. "I never wanted to be your enemy. Good luck. I mean it, truly. You'll need it."

THE UNEXPECTED

C azar peeked his head over the snow drift. In the bowl below, the troll camp sprawled like black barnacles sprouting from the snow. The air at this elevation was thin and the wind dreadful, even on such a blue summer day.

He squinted against the sun's reflection. On the ridge across the troll camp, Cazar saw a flash of light. *Polished steel.* It was the signal he had been waiting for. He turned to the man at his side. "They're in position."

Gjarn, the wild mountain guide, nodded back. "Good, good."

Cazar lifted his head over the snowbank to survey the field once more. The muscles of his back tightened as he readied for the coming battle.

After leaving Turion in the cave near the Ruined City, Cazar had returned to the camp with Jonny and Alyk. They met with the lords and officers and quickly split the army. Cazar assumed command of the detachment charged with lifting the siege of Mowka. With many of their best soldiers, including the cavalry and most of the highlanders from the lands around Mowka, Cazar had departed the camp the following day. Klorvone, a native Mowkan, had accompanied him, as had Rard, who begged the chance to go by saying, "I joined for two reasons only: free beer and killing trolls. And it seems I've already drank through most of the beer in camp."

The highlanders—Klorvone among them—knew the high passes and treacherous trails of the Great Mountains and led the army efficiently through the massifs north of Mowka. The larger part of the army stayed with Jonny, but Cazar's host constituted several thousand of the most experienced and capable soldiers. With only minimal necessary supplies weighing them down, the troops tolerated long marches and short nights. Furthermore, the highlanders were desperate to defend their home city and pressed the others forward with a hell-hastened pace.

True to Turion's word, the trolls had emerged from the shadowy passes of the Great Mountains on the tail of an early summer snowstorm that had blanketed the peaks in fresh powder. They had quickly set up camp at the edge of the cliff overlooking the city and settled in for a prolonged siege. With great trebuchets erected, they began bombarding the vulnerable city with boulders and blocks of ice mined from the peaks. Houses, taverns, shops, and churches were crushed beneath the barrage, while Lord Hillan, left with too few men to break the siege, had been forced to hovel with his people in the catacombs beneath Stonehearth.

And thus, Cazar's army penetrated the Great Mountains and arrived to find the siege long underway. To the south, the mountains dropped away in the form of a dizzying, terrifying cliff. At the base of the looming cliff, the city of Mowka was nestled. And while the rest of the realm was comfortably wrapped in the warmth of summer, atop the sheer mountain cliff a mile above Mowka, ice still clung to the stone, and thick clouds conjured up swirling snows that fell deep and heavy.

Coming from the north, the soldiers were at the trolls' rear. Undetected, they wasted no time preparing for the ambush. *We'll have them before the sun sets,* Cazar thought as he peered over a snowbank from a low ridge above the troll camp. The blinding sun still sat high in the sky.

From the moment he had laid eyes on the troll camp, he was pleased. Turion had claimed there would be four thousand trolls, among them Darvor's best units. But the camp looked smaller than Cazar had expected, and what trolls he could see were sickly and small. Even better, the men had succeeded in catching their foes unaware. Klorvone and Rard had taken half the troops around to the far side of the camp. Once in position, they planned to flash polished steel in the sun to signal to Cazar and the surprise attack would begin.

With his belly pressed against the snow, he surveyed the camp and waited for the flash from the ridge across the camp. His breath escaped in puffs that swirled in the frosty air. The soldiers behind him fidgeted in silent anticipation, the cold creak of their weapons and armor the only sound. He squinted against the glare of the sun. He feared he would miss the signal flash among the blindingly bright snow. If the ambush was ruined, the battle would be a far bloodier affair. At last, he saw the quick flit of reflected light from the distant ridge.

They gave the signal, Cazar thought. *It's time.* He exhaled deeply against his hands, trying to warm them. He hated fighting with cold fingers; it was harder to hold a sword. *And I move slower.* He closed his eyes for a moment and muttered an old prayer. Though far from a warrior-priest, Cazar knew the brink of battle was not a good time to practice atheism. With the prayer still hanging on his lips, he stood with a shout and charged forward.

Behind him, two thousand soldiers spilled over the snowbank. On the ridge across the camp, Klorvone emerged, and next to him, Rard. On their tail, another two thousand howling warriors joined.

Cazar was the first to reach the trolls. Ethwayl sang in the crisp air as he cut his way into the camp. Despite the countless melees he had fought in, the energy of battle never waned. His ears were filled with the white-hot noise of screams and clashing steel. His heartbeat pounded in his head and visions of Delena fluttered before his eyes between every swing of his sword.

A troll appeared from behind a tent, thrusting a trident with a hiss. Cazar caught the blow with Ethwayl and slid the blade between the tongs. With a twist, he threw the weapon from the creature's hands. A second troll emerged from behind, brandishing a broad-axe. Cazar spun, flashing his sword again. In the same swipe, he slashed through the chest of the first troll and deflected the axe blow of the second. He drove his knee up into the hip of the second troll. Off balance, the troll careened backward. Ethwayl flashed, and the troll was dead before he hit the ground. Cazar shook his head. *These are certainly not Darvor's best trolls.*

At last, he reached the middle of the camp, and Klorvone and Rard joined from the other side. Klorvone spun and twirled his long poleaxe, stabbing and hacking at any troll brave enough to challenge him. Nearby, Rard was fighting shirtless and bare-knuckled in his usual style. With blood dripping from his fists, he punched his way through the trolls.

An arrow whistled over Cazar's head and planted itself in Rard's shoulder. The man roared with enough strength to shake an avalanche from the mountain peaks. The blow would have felled any other man, but against Rard's immense size, the arrow looked a toothpick. The man's rage stirred, he grabbed the nearest troll and lifted the hapless creature high overhead. With a violent crunch, he twisted the troll and tossed the lifeless body aside.

"Are you all right, Gerard?" Cazar shouted.

"Call me that again, and you're next!" Rard bellowed.

Klorvone laughed before pointing forward. The trolls were being driven back against the cliffs. The three men exchanged nods and charged after them to finish the fight.

The battle was short and bloody. The last trolls were pushed back to the edge of the infamous cliff where legend held a brokenhearted Trystin threw himself to death. Many were slain, others were driven over the edge by the panic of their brethren. By noon, all that remained were smoldering tents and broken trebuchets.

Cazar paced among the remnants of the conquered camp, catching his breath and wiping the blood off Ethwayl. His steely eyes surveyed the chaos. Something seemed off, but he could not place it.

"Woot! What a victory!" Rard approached, unfazed by the half-dozen wounds on his bare chest and arms.

Klorvone joined them, trailing his poleaxe like a leaden tail.

The trio neared the edge of the cliff and peered down. From this height, the ruined buildings of the city looked comically small. The bodies of the trolls who had been driven over the edge were indiscernible.

Cazar gave a tired sigh. Once before, he had stood at the same spot with Jonny as the young boy had fearfully peered over the edge. *That was only seven years ago.* He found it hard to believe—it felt like a lifetime. *Now that boy is a man grown, the Cup of Power is destroyed, magic is real, and the love of my life is heavy with our second child.* He didn't know which was hardest to believe.

He turned from the cliff and looked back to the smoking remains of the troll camp. "How many trolls do you believe were here?" He thought back to the encounter with Turion. Four thousand, his old friend had promised.

Klorvone clicked and held up two fingers.

Rard nodded. "Aye, I reckon two thousand."

"Where are all the rest?"

"You're stalling!" Jonny exclaimed.

"I am not. It was a serious question!" Alyk looked up.

Jonny pointed to the gameboard between them. "I've captured two of your lords, and most of your cavalry is gone . . . you're stalling. Besides, that is too ridiculous to dignify with a response."

"It is not! Seriously, how long do you think you would have to hang someone upside down before the flow of food through their body would go the other way? So instead of putting food in the mouth . . . you know . . ."

Jonny blinked. "That's not how it works. Not even close." He looked at Eibbor, sitting in the corner of the tent. "Help me on this one."

Eibbor shook his head in disbelief. The empty space where his arm should have been ate up the shadows of the night air. "Is that really the stuff that goes through your head?"

Alyk brushed one of the pawns with his fingers. "I think about lots of important stuff. For instance, if you took a mountain goat out of the mountains, is it still a mountain goat? What about if you took a cave bear out of its cave?"

Jonny rolled his eyes. "Please stop talking and take your turn."

"Oh, what about this one Siley asked me: Would you rather have fingers as long as your legs or legs as long as your fingers? Go ahead and stew on that."

Jonny laughed. "You two are perfect for each other."

Alyk smiled, his eyes catching the candlelight. "She's too good for me; she just hasn't realized yet." He slid one of his lord pieces back a square. "Now if you would excuse me, nature calls." He sprung to his feet and slipped from the tent.

Turning his chair to face Eibbor, Jonny yawned and stretched his bare feet out, rubbing his toes on the rug. The night was warm, and he had changed out of his usual clothes in favor of a light tunic and thin pants. He gave Eibbor a long stare. *He's changed so much.* Jonny was always unsure how to initiate any meaningful conversation with the brooding man.

"We've made good time across Lydie. It won't be much longer until we meet up with Cazar again and, soon after that, with Lord Jocum. Then it's on to the troll lands.

Eibbor grunted in agreement.

Like talking to a wall.

"You've been there, you said."

Eibbor reached across his chest to scratch at the stump of his arm. "Aye."

"What do you know about it?" Jonny pressed.

"I know it is a place best avoided."

"I need more than that."

Eibbor grimaced at the memory. "Most of the lands are rugged, unkempt wilderness. The trees are bigger than some, the forests darker, the streams swifter. The meadows—and much of the land is meadow-land—is thistled and thorny. The wilderness is fouler than some places but not wholly sinister.

"But it is the cities you need fear. The trolls have few towns and cities, but what settlements exist are terrible places. The air is rank, and the buildings are built from bone and leather and twisted things. In black pits, their shamans work dark magic day and night. And the air is filled with the screams of tortured souls and unnatural creatures."

Eibbor shuddered. "Worst of all is their great city. Deep in their lands, in the shadow of the mountains they call Goulmcarn, is the black city they hold above all others. That's where you'll find Darvor . . . if he doesn't find you first. That's where it will end. If the black city does not fall, none of this matters."

Jonny let the words hang in the air for a moment. "Then that's where we go."

Eibbor looked away. "If you must . . ."

The tent flap lifted, and Alyk slid in, still lacing up his trousers. "Now, are you ready to lose this game?"

Jonny laughed. "Don't get your hopes up."

Outside, the night air was broken by a series of shouts.

"What's that?" Alyk paused.

The shouts were growing louder. A horn sounded in the distance, followed by another.

"Something's wrong," Eibbor muttered, drawing the long knife from his waist.

Alyk pushed to his feet. "You're in luck, Cupbreaker. Seems we won't finish the game."

The three men abandoned the tent and were greeted by chaos.

Fear and panic were spreading like wildfire through a dry field. Men and women raced about in disarray, pulling on clothes and grabbing weapons. In the confusion, tents were knocked over and fires flared.

"Trolls!" a man screamed, running toward them. "Trolls! They're in the camp!" He darted past.

A surprise attack! The blood drained from Jonny's face. "Where? Where?!" He raced forward. *How did they get past the sentries?*

A woman dashed by, pale and wide-eyed. "That way! They're coming from that way!"

"Jonny!" Alyk stopped. His bow was in his hand, an arrow already nocked. "Siley . . . I have to find Siley!"

"Go!" Jonny waved him off, stepping away from a panicked horse charging through the tents.

"Follow me!" Eibbor motioned. "This way." He pushed through the fleeing crowd.

The chaos worsened closer to the fighting. In the night air, the trolls appeared out of the shadows, lunging between tents, hacking and slashing their way through camp. Those soldiers brave enough to fight and those unable to flee were cut down all the same.

Eibbor rounded a wagon and came to face a large, snarling troll. The beast slashed with its axe, but even one-handed, Eibbor proved the greater match. His knife sang and the troll fell. Behind them, two more of the creatures charged. Jonny launched a pair of fireballs and the trolls dropped with sizzling holes in their chests.

Without hesitation, the pair plunged into the fray. Jonny quickly lost track of Eibbor as the warrior slipped and spun his way deeper into the battle, leaving a trail of slain trolls in his wake.

Jonny's mind raced. *Where did they come from? How did this happen?* All the while, he flung spell after spell, spraying the trolls with jets of flame. For every troll he killed, another stepped forward to take its place. His strength would not last forever, he reminded himself. Already, his lungs were burning.

And then he froze. Across the burning remains of the camp, Jonny saw him. In the red light of the fire stood Turion, staring back with hollow eyes. Shadows stretched his face into a ghastly scowl. In his hand, the thin blade of Filwain dripped scarlet blood.

As Jonny watched, Turion turned and barked an order to the nearest troll. A knot formed in Jonny's throat, and he wanted to scream. *Traitor!*

Turion again met Jonny's gaze, and a taunting smile spread across his face. With a shout, Jonny launched a ball of fire as hard as he could. The distance was too great, and Turion stepped away from the spell with a laugh.

Before Jonny could make another move, he heard a child shriek. He knew it at once. *Lord Brenton.* Spinning, he saw the young boy a hundred yards away. Encircled by a dozen of his loyal guards, the boy was attacked by a swarm of trolls, outnumbered and cornered.

Jonny looked back at Turion. To his dismay, the traitor stood opposite Eibbor. The breath seized in Jonny's throat. Turion loomed tall and poised, Eibbor bent and small. Eibbor, Jonny knew, could not defeat Turion. With two arms and some luck, the old Eibbor might have stood a chance. But crippled and frail as he was now, the duel was already decided. The pair exchanged unheard words and started toward each other.

Jonny's rage swelled as he realized his dilemma. He could not save them both. And without Lord Brenton, the Forest Folk would abandon him. He needed the Forest Folk and thus needed Lord Brenton. But Eibbor was his friend. Old words echoed in his head. First was Lady Arthin's threat should her son be harmed: *Even with all your magic, there will be nowhere you can hide.* And then Swarlar's: *But your decisions will come at a cost.*

He had only a heartbeat to weigh the predicament, but under the gravity of the moment, his mind whirled in overdrive. His choice would carve a deep wound upon his soul regardless of the path, and yet the most abhorrent choice was indecision. To abandon Lord Brenton was to abandon the cause. The Forest Folk would leave, and others would follow. The army would be doomed. But to cast aside Eibbor—the thought left him spinning.

Already the trolls were bearing down on Lord Brenton's outmatched guards. And as the guards fell one by one, the noose tightened around Jonny's neck. In the other direction, Turion had closed half the distance to Eibbor. The traitor's face was twisted in a snarl, and Filwain gleamed in the light of the burning camp.

There was no right decision, and Jonny was out of time. For a single flickering stitch in time, he wondered if there was some way out of the trap. But no. There was no time to hesitate. His mind was made.

He turned to Lord Brenton and the beleaguered Forest Folk, and from behind, he heard the clash of steel. Running toward the Forest Folk, he summoned a spell, pouring in the last of his fading strength. He released a pillar of fire and the trolls wilted under the flames. Lord Brenton and his guards were safe. Without stopping to be thanked, he spun back. Turion was gone.

Around Jonny, the battle died away. The soldiers in the camp had regrouped from the initial surprise and regained the advantage. The last trolls were retreating into the night. The attack was over.

Eibbor lay on the ground across the clearing. Numb to the world, Jonny staggered forward. He fell to his knees next to his friend. Eibbor was already gone, his eyes open and empty, locked on the stars above. Jonny pressed a hand onto the man's chest, where a pool of blood was bubbling up.

"No, no, no . . ." he wailed as hot tears seared his eyes. "Please, no!" He shook the man's shoulders. "No, you can't . . . you're supposed to see E'alith again . . . wh—No!"

"Jonny!" Alyk's voice was far away.

The world came flooding back. Jonny looked up. *Turion's getting away!* His rage breathed new life into him, and he sprung to his feet. He shouted to the nearby soldiers. "After them! They're getting away!"

Alyk grabbed him by the shirt and pressed his face close. "Jonny . . . Jonny! We can't. Listen to me . . ." The archer's face was streaked with dirt and blood, and tears softened his eyes. "We can't go after them. Not now. It's the middle of the night—our camp is in chaos. We only barely chased them off. We'd be slaughtered."

"No!" Jonny tried to push back. "Turion . . . he's getting away! We can't let him get away."

Alyk pulled him closer. "I know. In the morning . . . but not now. Not now."

Jonny sank his head into Alyk's shoulder.

"I'm sorry," Alyk whispered.

And Jonny cried.

The Hunt

Jonny stood before the mound of dirt—one of hundreds scattered over the hills. Like stains, each grave left a mark on the green fields of Lydie. The grass would cover the field again in time, but the wounds of the heart would not heal so fast.

Denial, anger, bargaining, depression . . . Jonny spit out a hollow laugh. He had heard of the stages of grief, but he could not see past the second. *These deaths were Turion's fault.*

Most of the graves had been marked by cairns or tokens, but Eibbor's was naked—a heap of soil a foot deep. He had no grieving kin to receive his belongings, no neighbors to toast his memory for years to come. *After all, he died years ago,* Jonny reminded himself. *A hero of Guard Tower Island.*

Still, the unmarked grave looked wrong, and Jonny's heart burned with fury. He knelt and, placing a hand on the ground, poured his sorrow and rage into the earth. The dirt beneath his fingers grew warm, then hot. The tips of his fingers seared in the heat, and he poured more of himself into the spell. The soil glowed and bubbled. At last, with his strength failing and the skin of his palm blistering, Jonny stepped back. Tendrils of smoke rose off the grave and, once they cleared, revealed the masterpiece. The earth had melted into a slate of opaque, gray-brown glass. Polished and smooth, it would reflect the clouds by day and the stars by night.

A tomb fit for Eibbor, son of Lyam.

"It's beautiful," Siley said, pulling Jonny from his waking dreams.

She stood behind him with an arm around Alyk's waist. The couple wore cheeks wet with matching tears.

"That glass will last a thousand years," Alyk said.

Jonny pushed past them to return to the camp. "Are the men ready?" he barked over his shoulder. "I'll not wait another minute."

The night had been spent recovering from the surprise attack. By morning, Jonny had set in motion plans to pursue Turion. He had permitted a few hours for graves to be dug, but it was already noon, and every moment he waited, Turion fled further. Most of the best soldiers had gone south with Cazar to rescue Mowka, but he still had more than a thousand good fighting men. *More than enough for that bastard.*

They were leagues behind Turion and his trolls and would need to move quickly to catch them before they disappeared across the East River into enemy lands. And so, before the sun reached its zenith, Jonny rode out of the camp at the head of a column of his best men. The other soldiers, as well as the camp women and wounded, would remain with the camp and supplies. Those left behind would continue east at a slower pace and meet up again with Jonny at the shores of the East River, where they would join Cazar's triumphant cohorts and Lord Jocum's fresh legions from Guard Tower Island.

Turion's army was traveling light and swift, and Jonny knew his force must do the same. He permitted the soldiers few supplies and only what food they would need for a few days' time. They made long marches with few rests. "You're stretching us too thin," Alyk whined, but Jonny would hear none of it. The tracks of the trolls were obvious to follow, and follow Jonny would.

It was not until the morning of the third day that the hunters caught scent of their prey. One of Jonny's outriders returned at a mad gallop, shouting the news. The rider was breathless and the horse in a lather.

"Cupbreaker, I've spotted them!" the man gasped, drawing on the reins. "Three leagues to the east and marching quick."

"How many?"

"Little more than half our number."

"And Turion was with them?"

"Aye, Commander. At the front of their column."

Jonny twisted in his saddle and shouted to the rows of men behind him. "We have almost caught them. Onward! Faster!"

A silvery lieutenant at Jonny's side sniffed. "If we march the men any faster, they'll not have feet to march on."

Jonny shot the man a murderous glare. "The trolls will be tired too. We must avenge our dead."

Alyk sighed. "If the dead care for anything, I doubt it's vengeance."

By nightfall, another outrider returned with news. Two leagues. *We're catching them,* Jonny glowered. But with more grumblings from his officers, Jonny was forced to relent and break the chase for the night.

"The men will fight better rested," Alyk assured him.

The pair took a seat beneath the whitened remnants of a long-dead tree. "He murdered Eibbor," Jonny replied. "And how many others?"

"Aye, and I'll not forgive him for it. But we must remember, you and I and a few of the officers are on horseback, but the rest of the soldiers aren't." Jonny had sent most of the cavalry with Cazar, a decision he had regretted since Turion's attack. "They need their rest, or they will be slaughtered."

"I hate him," Jonny growled through clenched teeth.

"I know, but we can't lose sight of the bigger picture. This is about Darvor."

"But if Turion gets across the river, we'll lose him. And he'll come back to haunt us. I promise you that."

Alyk produced a folded parchment from his bag. "We know where he's going," he said, unfolding the parchment. The map was faded but most of the features were legible. "The Thundering Ford." He tapped the squiggly line representing the East River.

The Thundering Ford, Jonny knew, sat nestled between steep riverbanks less than a mile upstream from an immense waterfall. The roar of the cascade had lent name to the crossing. "It's a hard crossing," Jonny said. "This time of year, the water will be flowing fast and deep. That's why Lord Jocum wanted us to meet him to the north by Tannery Ford; it's an easier crossing there."

"Aye, but for that very reason, Turion must go to the Thundering Ford. Ol' Jocum's got the Tannery closed."

Jonny scratched his chin. Alyk was right.

"If we start after him first thing in the morning, we can close those last two leagues by sunset." Alyk folded the map. "Let Turion enjoy his last night in this life."

Before the sun had chased away the stars, the hunt had resumed. Two leagues were no small distance when the prey was on the run, and Jonny drove the men hard.

Visions floated before Jonny's eyes—Turion's handsome face, twisted and sneering, painted in the light of the burning camp. Jonny had distrusted the warrior from the moment they met. It was he, after all, who had sold ancient secrets to Darvor and rode the Black Beast into battle at Guard Tower Island. But Swarlar claimed Turion did those dreadful things under the sway of Darvor. Jonny scowled, thinking how he had trusted Turion. *How could I be so foolish?* It would make no difference; he would have his vengeance by sunset.

As the afternoon swelled, they finally saw their foe. Cresting the next hill, Turion rode at the head of a ragged host of trolls. Beyond the hill, white clouds of mist billowed, carrying the roaring sound of falling water.

"They are nearly to the Thundering Ford!" Jonny shouted. "Forward!"

"They are still nigh a quarter league ahead," a petty lordling protested. "I do not know that we can catch them."

"We can and we will!" Jonny fixed his eyes on the enemy. *They are so close.* He could see Turion's golden hair reflecting the sunlight, and for a moment, he felt Turion's eyes fall heavy on him. The trolls disappeared over the crest of the hill, and Turion with them, descending toward the East River and the turbid crossing of the ford.

With their foe in sight and the end of their long march nearing, the men summoned the last of their strength and doubled their speed, desperately racing to catch the trolls before they could cross the river.

"Cupbreaker, look yonder!" One of the soldiers pointed behind them. Two riders were approaching from the southwest at a mad gallop.

"Alyk, who goes there?" Jonny asked, trusting his friend's keen eyes.

The archer squinted. "The son of Aazar and Klorvone of Mowka."

Jonny nearly smiled. *Just in time, my friends.* "We cannot wait for them; time is of the essence. Look how fast they are coming; they will catch us soon."

He turned back to the chase. Turion's army had again come into view. They had reached the shore of the river, but none had yet crossed. Jonny grinned.

He motioned the troops forward as he surveyed the scene. The earth sloped down from his position toward the river, falling almost two hundred feet over the half mile to the water. Across the river, the far shore rose steeply again, disappearing into the eastern plateaus.

For most of its length, the East River ran wide, a slow, lumbering behemoth of lazy bends and black ripples, but here near the Thundering Ford, the river cut between looming hills, picking up speed and anger as it went. The ford itself was three hundred feet wide, and waist deep at its shallowest point. The water flowed swiftly, spraying over great boulders and swirling in a froth of whirlpools and eddies. Anyone daring to cross needed to do so carefully, lest a misstep sweep them off their feet and away. If that happened, their doom was certain—just downstream, the river vanished entirely, falling away in a roar.

The waterfall was a beast. The whole river's volume dumped into its hungry gullet, falling three hundred feet into a maelstrom louder than any storm. The churn of the cascade stirred up immense clouds of mist that drifted up and down the river, a mile in either direction, sometimes obscuring the far shore.

To the north and south, stout hills loomed, blocking most of the river from view and even some of the waterfall. But the path ahead was clear.

Jonny glanced back over his shoulder. Cazar and Klorvone would catch them soon, but there was no point in waiting. He had Turion in his grasp. He turned back to the trolls. The miserable creatures huddled with their backs to the water, forming themselves up to fight. In their center, Turion stood tall and proud. *You have picked a grand place to die.*

Jonny raised his hand, preparing to command the charge. His own troops outnumbered Turion's trolls almost two to one. They could drive the trolls back into the river and slaughter them. The battle would be quick.

Through the mist, Jonny could see Turion staring back with eyes unblinking. His cold expression sent a shiver down Jonny's spine. There was no fear—instead, he was calmly confident. Something was wrong.

The warrior lifted a horn and brought it to his lips. He sounded a long, doleful note, loud enough even to break over the roar of the waterfall. Jonny's stomach dropped.

To the north, a swarm of trolls appeared over the adjacent hill, charging down the slope to Jonny's flank. *Another ambush,* Jonny realized with growing panic. The hunters had become the hunted.

A THIRST NO BLOOD CAN QUENCH

The swarm of trolls sprung over the hill with war cries wet on their lips. They bounded down the slope to swell the ranks surrounding Turion. Beyond them, the waters of the ford swirled and sprayed.

Alyk and the other lieutenants shouted orders while the tired men hustled into battle formation. Jonny's horse whinnied in fright and reared, threatening to throw him. But he was elsewhere, lost a thousand miles in his own head. The surrounding noise and chaos were quiet and distant. *I was wrong again . . . I walked into the trap.* What had promised to be an easy victory was now a fight for survival.

"Forward! Forward! All forward!" Alyk's order pulled Jonny back.

The soldiers charged forward with a shout. A half mile ahead, the trolls did the same. Jonny surveyed the clashing armies. With the troll reinforcements, they were nearly the same size. Many of the trolls were tired and battered from the long chase, but Jonny's men were as well.

"We'll have need of your magic, Cupbreaker!" Alyk quipped.

Jonny set his jaw. "We have the high ground."

"What did we miss?" Cazar said, appearing breathless at Jonny's side. Klorvone rode up a half moment behind, brandishing his gleaming poleaxe.

"Where's Rard?" Jonny asked.

Klorvone clicked and gestured.

"Too big to ride a horse," Cazar translated.

"Turion!" Alyk pointed.

The warrior stood at the rear of his advancing trolls with his back to the river's edge. He had taken the bridle of a black stallion in hand and, with his usual lithe movements, swung a leg over the saddle.

He means to cross the ford. Jonny's eyes grew wide. But, again proving Jonny wrong, the warrior turned his horse and broke south, tracing the river's edge and disappearing into the mist.

"I'll be damned if he gets away!" Jonny raised his reins in a white-knuckle grip.

Cazar held up a hand. "No."

"Your magic is needed here," Alyk said, waving toward the imminent battle.

"He killed Eibbor!"

Cazar drove down on his spurs. "Leave Turion to me." And before Jonny could raise a protest, the old Guard was gone.

Cazar left the sounds of battle behind as he galloped after his quarry. The water shaken free of the river by the angry falls rose in billowing swirls of mist. It swallowed him and blinded him to all that lay around. If the foe had been anyone besides Turion, Cazar would not have pressed the hunt. The low visibility made the landscape ripe for an ambush. But Cazar had known Turion since childhood. *He won't ambush me or cut me down through trickery and deceit.*

He squinted at the ground. The mud held the hoofprints of Turion's horse. *Where are you going, old friend?* It was not like Turion to run from a fight. The tracks led up the hill, and Cazar followed.

Cazar had realized Turion was not true-faced from the moment the old Guard lifted the siege at Mowka. There, he had found less than half the promised force of trolls. Wheeling his army around, he had tried to catch Jonny before the trap could be sprung. But sleepless days and nights of hard riding had not been enough. By the time he arrived at the Thundering Ford, the battle was already set.

Cazar leaned forward and his horse climbed the slope. Something did not sit right with him. One look at the battlefield and Cazar had found a question circling his mind. *Something doesn't fit . . .*

The mists parted and Cazar rose over the crest of the hill. Turion stood waiting to greet him.

The hill buttressed the west edge of the falls, standing like a sentinel over the crashing water. At its edge, it dropped a thousand feet to the tumultuous froth at the base of the falls. Dry and windswept, the hilltop was littered with stunted trees, thorny shrubs, and the cleaven boulders of a long-forgotten watchtower.

"Hello, Cazar," Turion said, sliding Filwain free of its sheath.

Jonny's throat went dry as his friend disappeared into the mist after Turion. With his magic, he could have defeated Turion; he had no doubt about that. But in honest combat, sword against sword, Turion was revered far and wide as the greatest of any generation. *Goodbye*, Jonny wanted to say as Cazar broke away, but the word stuck at the back of his throat.

For a moment he wanted to order Cazar to stop, but he knew he had no power over the old Guard. And Alyk was right—the battle hung in the balance, and Jonny's magic could tip the scales. He needed to join Klorvone, Alyk, and the soldiers. If Cazar did not go after Turion, the great warrior would escape, only to haunt them again.

It seemed a waste to Jonny as Cazar disappeared into the mists, but of all the warriors in all the ages of man, Cazar was the only one Turion ever respected. If there was anyone Jonny could hope for, it was the Son of Aazar.

With a heavy heart, Jonny wheeled back to the impending battle. His troops ran toward the horde of trolls, shouting battle cries and brandishing swords and spears. Klorvone was among them, a full head taller than any of the others. Alyk had taken up position behind the ranks with a dozen other archers. Jonny scowled and spurred his horse into the fray.

On horseback, Jonny quickly caught the other soldiers and met the trolls at the same time. He sprayed down a dozen of the beasts with a burst of flame. On either side, man and troll collided with a thunderous clash. The air was filled with splitting steel and cracking bones, pained cries and dying horses.

Jonny melted a score of the brutes with a wave of his arm, and feeling the magic pull the strength from his core, he pulled back. He could not be as foolish with his magic as in the past; he knew his limits. Klorvone stepped in front of him and split a troll from head to toe with a swing of his axe.

Catching his breath, Jonny straightened in his saddle to survey the chaos. The combat was vicious, bloody, and intense, but an odd feeling settled in the back of Jonny's mind. He could not pin it, and in the thick of the fighting, it slipped beyond his grasp like a dandelion seed in a gale. Something about the battle and its circumstances was off. Not wrong, but off. He scanned the battle, trying to place it. The armies were of equal size, but with the gentle slope of the riverbank playing to their advantage, Jonny's troops slowly drove the trolls back toward the river. Meanwhile, the two hills that hemmed either side of the ford kept the combatants locked in, unable to maneuver or run.

With a laugh, Jonny realized what he was missing. He launched another flurry of fireballs at the trolls and let out a hoot. "Ha! He messed up," he shouted to Klorvone. "Turion triggered the ambush at the wrong time. He sprung the trap too early!"

⸻

The waning sun caught the edge of Filwain, painting the blade in a blood-red sheen. Turion's face was dark, and his lips bent in a scowl. "I knew you'd come." His voice cracked like the first frost of winter.

"Stay your sword, Turion, and put an end to this madness." Cazar swung off his horse.

"No."

The finality in the word froze Cazar in his tracks. "So that's it? You've thrown your lot in with Darvor again. What is it this time? Has he clouded your mind again? Enslaved you with his black words?"

Turion raised the corner of his lips. "My mind is clear. It has been these last seven years."

"Then what's your excuse?"

Turion stayed silent. His fingers tightened around the hilt of his sword.

"Darvor's blood!" Cazar swore. "You've betrayed us again." Unable to control his anger, he burst, "You cut down Eibbor! You killed a hundred men in that attack on Lydie! Hundreds more will die in your ambush today—"

"You're better than that, Cazar!" Turion's voice was strained. "I expect as much from that arrogant boy-warlock to whom you've sworn your sword. But I expect better of you."

Cazar stepped back and narrowed his eyes.

"Look around you, Cazar. Look at the landscape, at the battle down there." He pointed to the dale below them, where the first sounds of battle had erupted. "See it not through the glint of passion but rather with those cold military eyes of yours. Understand what the Cupbreaker was too foolish to. Then name me a traitor, if you will."

Cazar looked down the slope of the hill, past the thick mist of the falls. He saw the narrow strip of land between the two hills and the two armies locked in battle. He saw the flashes of Jonny's magic and knew that, somewhere in that distant chaos, Klorvone and Alyk fought with him. He saw, too, the swirling waters of the Thundering Ford and the churning rapids that paved the way to the gluttonous falls. The steep banks of the river and the clouds of mist and fog, he saw it all. And then he saw it differently.

His eyes widened with realization, but he turned back to Turion with a suspicious stare. "You killed Eibbor."

"I had to." There was a hint of pain in his voice.

Cazar shook his head. He saw Turion now in a different light. With new insight, the events over the last weeks coalesced into a new form. The realization crashed around Cazar in a wave, the weight of which threatened to drown him. Turion stood before him not only as a traitor and murderer—though he was those things—but as a friend and a fulcrum upon which the fate of untold thousands rested. "There had to be another way," he said with a strained voice.

"Not against Darvor. You won't have another chance like this."

"So join us now. Help us finish this!"

Turion continued, ignoring Cazar's plea. "The way ahead is clear. Darvor has withdrawn an army of his finest trolls to defend his throne in their black city. He put all his remaining forces into this plan and this attack. You'll meet no other resistance until the end."

"You'll be there with us, walking through the conquered ruins."

Turion shook his head. "No. Even if Jonny could accept that I am not the villain he claims me to be, Darvor would not let me live. You do not know his power like I do. You do not fear him enough. He walks among your camp at night. He whispers unseen in Jonny's ear. While you liberate Mowka, he watches your son sleep in Delena's arms. He is everywhere and nowhere. He builds his web of lies and traps and, like a puppet master, watches us dance on our strings. No, Cazar, he will find me, and he will do far worse to me than you can imagine."

"What will you do?" Cazar asked.

"No, my old friend, the question is, what will *you* do? You see, I cannot let you leave here. Not while my soul's great question remains unanswered."

"You have answered that greatest of questions. You have shown yourself to be true, to be marked with iron morals. No one can claim to have done more for the cause of good."

"That was never my question." Turion's eyes burned black. "I know where I stand, where I have always stood. But alas, my soul needs something more."

Cazar took a step back and raised his hand. "We've been through this before."

"Only once in true battle. Every other time has only been on the training yard."

"You are a better swordsman than I. I'll not fight you again."

Turion growled and swung his sword. "You will! Last time, you fought with a broken rib, bruised, bloodied, and tired. We are evenly matched this time. And before I go to my endless sleep, I must prove I am the greatest."

Cazar started to protest, but Turion silenced him. Stepping aside, he revealed a bow and quiver resting on the rock behind him. "Run and I will put an arrow through your heart." His tone broached no argument. "If you want to see Delena again, if you want to see your son and your unborn child, you must fight me."

"I can't," Cazar's voice wavered. A fear coursed through him he had never known.

Turion hoisted Filwain. "I have loved you almost as much as I have hated you. And for that part of me that still sees you like a brother, I hope you are wrong."

◆——————◆

Beside Jonny, a young lordling fell with a troll arrow protruding from the sight gap in his helm. The battle had not lost any of its ferocity, but since Jonny's realization, the outcome had become inevitable. Klorvone had joined a handful of Lanaki in driving the troll's flank back toward the water while Jonny stayed with the vanguard, strafing the enemy as his strength allowed. At some point, Jonny's horse met a troll spear, and he was thrown to the ground. But bruised and muddied, he fought on, gaining inch by inch.

The troll numbers dwindled as they fell back. When at last they were pushed into the river, their ranks fell into chaos. Trolls tripped over one another, struggling to maintain their footing in the river's swift current. Those who fell were swept downstream toward the roaring falls; those who did not met the arrows of Alyk and his archers.

When all was said and done, a single troll reached the far side of the river. He splashed ashore, staggering like a drunk. Alyk laughed and drew back on his bow. Only pausing for a moment to weigh the wind, Alyk let the arrow fly. Over water and through mist, the dart flew, and where it stopped, the troll did too.

A hearty cheer went up from the soldiers, and Alyk flicked Jonny a wink.

Jonny did not pause to join the victory celebration. He wheeled, still fighting for breath, and fixed Alyk with a somber expression. "Cazar . . ."

--- ◆ ---

Cazar drove the hilt of his sword forward with a shout. Turion adjusted, shifting his foot to not be caught off balance. Cazar pivoted and his sword caught Turion's. The polished blade of Ethwayl slid down the pale steel of Filwain with a shower of sparks.

Cazar slashed wildly, but again, Turion was quicker, moving with the poise of a dancer. Cazar's sword bit only air and he staggered to regain his balance. Turion strafed back to a safe distance and laughed.

"The years have not slowed us," Turion said. If he was tired, he did not show it.

Cazar ran a hand across his mouth, wiping away the blood that ran from his lip. "Please!" he panted. "Stop!"

"Do not waste your breath."

Cazar's mind was a maelstrom of fear and rage. For what felt like an eternity, he had sparred with his former friend. He had succeeded in drawing blood from Turion's shoulder and cutting a wisp of the warrior's golden hair but nothing more. Meanwhile, Turion had dealt him a gash on the thigh, split his lip, and severed part of his ear.

It was too much to bear. Like steam escaping a boiling pot, Cazar's emotions bubbled over. He screamed, long and loud.

"That's it." Turion smiled. "Get angry. Hate me."

"I will never hate you." Cazar raised his sword.

"Then you will lose."

The warrior lunged, driving Cazar back toward the toppled ruins of the watchtower. Seven years had passed since their last duel, and both were seven years wiser. Like a chess match, they fought; every move calculated, every parry part of a grander strategy. Turion was stronger and faster, and his reach was precious inches more, but Cazar fought back with frenzied determination. *Delena . . . Dazar . . . home . . .* Every blow brought memories of warm summer nights, gentle kisses, sweet wine, and soft music. And so he fought.

As a boy at the Guard's Academy, he had sparred with Turion time and time again. Every time he had marveled at Turion's skill. There was no one with his natural grace nor his unfettered drive to improve. Their practice sessions drew crowds, but most often, they ended with Cazar on his back in the mud. There was simply no one who fought like Turion. But this was not the training yard, and there would be no handshake at the end.

In the dale below, the sounds of battle were fading. But the duel only swelled to fill the void. Turion pressed the attack, beating Cazar back toward the cliff and the falls' roar. *It's over,* Cazar realized with growing despair. He was tired and growing slower, and no amount of will was enough to match his foe's speed and skill. He brushed aside Turion's thrust with one of his own but only just turned aside the counterattack. A thousand times Cazar had faced death, and a thousand times death had been cheated. *And now my debts are due . . .*

But then he saw an opening. Turion slashed and Cazar ducked. The steel whistled over his head. He thrust his shoulder up, forward, right at Turion's chest. But Turion pivoted. *That's what he wanted,* Cazar realized too late. Turion's feint had worked. Cazar fell off balance; his heel caught an upturned rock. He crashed to the ground and the fall drove the breath from his lungs.

At once, Turion was on him, swatting aside Cazar's meager defense. With a flick of the wrist, Ethwayl flew from Cazar's hand and clattered across the stones.

Turion stood over him, face bent in a sneer. There was no time to even consider how it would feel to die. Turion brought the sword down with a shout. Cazar closed his eyes.

Delena . . .

The world went quiet.

There was no pain. Slowly, Cazar opened his eyes. The sunset sky above was purple, orange, and gold. He blinked.

Next to his head, Filwain protruded from the ground, the tip buried in the dirt next to his ear, the blade rising away from him. The handle rocked back and forth, coming to a stop.

Cazar raised himself up. His eyes fell on Turion, standing on the edge, his back to the looming cliff.

"I won." His words were soft and threatened to break under their own weight. "The songs will never sing of this. The minstrels will never remember me as a hero. Jonny will even smear my name as a villain, but you know, and I know." He shook his head. "I killed more trolls than can be counted. *Grevices*, giants, spriggons, wolfmen, *tentali* . . . a hundred strange beasts and ten times as many grand adventures. There has never been anyone like me, and now there is no doubt—I am better than even you. I stand alone atop a pantheon of great warriors. Why does it still feel so empty?"

"Turion . . ." Cazar extended a hand.

"No matter. Now I can go—now that I know I was the best." He took a step back and fell out of view.

Jonny reached the hilltop first, followed soon by Alyk and Klorvone. They found Cazar alone. The warrior knelt next to the fallen remains of a wind-battered watchtower. His broad shoulders shook as he sobbed. Jonny took a step forward but stopped. He did not know what to say.

Cazar's shoulders grew still, and a long moment passed. He turned to face them. "He's gone." His eyes were red. "Over the falls." He raised his hands and in them rested Filwain, glowing red in the fading sun. "He bought us this victory today with his life. Darvor laid this trap for you, Jonny. He knew you would be stirred into a rage and run right into his ambush. If Turion had crossed the river like Darvor planned, you would have chased after him. Then the ambush would have fallen on your rear. You would have been trapped in the river, fighting trolls on both sides. The soldiers that stumbled would have been swept over the falls by the current. And the river's water would have quenched your fires and eaten up whatever magic you tried to use."

"What do you mean?" Jonny asked, his blood still running hot.

Cazar climbed slowly to his feet. "It would have been a slaughter. This war would have ended here today. Darvor would have won if not for Turion." He fastened Filwain to his belt. "Do you understand?"

Jonny said nothing.

"Turion was once a pawn of Darvor's. He allowed Darvor to believe he still was. Darvor used him to incite you into a rage and lure you into a trap. But Turion triggered the ambush at the wrong time, so you did not fall into Darvor's trap. He knew that doing so would bring Darvor's fury down upon him, but he did it anyway. And rather than face Darvor's wrath . . ." He looked to the cliff. "Remember that when you remember him."

Cazar's words summoned a strange mix of emotions in Jonny. A deep hatred of Turion still rested in his heart but was suddenly tempered with shame, pity, and a thousand other emotions that did not carry names. "He killed Eibbor," Jonny mumbled.

"Aye, he did that too." There was sadness in Cazar's voice and deep weariness. He started forward and brushed past them on his way down the hill. "I'm tired . . ." Then, over his shoulder, he added, "Let's go—it's time to finish this."

ALL ROADS LEAD

"My boy, how you've grown!" Jocum threw his arms wide and pulled Jonny into a tight embrace. The aging commander of Guard Tower Island was a grizzled man who smelled of ale and cheese.

"Seems you haven't shaved since the last time I saw you," Jonny chided, freeing himself from the man's arms.

Jocum rubbed at his gray-streaked beard. "Aye, hides the scars." A grim shadow passed over his face, and Jonny knew his thoughts returned to the bloody battle fought at Guard Tower Island years before. The fight had cost Jocum an eye and five thousand other men their lives.

"I don't have that luxury," Jonny said, putting a hand to his own smooth cheek.

Jocum laughed. "Not yet, but I see some fuzz sprouting. Maybe one day . . ." He turned to Jonny's companions. "Son of Aazar! Every day that passes, you look more like your father." Cazar stepped forward and the two shared a warm greeting.

"Commander—pardon me, it's Lord-regent now, isn't it?" Jonny corrected himself. "Lord-regent, allow me to introduce my companions: Alyk, son of Alyn; Klorvone of Mowka; and Rard of the Lost Lands."

At the last of the introductions, Jocum strained his neck to look up. "Rard, you say. My, you're a big fellow. Were I to climb my own shoulders, I might still not be able to put a hat on your head."

"Dare you to try," Rard growled.

"His bark is worse than his bite . . . unless you're a troll." Jonny waved his hand.

"Right, right," Jocum said. Looking at Jonny's companions, he nodded. "Glad to have you." He swept out his hand. "If you'd follow me, the camp is this way. The men you hoped for, I've gathered all and more."

Jonny and his friends fell into step behind the Lord-regent and were soon shown to the camp. As planned, Jocum had gathered the willing and able fighting men of Guard Tower Island and its hinterlands and marshaled them at the shores of the East River near its easiest crossing. Since the battle at the Thundering Ford, Jonny had salvaged the scattered pieces of his army and marched north to join Jocum. Now, reunited with the cohorts Cazar had taken to break the siege of Mowka and the units left behind after Turion's ambush, the army was again approaching something formidable.

The sun was high in the sky by the time Jonny's army began filing into the camp. "Lord Voramandier sent messenger birds to all the lords of Guard Tower Island, bidding us not to lend you our arms," Jocum said, standing next to Jonny on a low hill outside the camp. Together with Cazar, the three men watched Jonny's army file into Jocum's camp. "It seems that cantankerous old fool is not rooting for your success." Jocum grinned. "But ever since that battle, stories of the two of you have passed from lip to lip through every hearth and tavern in these lands. The young Lord Leyne even commissioned a song of your exploits. The vassal lords of House Leyne were quick to burn Voramandier's letters and call their banners. Long have we lived under the tyrannous threat of the trolls. But no more."

"You've done well," Cazar commended. "Your men nearly double our strength."

Jonny nodded his agreement. The camp stretched toward the horizon in orderly rows of tents pockmarked with campfires and supply wagons. Lord Leyne's forces alone counted in the thousands. And from where he stood, Jonny spied the flags of a dozen other lesser houses fluttering in the wind. The blue and silver of the Estermonts, the orange and blue of the Fastricks, the yellow and purple of the Rosmars, the plaited brown of the Lethhulls. *We're coming for you, Darvor.*

"Our rangers have reported the troll lands have largely emptied," Jocum continued. "Many of the trolls went west to meet you on the plains of Lydie. The rest have fallen back to their cursed city in the shadow of the Goulmcarn Mountains."

"So, we've heard," Cazar said. "The way ahead is clear. We'll meet little resistance until we're outside their walls."

"And then?" Jocum raised the eyebrow over his blinded silver eye.

"Hell."

The word sent a shiver down Jonny's spine.

"Your soldiers and camp followers have come a long way these last few weeks," Jocum attempted to change the mood. "We have food enough to feed them; oats and hay for the horses too. I assume you'll want to stay here a time and rest."

"Three days," Jonny replied. "Three days and no more." And somewhere in the back of his mind and a thousand leagues away, Jonny heard an evil laughter.

Cazar unfastened the clasp on his cuirass and dropped the armor to the ground with a clang. Underneath, his tunic was dark with sweat. He had spent the afternoon training a batch of young soldiers, and his muscles ached from the effort. His lessons had drawn almost a hundred to a small clearing beyond the camp. Many of the men Jocum had enlisted were green and had never fought in real combat. They had been boys when their fathers died defending the walls of Guard Tower Island. *What had been their mother's reactions when they answered the call to enlist?*

He looked the soldiers over, taking in the wide range of emotions. Doubt, apprehension, and fear lurked behind some eyes. Most seemed fiercely proud. A few months before, most had been farm boys, apprentices, and shepherds, dreaming their lives away. Now they had been given a chance at a glory they had not thought possible. It had been many years since Cazar had been that green. A pupil at the Academy of the Guards of Gluton, he stood where they now stood. His instructors' lessons had kept him alive through all the adventures since, with great help from luck and chance. He was painfully aware of the responsibility he now bore as an instructor to the next generation, and it weighed heavy on him that no matter how well he drilled them, not all his trainees would survive the battles ahead. *If my lessons save even one of them, it will have been worth it.*

Cazar dismissed the trainees with a wave. The sun was setting, and tomorrow morning they would cross the East River and begin the long march into the land of the trolls. They would need their rest. *I do too,* Cazar admitted, rubbing the scab on his lip. The fight with Turion had drained him, leaving him feeling like tattered sinew stretched over a wicker frame. And something Turion had said still haunted Cazar: "*He watches your son sleep in Delena's arms.*" He grimaced and felt the scab pulling his lip. *What kind of foe are we up against? Is Jonny ready?*

Cazar set down the blunted training sword he had been using and picked up Filwain and Ethwayl, fastening them both to his belt. With tired bones, he started back toward camp, winding through the rows of tents. *Dinner will be served soon in the command tent. Maybe pork . . .*

He parted the tent flaps and stepped inside to the smell of smoke and mead. A swell of hushed whispers died at his entrance. He blinked back the darkness, and the figures came into focus. Alyk was there, as were Rard and Klorvone and a dozen other lords and officers.

"Perhaps the son of Aazar knows," one of the lords said.

"Aye, see if he makes sense of it," Rard growled.

"Makes sense of what?" Cazar asked.

The lords stepped away from the table. Alyk swept a hand across the wood. "This."

Cazar stepped closer to inspect the tabletop. Deep black scars were seared into the wood. In some places, the wood still smoked, and the ashes glowed red. The scars formed numbers and letters written in slashing script.

"Who did this?" Cazar asked.

"We don't know," an officer replied. "Nobody saw anything."

"What does it mean?" Alyk asked.

"Does Jonny know?" Cazar demanded.

"Do I know what?"

Cazar spun to see the boy standing at the door. His hair was still wet from washing in the river.

Jonny approached and scanned the table. He stiffened, and the blood ran from his face. For a moment, Cazar feared he might collapse, but the boy steadied himself and looked up. "Question the guards stationed outside the tent and anyone known to have passed the tent this afternoon. Someone must know something."

"We have," Alyk replied. "No one knows how this got here."

"No one was seen coming or going from the tent," an officer confirmed.

"I was in here an hour ago and the table was untouched," Rard added.

"What does it mean?" a stout, bearded lord piped.

"Nothing, it's nonsense." Jonny swayed. "Take the table outside and have it destroyed. Find us another to use." Jonny's fingers curled into fists. "After that, my lords should get some rest. We have a long road ahead of us."

Rard and Klorvone hauled the long table out as the remaining lords and officers followed, leaving only Cazar, Alyk, and Jonny.

"Lie to them, but not us," Cazar said. "What did that writing mean?"

The facade of the confident commander had melted, and Jonny stood before him a scared boy. Looking every bit as afraid as he once had in the dark of Sliok, Jonny sank into a chair. "Those numbers and words . . . that's my family's address. He knows where they live."

—◆———◆—

Jonny wandered among the rows of tents with his cloak pulled around his shoulders. The night was not cold, but Jonny felt a chill, nonetheless. The summer stars still glimmered above, but with each night, they crept closer to the horizon, just as Jonny knew he crept closer to Darvor.

They had crossed the East River a few days prior and were making their way into the land of the trolls. So far, they had seen little sign of the enemy save for a few burnt-out villages and abandoned outposts. But that only made Jonny more nervous.

He rounded a wagon and came across Siley sitting beside a crackling fire. Alyk was not in his usual position at her side, but despite her solitude, she did not seem lonely. The tune of a dancing ballad drifted in the air from a few tent rows over, and Siley swayed to the melody, tapping her foot.

"It's coming this way, oh, an angry horde,"
Said the boy to the mighty lord
But he wasn't Tomler and wasn't a fool
Said the other, "I've come to rule."

"Have you heard it?" Siley said, twisting to look up at him.

"Bits and pieces," Jonny replied. "It's mostly wrong. I never killed the Black Beast; that was Eibbor."

She patted a stool beside the fire, bidding him to sit. "I know, but it's a lovely song, nonetheless. Like the heroes in all the stories I heard as a wee lass. Tomler the Fool, Tomm o' the Hills, Glu Voramandier . . . and now Cazar and Jonny." She covered her laugh with a slender hand. "The singers from Guard Tower Island introduced the song to the rest of us, and now men ask for it every night."

Jonny took a seat. "They don't mention all the blood."

"They never do. The songs, the stories—they're always polished. That's all right. Sometimes the world needs polish."

"Where's Alyk?" Jonny asked, stomping an ember that had settled near his boot.

"It was his turn to take the watch tonight." She raised a mug of cider and drew a sip. "Do you know the meaning of those stones?" She pointed across the fire from them to a stone pillar standing on end.

It was not the first Jonny had seen. The wilderness east of the frontier was scattered with them. The pillars were about the size of a fencepost, cut from gray stone and marked with ancient runes. Many were toppled and smashed, some were grown over by vines, but a few, like the one present, remained undefiled.

"They mark the old roads through these lands."

"They might if there were ever real roads here," Siley replied. "I've heard the lords talk—they say the stones were erected by tribesmen that inhabited these parts long before the trolls, perhaps even before the Broken Ages and the War of the Giants. But they're wrong."

She brushed a wisp of copper hair behind her ear. "They're fae stones, raised by fairies long before the first men arrived. They were once found in every corner of the land, but now—"

"What happened to them?"

"Toppled, buried, stolen . . . they're all but gone from any place where men are found. There is one in the village I grew up in, but I knew of no others until we came here, to the land of the trolls."

"I don't mean the stones. What happened to the fairies?"

Siley shrugged. "Wise men claim there were never fairies. But when I was young, there was an old smith in the village—you know the sort: beard down to his knees, so old that even the grandparents in the village couldn't remember him ever being young. He claimed the fairies were remnants of the Old Magic with which the Creator wove the world into being. They settled to earth like sparks from a campfire." She stretched out her hand and touched a floating ember from the fire. "They danced in the fields, sang in the forests, and bathed in the waterfalls. Powerful beings, they had but a single weakness: hate. When the first men arrived, they carried a drop of that hate in their hearts. And, like all foul poisons, it only took a drop to spread. Everywhere people went, the fairies died, and with them, the Old Magic faded."

Jonny thought about his own world, of the hate and violence on the nightly news, and wondered what magic might once have been. "Can it be undone?"

Siley offered a warm smile. "There's an antidote to any poison. But you're a smart one—I don't need to tell you what it is."

Jonny looked back to the fire and let his mind drift. It was a charming story, but like the singer's version of the events in the battle of Guard Tower Island, it certainly wasn't the whole truth. Anyone with eyes could see the "fae stones" marked the trolls' war trails, one of which they'd been following for days. And in this wilderness, he knew all roads led to a single place . . .

As if on cue, Siley spoke. "Alyk has told me about Darvor."

The name stung Jonny's ears and he fought to steady himself.

"He really cares about you, Jonny. Alyk . . . he's worried."

Plagued by a sudden chill, Jonny tugged the corners of his cloak, pulling the cloth tight around him. "What's to worry about?"

"That." She leaned forward. "That right there—you're terrified, but you won't even let yourself admit it. We all see it. You barely eat, you're up walking this camp at all hours of the night. I know you've noted your clothes are getting looser . . . you're wasting away."

Jonny swallowed hard, blinking back tears. "Truth is, I don't know if I can stop him. I think I can, but I have my doubts. It will take everything I have to defeat him, every ounce of strength. And he has thousands of his best trolls guarding him now. I can't get through them and still have the strength to fight."

"You're not alone." The earnestness in her eyes gleamed like a second moon. "None of us can get through this life on our own. You've got a lot of friends, Jonny. That's what friends are for—shouldering the burden this life puts on us."

Jonny turned away, afraid that if he spoke, his voice might break, and tears might flow.

But the moment was shattered by the shouts of an approaching lieutenant. "Cupbreaker! Cupbreaker, this way!"

Jonny stood and hailed the lieutenant. It was Davinnof, a familiar face from Jonny's long-ago quest to the Vale of Joy.

"To the northeast of camp," the man gasped. "Half a league."

Sparks danced at Jonny's fingertips as he tensed for battle. "Trolls?"

"Perhaps, or something fouler—you'll have to see."

Jonny heard no battle horns, and something about the man's countenance alerted him it was not a battle. The fire vanished from his fingers.

He started after the lieutenant and was joined on the way by Cazar and later by Klorvone and Rard.

"Some of Lord Arthrin's men found it," Davinnof explained as they walk-ran toward a hill beyond the camp. The wild forest pressed in around them, and thick trees drowned out the moon.

"What? Found what?" Jonny demanded.

Davinnof only shook his head. "Right here, just ahead."

The young Lord Arthrin stood in a small circle of torchlight with a gaggle of his household guards. Jocum and Alyk were with them.

Silently, the crowd stepped aside. Jonny's stomach twisted at the sight, and he pressed his hand to his mouth to stifle a cry. Six bodies were mounted on the trees, impaled by iron spikes driven into the wood. All were the bodies of men, but little of their humanity remained. Mutilated, some were missing limbs while the entrails of others hung free, dripping to the ground. Their eyes were burnt away, leaving only blackened sockets, while their tongues were replaced with ash.

Behind Jonny, Rard let out a curse and stomped at the ground. "What devilry!" The other men stood pale-faced and quiet.

"These men were some of our outriders scouting the next day's march. This was found hanging from the neck of one of them," Jocum said, handing a wooden plank to Jonny.

Jonny turned the sign over and read.

These men died because of you, Jonny. Turn around and go home. If you do not, more will die. Many more.

Jonny was shaking by the time he finished reading. Every word on the sign carried the haunting melody of Darvor's voice. The storm that had long bubbled in his soul broke forth, his sleepless body powerless to hold it back. "He's mocking me! He's out there and he's mocking me!"

He saw the surprise in the men's expressions. He was aware how he must appear, wide-eyed and haggard, screaming and flushed with panic. But he could not stop himself. He cried, the tears hot on his cheeks. "It's him; it's all him! What do we do?!" He spun, throwing his arms wide. "He's here, walking amongst us, in the shadows! We are—"

The strong weight of Cazar's hand came to rest on Jonny's shoulder, steadying him. A heavy calm permeated the steadfast grip.

"If we turn back now, these men . . . all of them will have died for nothing," Cazar said. "We are so close to ending this. So very close. Do not let him break you now."

CLOSER

Jonny cast the shovel aside and sank to one knee, staring blankly at the six mounds of dirt. The sun was beginning to rise, weak and gray, behind a thick blanket of clouds. Jonny rubbed at the back of his neck. With Cazar and Alyk, Jonny had spent the night digging graves for the remains of the mutilated soldiers. The soil in the forest had been thick with roots and the digging was exhaustive. Jonny's back and shoulders burned, and the shovel had rubbed raw the skin of his hands.

Alyk set down his shovel and stretched, twisting his arms behind him. Cazar gave the graves a final smoothing with the back of his plow before dusting the mud from his hands and knees. "This is a peaceful place," Cazar said, looking up at the thick canopy of trees. "When this is finished, we can return and construct a better monument." He extended a hand to Jonny.

Jonny looked up and, taking the offered hand, rose to his feet. Ignoring Cazar's remark as though he had not heard, he remained quiet for a long moment, staring at the six graves. "He's right—Darvor. He was right when he made that sign. Many more will die." *Perhaps we should turn back.* The thought had echoed in his head all night, rumbling with each heave of the shovel.

"Aye," Cazar said. "He's not wrong. It does not take a fortune teller to predict more men will die if this fight goes on." He grabbed a hold of Jonny's shoulders with a steadfast grip and met his eyes. "Do you doubt what we have set out to do? There can be no room for doubt. We turn back, or we press ahead. But whatever path we embark on, we do not doubt ourselves."

"I doubt if it's worth it," Jonny replied. "The cost."

"You once said you would bear any cost."

"Then I was a fool."

"Do you doubt what we are doing is right? Ending the threat of Darvor and his trolls—do you doubt that is right?"

"No." Jonny wiped his eyes.

"Then what of the cost? Weigh the cost when you are buying a pie. Consider if a new pair of boots are 'worth it.' But when deciding between doing what is right and what is wrong, the cost must have no role in your mind. What has changed? You have seen others die. Years ago, at Guard Tower Island, you saw thousands die. These are not even the first to die under your command. What has changed in you? Has your resolve weakened? Are you less than the person I thought?"

Jonny shrugged off Cazar's grip and stepped back. "He has been mocking me since the first battle. He has come and gone from our camp with impunity, leaving me messages all the while. First, the burned carcass. Then my family's address burned into that table. These soldiers." He swept a hand toward the fresh graves. "In the quiet moments when no one is around . . . I hear him laughing."

Alyk had drawn up next to Cazar, and the two stared at him wide-eyed.

"I was so confident I could defeat him when we started. I hoped Swarlar would be here because I know that with his help, Darvor wouldn't stand a chance. But even without Swarlar, I thought I could beat him. I'm so much stronger than I was when I was a boy. Now, I don't know . . . I don't know . . ." He turned away from their gaze, raising his hands. "I mean, he would have won already. At the Thundering Ford, he would have ended our campaign there and then, before we even entered the land of the trolls. And he would have done it without even raising a finger himself. Turion saved us, not me. He was the one who foiled Darvor's plan. I took the bait like a fish going after a worm on a hook."

Jonny turned back to face them. For a moment, he thought he saw the same doubt in his heart mirrored on Cazar's face. But the old Guard swallowed, and it was gone.

Alyk nodded knowingly. "Aye, it would be a real downer if we marched you all the way up to Darvor's door only to have him blow you over with a sneeze." He smiled and shrugged. "But if you do get knocked over, we pick you up. If you ask me, I think he is afraid. I think the trolls—they're afraid too. We defeated them on the Plains of Lydie. Cazar defeated them at the siege of Mowka. We beat them again at the Thundering Ford. Now they've fled to their sacred city, praying their high walls will protect them. Darvor is probably desperate, hoping you will give up. Wild with fear." Alyk looked at them both in turn before surprisingly laughing. "I mean, come on . . . I can't be the only one who thinks we've got this in the bag."

Jonny had felt himself teetering, tears in his eyes. But Alyk's remarks buoyed him. Jonny grinned despite himself. *Let the rest go . . .*

Even Cazar laughed. "You've got confidence for the lot of us, there's no denying that."

Grateful for his friends and in a better mood than he had been overnight, Jonny gathered the shovels and plows. The doubts and gloom had not gone, but they had receded under the glow of Cazar and Alyk's companionship. By the time they reached the camp, he was ready to press on despite the sleepless night.

With Rard and Klorvone, the lords and officers had already organized the army for the day's march. "Breakfast will be in the saddle for you three," Siley said as they drew near. She offered Alyk a kiss on the cheek before turning to Jonny. She took his hand. "We're with you, Jonny. We're all with you."

"Thank you. I really mean that."

Before long, the three had found their mounts and some bread to fill their stomachs. With two blasts on the fore sergeant's horn, the army advanced, and the night's grim events were left without another word.

On the move again and busy keeping the army moving, Jonny was glad for the distractions. In much the same way they had crossed the Plains of Lydie, the army wound through the lands in a long column, stretching beyond sight. They moved slowly, only as fast as the slowest wagons could be guided, but they made progress, nonetheless. Slow and relentless.

The air was filled with the noise of a city market. In addition to the soldiers, most of whom were on foot, they still possessed over a thousand good cavalry and hundreds of wagons and carts hauled by oxen and donkeys. There were cattle and sheep kept for food and driven by the stockmen and camp boys. Goats were tied to the backs of wagons, and chickens were crammed in cages on top. Bleats, moos, and caw-caws filled Jonny's ears as he rode down the length of the column, surveying the ordered chaos.

As loud as the animals were, the marching songs were louder still. No line of men stretched over such a distance could maintain a single tune, so every battalion sang their own. There were variations of popular tavern songs, famous chants, and unique regional carols. Lord Kenna led his troops in a spirited take of "The Storm that Breaks the Dawn." A group of Lanaki spearmen echoed with "The Women of Washing Wyls." The loudest, Jonny noted, were the highlanders of Tommdale Castle who belted a well-known, if not profane, ballad:

> *Don't get me wrong, three is no bore.*
> *But I prefer two or four.*
> *So, I'll always be home to you,*
> *Oh, I'll always be home to you.*

Jonny did not stay to listen to more. Years before, a traveling bard in the Great Forest taught Jonny the song about a famous innkeeper, and Jonny knew the later verses only got fouler and more ridiculous. He rode further down the column, calling out words of encouragement to the rank and file and exchanging the occasional pleasantries with some of the lords and officers.

He found Lord Brenton and Jocum riding near the front of the column. The pair made an odd sight—the one barely old enough to ride his own horse, the other a grizzled veteran half a century older.

"I should very much like to see it someday," Jocum said with a gracious nod. "If it is as beautiful as you say, it is surely a sight to behold." His deep voice boomed.

"I think Willow-water is the most beautiful place in the world," Lord Brenton responded, his voice impish by comparison. Noticing Jonny falling into place beside them, the young lord added, "You were there once yourself, were you not, Commander Jonny?"

"I was," Jonny affirmed. "Years ago. Under very different circumstances than you know it, I'm sure."

The boy stared back blankly, expecting more.

Jonny bit his lip. "It was very beautiful. Words don't do it justice."

"And what"—Jocum cleared his throat—"what do you think of these lands?"

Jonny looked around. They followed a heel-beaten path through rolling hills, thick with low shrubs and windswept heath. The landscape had been much as Eibbor had described—wild, raw, and rugged, but not inherently sinister or evil. The lowlands and dales were shrouded with dark forest, but much of the land was barren hills and moors. Well-worn paths—like the one they currently trudged along—streaked the landscape, connecting the remains of the troll forts. And though those settlements had been vile places, the open lands between whispered of a distant beauty long oppressed by the melancholy of troll rule.

"I think it was once vibrant," Jonny said. "And if I could make myself forget that evil has lived here for a thousand years, I might think it was still beautiful. But as it is, every step I take, I feel the thousands of trolls who have trodden this way before. It makes the land feel stained."

"It will be beautiful again one day," Jocum sighed.

Lord Brenton tugged the reins of his horse. "My mother will be so proud that we have purged the trolls from these lands."

"We haven't purged them yet," Jonny said. The familiar burden of battle settled over him like a wet blanket.

That blanket wrapped Jonny tightly as the leagues and days fell away. Each morning, he rose with Darvor on his mind. Each night, he unwillingly welcomed the enemy into his dreams. Food had lost its pleasure and sleep was no solace. His only true respite was the companionship he found in his band of comrades. Cazar, Rard, Klorvone, Alyk, and Siley did not often allow him solitude. Whether they had conspired to be that way, he could not be sure, but at every halt in the march or every night by the campfire, they were there. And though he did not often say it, he was thankful for it. There was a warmth in their comradery that lifted the burden, if only for a few moments.

The moments never lasted long enough. Reminders of Darvor and the coming battle haunted the trail. They once encountered a grand oak tree with a dozen skeletons hanging from its looming branches. The sign nailed to the trunk read:

Right this way, fools. It is not much further now.

Not long after, from a weathered scaffold hung two more skeletons and another sign.

You're almost there. We're waiting for you.

The worst, though, was when they came across the body of a dog tied to one of the fae stones along the road. The dog was long since dead, all sloughing fur and bones, but around its neck hung a crudely fashioned tag on a leather string. Even before he read it, Jonny knew the name on the tag: his family's pet retriever. The remains were not his family's dog and instead belonged to some wolf or wild hound, but the discovery left him shaken, nonetheless. Alyk had been quick to yank the tag from Jonny's hand and pull him in for a hug. "Let it go," he whispered. "Hold on to just enough and let the rest go."

After the discovery of the dog remains, they made good time, each day putting more leagues behind them. They continued to encounter the burnt remains of troll settlements but, since the Thundering Ford, had not caught sight of a single troll. This bothered Rard but seemingly no one else.

"I signed on to kill trolls and get free ale," Rard complained loudly as they lumbered along one day. "But I finished the last ale in the camp two days ago . . . except that victory barrel we're saving for the end. And Jocum, that ol' hound, won't let me near it. When the hell are we going to get back to killing trolls?"

"Soon," Cazar replied flatly.

Klorvone clicked and shook his head. The companions were near the front of the army. A hundred yards ahead, Jocum was taking his turn riding at the head of the column. The rows of soldiers, wagons, animals, carts, and camp followers stretched behind them out of sight.

"If Eibbor's description holds true—and he hasn't been wrong so far—it can't be more than another two days to their city," Cazar said.

"I know no one asked," Alyk started, "but I think—"

"If no one asked, no one cares," Siley quipped before he could finish. She sat behind him on his horse, arms wrapped around his waist.

"Ouch," Alyk said with a laugh. "I don't think you're right." He looked at Rard. Even seated on his horse while the immense man walked, the archer had to look up. "You care what I think, right?"

"Not even a little," Rard grunted.

Alyk turned. "Jonny? You—"

A single horn blast sounded in the distance. Jonny looked up the column of troops. *Now what?* He was in no mood for another delay. Each interruption only prolonged his dread.

One blast of the horn was no cause for panic. It had come from one of their scouts, riding a mile or more ahead of the main army, and signaled something of interest rather than an imminent threat to the column. It had been with a single blast of the horn that a scout had alerted the command about the tree adorned with skeletons and the dog tethered to the fae stone.

As the order came down the line to halt the march, Jonny and his companions broke away and galloped toward the front. Rard jogged behind, cursing that no horse was big enough to bear him.

"It only sounded once," Jocum shouted as Jonny drew near. "Not thrice." He pointed ahead. "See the column of smoke beyond the trees?"

"Aye," Cazar replied from over Jonny's shoulder. "Here comes the lad who blew the horn now with news." The old Guard gestured to a rider emerging from a grove of trees. In the distance, beyond the forest, a thin wisp of smoke rose, spreading and softening until it blended with the blanket of gray clouds.

"Tell the lords and officers," Jocum said to the lieutenant at his side, "not to let the men get too comfortable. Hopefully, this won't take long to sort out." The young officer nodded and rode off to carry out his order.

"Wait here, Jonny," Cazar said firmly before riding out with Jocum to meet the scout.

Jonny grimaced. *He's trying to spare me if it's more of Darvor's taunts.*

"It's nothing Cazar can't handle," Siley said softly, doing little to hide that she had seen Jonny's expression.

Jonny returned a wry smile. *I can't take any more of Darvor mocking me.* He watched the old Guard and the Lord-regent engage the scout. For a few moments, the three talked beyond earshot of the army. The scout was collected and not wide-eyed with fear, but he gestured with a fervid intensity. Whatever he had discovered was of greater magnitude than a dead dog beside the road. The conversation carried on until Jonny could bear the suspense no longer. *I have to know what's going on.*

He started to stir his horse forward when the three turned and approached him.

Jocum waved to Jonny. "The lad spied some trolls ahead." The lad, Jonny noted, looked to be his own age.

"It was only a couple troll grunts," Cazar said.

"Three, Commander," the scout clarified.

"There's a troll fort on a low hill beyond the forest ahead," Cazar continued. "They were idling by the fort. They ran off as soon as they were spotted."

"You were on horse and they on foot?" Alyk asked. "And you didn't run them down?"

Cazar raised a hand. "He was one against three. He did the right thing."

"And the fort?" Jonny asked, looking to the forest ahead.

"Burnt out and abandoned," the scout replied.

"Like all the rest," Jocum added. "Only it looked to be more recently burned. He didn't investigate too closely. But smoke was still rising from the ruins and some of the ash still bore glowing embers."

Cazar rested one hand on the pommel of his sword. "The three trolls were likely the ones left behind to burn the fort after the garrison abandoned it. We're nearly on the tail of the retreating trolls, it would seem."

"Excellent. If we press ahead quickly, we can still catch them," Rard said, beating a fist on his chest.

Cazar shook his head. "We've made good time since crossing the East River. Now is not the time to get hasty. It could still be another trap."

Lord Rosmar approached the companions with a handful of fellow lords and officers in tow. "My good men, what news?" the nobleman hailed.

"Some troll outriders," Cazar said with a courteous dip of the head.

"Are we continuing the march?"

Cazar's eyes fell on Jonny. For a moment, the Guard remained silent, thinking. "We'll pause here for the day. There is an abandoned troll fort ahead. I'll take a few men to explore it, see what can be gleaned. In the morning, we can continue."

"I agree." Jonny nodded. The gathered lords echoed the sentiment.

"Alyk, Rard, Klorvone. With me." Cazar wheeled his horse around.

A flash of confusion hit Jonny. He straightened in the saddle and squeezed the reins. He looked to Cazar with laughter wetting his lips. *He forgot me? How did he forget me?* "What—"

"Not you," Cazar said firmly. He raised his hand. "You stay here."

CHAPTER
19

The Fort

Cazar guided his horse between two weathered fae stones. The trees fell away beside him, and the blackened remnants of the fort loomed ahead. He stopped his horse and cocked his head to listen. The fort was surrounded by a wooden palisade, and though blackened, much of the wall still stood, forcing anyone entering to go through the gate. Within the walls, the collapsed roofs of the fort's structures were barely visible. A lone watch tower remained, rising high above the palisade. Tendrils of smoke drifted lazily over the fortress like the tentacles of some foul beast.

"Looks clear to me," said Alyk, drawing his horse beside Cazar. "I say we head in and check it out. The fire has burned itself out; I reckon it is safe for us to enter."

"Stop talking and listen," Cazar commanded. He pressed a finger to his lips.

"I don't hear anything."

Klorvone clicked and tapped his ear.

"Hush." Alyk rolled his eyes. "Just because you can't talk doesn't mean I talk too much."

"Shhh!" Cazar hissed.

"Again, I don't hear anything."

"Exactly." Cazar dismounted and tied his horse's lead to one of the fae stones. "No birds. No crows. Nothing."

Klorvone and Alyk slid from their saddles and tethered their horses. "Perhaps they haven't gotten here yet."

"Perhaps," Rard growled, cracking his knuckles.

The wind shifted and the smoke drifted down the hill toward them. It stung Cazar's eyes and carried a foul taste. Alarmed by the fumes, the horses reared and pulled at their tethered reins.

"Easy, easy!" Cazar calmed the horses before they could break free. "We'll only be a moment . . . easy, easy."

"Each of these troll settlements smells worse than the last," Alyk quipped, fanning the smoke away. He slid his bow from over his shoulder and flicked the string for good measure.

The smell was indeed noxious, and each of the troll forts seemed to have its unique fragrance. *The smoke here, however, carries a different smell buried beneath the fumes—something I cannot place. Odd.* The feeling left him unsettled.

"Let's make sure Darvor hasn't left anything more for Jonny." Cazar shifted the belt at his waist. It was heavy under the weight of two swords, and he hadn't yet grown accustomed to it sitting lower on his hips. "The clearest path to the Goulmcarn Mountains takes us through this way. To go around would take our army a day or more." He slid Ethwayl silently from its scabbard. Though he carried Filwain at his other hip, Turion's sword was still unnatural in his hands, and he wasn't ready to trust it with his life. "The sooner we are past this place, the better."

They started up the hill toward the gate. It was a gentle slope, and the hill was only two hundred feet high, but the climb took them time, nonetheless.

"Do you think Jonny has forgiven you for making him stay behind?"

Cazar grunted. "I don't care if he has." In truth, however, he did hope Jonny understood. "And I didn't make him. I'm not the one in charge."

"I know." Alyk swatted away a fly. "You're only with us as an advisor. But you sure made it seem like he had no choice."

Cazar grimaced. Jonny had protested, thankfully not loudly. With the other lords and officers present, Jonny had rightfully appraised that any stiff conflict between himself and Cazar would strain their position of leadership. Nonetheless, he had fixed Cazar with a scalding glare that still twisted the old Guard's stomach. They were friends, and he did not like to fight.

It's for his own good. With each successive message Darvor has left, Jonny has teetered closer to a breakdown. If Jonny's mind fails or his spirit breaks, none of this will have meant anything.

"I think it's the right move," Alyk said. "He could use some rest. Though, to be honest, I'm surprised he agreed to stay back. I never thought he'd relent—he's not the kind to sit these things out."

"If there is nothing here, it won't matter anyway," Rard said from two paces behind them.

They reached the gatehouse and paused. "I don't like how quiet it is," Cazar said. He scanned the ramparts. The hinges had fallen away in the fire and the gate doors hung askew. "And the air here is something foul."

He entered first, cautiously. Every muscle poised to spring at the faintest sign of trouble. Behind him, Klorvone followed, gripping the pommel of his poleaxe with white knuckles. Rard and Alyk came after, the latter nocking an arrow to his bowstring.

The fort would have once supported a garrison of two or three hundred trolls. And though the fire had gutted much of the fortress, what remained was still vile. Blackened timber and raw, twisted iron formed the remnants of the collapsed structures. In places, tattered hides and boiled leather had escaped the flames, stretched between posts, capturing shadows. Pens held the charred carcasses of livestock. Sheds were filled with the weapons and armor the retreating trolls had not managed to cart off. In the center of a small clearing, a wooden post was topped with iron manacles and stained with a tarry residue. *A whipping post.* Cazar shook his head, giving a wide berth to the thick, black stains on the earth around the post.

"They're long gone." Rard's voice boomed through the silence like thunder.

"Alyk and I will go this way." Cazar pointed Ethwayl. "You two swing that way. Just make sure there is nothing troubling for Jonny or the other soldiers to find."

Cazar ducked under dangling animal bones strung across an alleyway and beckoned for Alyk to follow.

"These troll settlements really are foul places," Alyk muttered, stepping over something rotting. He peeked over his shoulder to make sure Rard and Klorvone were out of earshot. "Can I ask you something? And be honest. Do you think Jonny can defeat Darvor, really?"

It should have been easy to say yes, but the word caught in his throat. He bit his lip. *Why is it so hard to say yes?* He looked to Alyk to find the archer staring back patiently. "I think . . ." Cazar paused.

"What are we doing here if Jonny can't win?" Alyk shook his head. "What's the point? It's all pointless if we don't defeat Darvor."

With his free hand, Cazar reached to his collar, undid the tie of his tunic, and pulled open his shirt. Of the half-dozen scars visible on his exposed chest, the twisted, silvery mark over his heart was the worst.

"In my honest opinion, I cannot say with any certainty. I encountered Darvor once and won this reminder, lucky to have my life. Jonny faced him more than once but couldn't even singe the toe of his boot. Yes, Jonny's magic is a hundred times stronger now than it was then. But . . . but in the fraction of a second when I saw Darvor, when I looked into his eyes"—he grimaced—"all the evil in the world lurked in those black sockets."

Alyk pursed his lips but remained silent.

"I have never known Swarlar to show fear," Cazar continued, lacing up his shirt. "Concern, yes. But never fear. Yet when he speaks of Darvor—only of Darvor—there is something that flickers at the corners of his mouth. I do not know what word to describe it, but if I had to choose, I would say fear."

Alyk's expression was somber. "So why are we doing this?"

Cazar shrugged and started walking again. "You must find your own reasons. I have mine; every person marching with us has their reasons. I can't tell you yours."

"Darvor is plotting his next move. That's why the trolls entered the Vale of Joy and took the water from that fountain."

"As you've said." Cazar peeked around a corner as they continued down the alley.

"Jonny would march right to the gates of hell by himself if he had to in order to stop him."

"Aye, that he would."

"And he does stand a chance . . . even if it's a long shot."

"He does. I wouldn't be here if it were hopeless."

"Then I guess my real reason is to help Jonny."

Cazar smirked. "To help a friend in need—that might be the truest reason there is to do anything."

"Well, that and the fame, riches, women, and ale."

". . . and you ruined it." Cazar rolled his eyes.

"He'll need every advantage he can get."

"Aye." Cazar lifted the leather flap covering the doorway of a low building spared by the flames. A butcher's tools hung from the ceiling, coated in old blood. On the table, a rump of meat lay covered in maggots. "He'll need every advantage," he said, moving on. "If it comes to a battle to take their city, we cannot have Jonny spending any of his strength in the battle before the right moment. Doubtless some lords will find that difficult to understand. But like we saw on the Plains of Lydie, his strength has limits."

"It will be for us to fight the battle. Get him in front of Darvor with all his strength saved."

"Yes, that is our best hope. And it may not be a lot, but the thing I've found with hope: a little bit is usually enough."

They exited the alley to find themselves in a small clearing. Ahead, the lone watchtower stood, and on either side, the remains of larger buildings—barracks or meat halls.

"Cazar, look." Alyk pointed to the door of one of the buildings. On each side of the doorway was mounted a human skull. They were too small to have belonged to adults.

Cazar scowled. *Beasts . . . damned beasts.* He thought of his son, Dazar, and his unborn child. His blood ran hot in his veins. "Eibbor would have been dragged to a place like this after he was captured at the battle of Guard Tower Island. Just think what he endured. The horrors."

"Poor soul." Alyk shook his head. "No wonder he came back a changed man. It is a wonder he survived at all."

"I don't care how slim the chances of victory." Cazar raised his sword toward the mounted skulls. "We have to make sure the world is freed from that." His voice was thick. *What if something like that happened to my family?*

"I'll bury them." Alyk crossed to the doorway and took down the mounted skulls.

Cazar scanned the surroundings. The wind had shifted again, blowing more of the smoke toward him. There was an odd scent in the air. It was buried under the fumes of the troll fort, but it did not belong there. It was a foreign scent, a subtle scent. He had smelled it before, but far away and long ago. As out of place as it was, he could not define it. *That smell is what spooked the horses.*

He looked back at Alyk. The archer knelt and scooped out a hole in the mud with his hands. The perpetual dampness of these lands left all soil soft and sloppy. The clearing in which they stood was paved in sticky mud. *That smell . . .* Cazar turned. *Where are the crows?* His eyes fell on a print in the mud two yards from where he stood.

His father had taught him everything about hunting and tracking from an early age. He knew every animal print from the westerlands to the Shrouded Island. The print in the mud was no bear nor wolf. His stomach twisted. He knew that print well.

"Cazar! Alyk!" Rard's cry echoed from the far side of the fort. "There's—"

A shape emerged on the roof above Alyk. In a silent blur, it lunged, bearing down on the archer still kneeling in the mud. There was no time to think, let alone call out. Cazar snapped into action, driven by instinct. He drove the pommel of his sword over his head, launching it like a spear with the whip of his arm. The sword whistled, glinting as it spun. For half a heartbeat, it was unclear which would reach its target first: the spinning sword or the falling *grevice*.

Alyk twisted in time only to see the predator crashing toward him, jaws snapping. The *grevice* collided with him in a blur. Cazar blinked.

Ethwayl had been fastest. Alyk grunted, buried under the *grevice*'s hulking body, but alive. The gleaming blade of Cazar's sword entered the now lifeless beast's eye and protruded from the opposite ear. Cazar breathed deeply. *That was close.*

"There's a bunch of them here!" Rard's voice echoed again. "Bloody hell! It's a whole pack. Where are you?!"

⁘────────⁘

Alyk struggled under the weight of the dead *grevice*. The impact had knocked the wind from him and trapped his arm under him at a painful angle. For an instant, he thought the beast had ripped off his arm, the pain had been so great. But he could wiggle his fingers and did not feel the wet heat of blood. He squirmed and gasped for breath under the shaggy monster. Searing pain raced from his shoulder down the length of his arm. He bit back a scream.

A bone-chilling growl split the air, followed by another. Alyk turned his head. With his face pressed between the *grevice's* shaggy coat and the thick mud, he could barely see Cazar.

The old Guard spun. Two more *grevices* emerged over the rooftops, lifted by the silent beating of leathery wings. The first tucked its wings and drove toward Cazar, while the other circled to attack from another angle.

Alyk tried to thrust his hips from where they were pinned. The attempt brought more pain, and this time there was no holding back the scream.

He had never seen a live *grevice* before. Once, as a boy, a traveling showman had come through with the stuffed pelt of one. Alyk's father had paid two coins, and they went into the large tent to see it. The lion-like body—twice the size of a man—was posed in an artificial position, the black wings suspended by string. It was a terrible-looking thing, and its long teeth, curled horns, and razor-sharp claws had given Alyk nightmares for weeks.

Those nightmares did not compare to this. He was trapped and helpless to watch Cazar defend himself against two of the monsters. Even the most skilled of hunters could not always best a *grevice*, and Cazar was confronted with two. Somewhere on the other side of the fort, he could hear the roars and crashes of Rard and Klorvone's battle with the creatures.

Cazar rolled away from the attack of the first *grevice*, sending a spray of mud. Ethwayl was lodged in the dead *grevice* on top of Alyk, but Cazar had already drawn Filwain. Turion's former sword traced a graceful arc over the warrior's head.

The second *grevice* swooped from behind. Cazar spun and slashed out with his sword. The *grevice* was too quick, twisting out of the way unharmed. The first took the chance to snap its jaws at Cazar's head. The warrior danced aside. Driving Filwain down, he caught only air.

Rard bellowed a string of cuss words, which were returned with the dreadful shrieks of the *grevices*. Their melee seemed to be going no better.

Cazar dodged another attack, this time, slashing one of the *grevices* on the wing. Filwain's razor edge tore effortlessly through the leathery webbing. In a fury, the beast lashed its tail around, catching Cazar's leg and knocking him to one knee. The warrior cried out but staggered back to his feet in time to parry the next attack.

Alyk's heart thumped in to his throat. He could not let it end this way. He tried lifting the *grevice* with his free, uninjured arm. More pain.

Alyk could only watch as a third *grevice*—mangy and larger than the others—emerged from the dark doorway of one of the burnt buildings behind Cazar. It strode slowly, silently, black wings folded close to its body. *No, no, no!* Cazar might have managed against two *grevices,* but three of the beasts was a hopeless prospect. Alyk's helplessness seized his heart. Thoughts of Siley flashed through his mind. *Not like this!* He threw his hips with all his strength, mustering fear and grit to heave the dead *grevice* off him.

"Aaghh!!" A blinding, white pain burst through every sinew in his body. It narrowed his vision and brought bile to his mouth. But the pain waned. Suddenly able to breathe, he drew in a lung full of air. He was free.

He rolled to his knees and reached for his bow. Snatching the weapon up with his left hand, he realized his right arm—the one used to draw back his bow—hung limply at his side. Even the thought of swinging it a mere inch almost brought him to his knees. His faithful bow was useless.

Cazar thrust toward the first *grevice* but pulled back to block the slashing claws of the second. The third *grevice* circled patiently. Alyk gritted his teeth; there was no hope of drawing his bow, but neither could he sit by idly. Cazar swung his sword wildly, keeping the circling *grevices* at bay. But he was tiring. His movements were slowing. Against three *grevices*, he stood little chance.

Alyk swore and scanned for a solution. His bow was the only weapon he had any skill with, and with only one arm, his bow was as dangerous as a handful of flowers. Next to him, Ethwayl remained buried in the head of the dead *grevice*. Alyk had never swung a sword before. *No time like the present.* Without hesitation, he cast aside his bow and wrapped the fingers of his good hand around the pommel. With a heave, he slid the blade free.

When the mangy third *grevice* had its back turned, Alyk made his move. In three bounding steps, he crossed and drove the sword into the beast's side. He threw his body weight into the blow and sunk the blade to the hilt.

With the force of the strike, the pain surged in his injured shoulder, dropping him to his knees. Like burning lightning, it tore through his chest and twisted his stomach. He keeled over and vomited.

Spitting up the last of the bile, he steadied himself. When he raised his head, the mangy *grevice* had collapsed and was gurgling its final breaths.

Cazar was somehow, inexplicably, straddling one of the two remaining *grevices*. With a flash of Filwain, the monster's head rolled off its shoulders. The lone remaining *grevice* recoiled. Cazar was already back on his feet and charging the *grevice*. With a hiss, the monster flapped its wings and took to the air. It snapped its jaws twice and retreated to a perch on the rooftop of the meat hall. It stared down at them for a moment, appraising the situation. Seeing its two dead brethren, the *grevice* gave a frustrated shriek and took to the skies.

A stillness settled over the fort. Alyk slumped back into the mud, too weak to stand. He panted, fixing his eyes on the blanket of clouds above. "My shoulder . . ." He closed his eyes and breathed in the silence.

⋄━━━━━⋄

Jonny bounded through the forest, carried by the swift gallop of his horse. Ducking under the low-hanging branches, he urged the horse faster. He had been in the saddle the moment the *grevices'* shrieks had come over the rolling hills. And now, as more piercing cries split the air, he could see the trees ahead give way. The fort loomed beyond from the crown of the hill. He made it past the fae stones, where the others' tethered horses fought at their bridles.

With a frightened neigh, his horse skidded to a halt and tossed its head. "Darvor's blood!" Jonny cried and leapt to his feet. There was no time to try to coax the horse any further. The sounds and the smells of the *grevices* triggered a primal fear in the horse that Jonny could not hope to override.

He sprinted up the hill. *I should never have stayed behind! I should have been the first to go to the fort!* He had remained on the far side of the forest with great reluctance, watching with simmering annoyance as the others disappeared into the trees.

Two *grevices* appeared above the walls of the fort. Their black leather wings beat silently as they climbed higher. They either did not see Jonny or were not interested. With a hiss, they fled the fort and disappeared beyond the hills. Silence spread over the hilltop.

I'm too late!

He reached the gate and charged through. The *grevices* were most likely a trap from Darvor. But he cared not if there was more danger in the fort. *Maybe there is still time . . .*

He surveyed the charred remains of the fort and the blackened buildings. *Where are they?* He blew past the bloodied whipping post, then ducked under the string of animal bones. He dodged the rotting heap in the alleyway.

At last, he burst into the clearing, sliding to a stop in the mud. Fire swirled in his palms. He was ready for whatever trap was waiting.

"Cazar!" He fixed his eyes on the warrior.

Cazar was squatting next to Alyk and looked up at the sound of his name.

"Jonny." It was not a question, but surprise flecked his voice.

"Bugger that." Rard emerged from the far side of the clearing, followed by Klorvone. "I hate those damned things." He dragged one of the dead monsters by the tail. "Oh, hello, Jonny. When did you get here? We could have used your magic a little earlier." He waved, and his thick hands were coated in blood—both his own and that of the *grevices.*

Jonny was speechless. He scanned the courtyard. Three dead *grevices* littered the space, plus the one Rard was dragging. One *grevice* was missing its head; another was sporting the hilt of Ethwayl sprouting from its flank. Alyk was lying on his back in the mud, but he was breathing. *I don't see any blood.*

"What happened?" he finally managed.

Cazar scratched his chin. "Got ourselves ambushed by some *grevices.*"

Jonny let the fireballs in his palms wither. There seemed to be no immediate danger, and the spells were draining him. "A trap from Darvor?" He glanced to the sky to make sure the *grevices* had not returned.

Cazar followed his gaze. "No, I think not. I think they were just scavenging."

Klorvone clicked and waved his poleaxe.

"Aye," Rard grunted his agreement. "We stumbled on four of them feeding in one of the trolls' rot pits." He wiped his bloodied hands on his trousers. "Bad luck, I reckon."

"You once said *grevices* were solitary animals, and they only came together in packs because they were bound to the will of Darvor," Jonny protested. "And I thought they didn't live this far north."

"They usually are, and they usually don't," Cazar replied. "Perhaps those *grevices* that Darvor brought to his side have not returned to their wild ways. Or maybe they have. There was food here for them. Maybe, like Rard said, it was that and bad luck. Not every cloud is a storm cloud."

Jonny remained unconvinced. It was possible, he admitted, that they were wild *grevices* and Jonny's companions had chanced upon them by coincidence. But it was just as likely to be another game of Darvor's. The dark lord of the trolls did have *grevices* under his command. And killing Jonny's friends would have been a devastating maneuver by Darvor. Perhaps he hoped to kill Jonny with the ambush.

"It makes no difference now whether it was chance or design," Cazar continued. "It happened; we move on."

Jonny nodded. On that, they could agree.

"Is Alyk all right?" Jonny asked.

"My shoulder . . ." Alyk moaned. He was still lying on his back, staring up at the sky. His face was pale.

"He dislocated it." Cazar looked down at the archer.

"I . . ." Alyk groaned again. "Ethwayl . . ." With his good arm, he pointed to the mangy *grevice* and the sword protruding from its side.

Jonny crossed to where the *grevice* lay and wrapped his fingers around the pommel. Setting a foot on the beast's shoulder to steady himself, he pulled, and the blade slid free. "What happened?" he asked, swinging the sword to shake the blood off.

Cazar shook his head and looked down at the sword in his hand. "Filwain has a complex history, but today it started to write a new chapter. The balance is good, its growing on me." He extended a hand and took Ethwayl from Jonny. "But I'm not giving this up yet either."

"It hurts . . ." Alyk whimpered from where he lay in the mud.

Cazar looked back to Alyk and set the swords aside. "Come on now, we've got to get it set right or it will never heal. The quicker, the better." He extended a hand, but Alyk waved him off.

"I can't . . ."

"Rard, come give me a hand. I'll need you too, Klorvone."

Despite Alyk's protests and cries of pain, the three men pulled him to his feet while Jonny watched. The archer's arm hung from his shoulder at an odd angle. His palm was turned out and his hand dangled lower than the hand of his good arm.

"Sit here." Cazar guided the archer toward a barrel on the edge of the clearing and began to inspect the limp arm. The Guard pressed a thumb into the flesh of his shoulder. Alyk cried out and the blood drained from his face. Rard and Klorvone steadied him and held him upright.

"This will hurt. Badly. But only for a moment." Cazar pursed his lips. "Bite this." He unlaced his sword belt and put the leather strap in Alyk's teeth.

Rard and Klorvone pressed him into the barrel, preventing him from running.

"Ready?"

Alyk's eyes were wide with fear, but he nodded with feigned confidence.

Jonny swallowed back the wave of nausea that washed over him. *I don't know if I want to watch this.*

Cazar took a deep breath. Alyk fidgeted.

Without further warning, Cazar gave a violent jerk and twist to the archer's dangling arm. There was an audible *pop* from Alyk's shoulder. Jonny flinched at the snap and grabbed at his uninjured shoulder.

Alyk's head rolled back, and his body went limp. The leather strap fell from his mouth. Rard and Klorvone held firm, keeping him from falling.

Cazar felt the archer's shoulder, prodding his fingers into the sinew and muscle. "There. Better."

Rard lightly slapped the archer's cheeks. "There you go. Wake up. Come back to us, boy."

Alyk slowly lifted his head. His eyelids fluttered. "It still bloody hurts," he said weakly.

"Aye, it will for some time." Cazar picked up his sword belt. "But it's back where it should be."

Alyk nodded. He stretched his fingers and cautiously gave the arm a soft swing. "Actually, it already feels a little better."

Cazar stepped back and wrapped his sword belt around his waist. "You won't be able to draw a bow for a fortnight or two."

"I'll be able to eventually?" Alyk gingerly held his shoulder with his good arm.

"With a little luck, I think yes. We should make you up a sling."

Jonny unfastened his riding cloak. "Here, use this."

Cazar took the cloak and began to fold and twist the fabric.

While he worked, Klorvone and Rard cleaned themselves up from their melee. They each sported a few minor wounds and bruises but had fared well overall. Jonny remembered the first time he had encountered Rard in the Lost Lands years before. The brute had saved them from a pack of *grevices*. Completely outnumbered and overwhelmed, they had given him up for dead. But it had not proven to be his end. With a few terrible scars and a good story, Rard had prevailed. And so they had today.

Klorvone gestured that he had once before encountered a *grevice* and barely escaped with his life. Fighting alongside Rard, he had claimed two today beneath the glint of his poleaxe.

"You fought well," Rard commended the mute while wrapping a swatch of cloth around his bloodied knuckles.

"I should have been here," Jonny said, helping Klorvone bind a laceration on his shoulder. "You shouldn't have left me behind."

Cazar looked up from his work. "What if there had been something worse than *grevices* today?"

"Then you all would have died."

Cazar straightened. "Better us than you."

On their face, the words were kind, but they stung Jonny.

"I'm no more important than any of you. I should bear the danger just as much as you. Just as much as any soldier in this army."

Cazar shook his head. "That's not true. It hasn't been true since you started this whole mess."

"Are you blaming me?" Jonny recoiled.

Cazar's expression hardened. "Far from it. You have wagered everything for a noble cause. You have acted when so many others would have done nothing. I commend you for that. But the truth is, in the end, none of us will be the one to defeat Darvor. That must be you. And so long as that is true, you are more important. You are more important than me, than Alyk, than Rard, Klorvone, any soldier in this army—lord or peasant."

"I'm not . . ." The words sounded coarse in his mouth.

"You are," Cazar affirmed. "You may not want to be, but do not fool yourself with humility. A king's life is not worth more than the lowliest beggar's, but in this pursuit—this war to end all wars—your life matters the most. You need to act like it. Without you, this is all for nothing."

Inside, Jonny knew Cazar's words to be true. The weight of that truth was smothering. When he and Alyk had first sat in the back-alley pub in Gluton, their schemes had felt more daydream than reality, too distant to be touched. But with every step, every day, every trial and tribulation, the tangible reality had drawn closer. Not only was he drawn closer to a fight he feared with every fiber of his being, but he was also dragging all those around him closer too. And that, in many ways, was the heaviest burden.

Jonny closed his eyes. "I don't want it to be this way. It's too much."

He opened his eyes to see Rard looming over him. The man rested a giant hand on Jonny's shoulder. "We're here to help you carry that burden. That's what friends are for. And I'm a strong fella, so fear not—I can shoulder some of it." He winked, and though it looked awkward on his face, it warmed Jonny all the same.

Alyk stood and adjusted his sling. "Hold on to just enough. Let the rest go."

The five stood for a long moment in silence, and Jonny did not have the words to break it.

At last Alyk found something suitable. "I will say you owe us all a few drinks when this is over."

Jonny gave the archer a playful shove.

"Hey! Watch the arm!" Alyk winced.

"You need to be more like Klorvone and talk less," Rard grumbled.

"Like him?" Alyk pointed. "He'd talk more than me if he had a tongue."

Klorvone flicked a rude gesture at the archer. And for the first time ever, laughter echoed through the fort.

As the laughter faded, Cazar took a step back. He scanned the burned buildings around them. "We should finish scouting the fort and get back to camp. This is no good place to be after dark."

"Klorvone and I didn't see anything of note on that side." Rard gestured with his thumb. "Besides the *grevices*, of course."

"Good. Alyk and I cleared our side." Cazar looked at the door of one of the buildings and two iron spikes that adorned the door posts. "I suppose we get a look from the watchtower and make sure the way ahead is clear."

"I don't think that ladder will hold my weight," Rard said.

"I'll go." Jonny looked at Cazar. "I can do this much, at least."

Cazar gave a permissive nod.

Jonny approached the watchtower. It rose four or five stories, twice the height of the surrounding walls. The ladder had largely escaped the flames that had razed most of the fort. He took the lowest rungs in hand and began to climb. With each step, charred wood further darkened the palms of his hands. He paused on the fourth rung and looked back. "The ladder is solid. It will hold."

He resumed the climb, and the fort fell away beneath him. Reaching the top, he hoisted himself onto the platform and dusted the ash off his hands and clothes. It was sticky with his sweat and left his palms streaked. He frowned and straightened to survey the view.

Immediately, his stomach twisted. The sensation weakened his knees, and he grabbed the parapet of the platform to steady himself.

"Afraid of heights?" Rard hollered from the ground below.

Jonny squeezed the parapet. It was not the height that was horrifying. His shoulders slumped. *Let the rest go . . .* He stiffened his jaw and forced aside the wave of dread.

"No," Jonny replied. "The black city of the trolls. I see it."

Beyond the low hills, the Goulmcarn Mountains towered. Their icy, white peaks were wrapped in clouds and shadows. And at the base of the mountains, dark and unyielding, rose the city of the trolls. It loomed over the moorlands like a sore, engulfing everything it touched in doom and despair. The sight of its walls and towers cast a dread over Jonny that seized the breath from his lungs.

"We're here. We've come to the end of the road."

KNOCKING ON THE
DEVIL'S DOOR

The pavilion flaps fluttered in the breeze, revealing glimpses of the city looming in the distance and the towering peaks of the Goulmcarn Mountains beyond. Jonny ran a palm over the rough wood of the armchair he occupied, his eyes fixed on the black walls. Around him, the lords and officers continued their heated discussion.

The day was hot and the air inside the command tent had grown stifling. Most of the lords wore their battle armor and dripped sweat beneath the steel. Why they had donned their armor, Jonny didn't know. There would be no battle today. *Not yet,* he mused. Perhaps the armor made them feel more important or more secure.

"I understand, Lord Lethhull." Cazar leaned forward. The former Guard had sensibly left his armor behind today and sat in his customary black and silver garments. Even still, the collar of his tunic was ringed in perspiration. "It is not something I take lightly, but a protracted siege is not the answer. They may have supplies enough to last many weeks, all winter perhaps. And maybe even longer. We do not." He stood and swept his dark hair from his face. "Our food supplies are dwindling, and we will find nothing to sustain us in these lands."

"Furthermore," Alyk said, reaching for a plum in a bowl on the table, "the autumn harvests are nearing. Many of the men need to be home by then. If they are not there to help their families with the harvest, their wives and children may not survive if the winter comes hard this year. They were promised a quick war, and they expect it." He rolled the fruit in his palm. "If we delay, desertion will plague our ranks."

Jonny turned his attention back to the doorway of the pavilion, where the flaps danced in the afternoon wind. The city in the distance loomed dark and menacing. They were still a full two leagues from the walls, but Jonny could easily make out the crenelations and fortifications. *Darvor's city*, he thought.

The reports from scouts that had ventured near the city were troubling. The black walls were polished and set together so smoothly that magic, they had concluded, was the only explanation; no one could hope to climb them. Towers were spaced every quarter mile, topped with ballistae, trebuchets, and other still more horrible war machines. A thick moat ringed the walls and towers, and within it, twisted spikes and rusted barbs threatened to swallow anyone who fell in. The only weakness was the lone gate, and even that was a monstrous thing. The arch of it loomed forty feet high, and the portcullis lowered across its mouth was a grate of solid iron, each link as thick as a man's torso.

The army had reached the city a fortnight earlier, and the days since had been spent planning for an assault. Detailed charts were mapped of the external defenses, siege engines were designed and constructed, and battle stratagems planned down to a single man. The engineers were finishing siege towers that could be wheeled to the walls and allow the assailants to scale the battlements. Mobile bridges had been built to traverse the moat, and catapults prepared for bombarding the trolls' defenses.

These preparations did not come easily. Soldiers toiled day and night to construct the siege engines, hauling lumber from distant forests, while teams of oxen lugged stone munitions for catapults from boulder fields a league or two away. An exhaustive enterprise that had employed every able man in the camp, it had not gone as smoothly as it might. A half-dozen men had been injured when one cart of lumber rolled off its path. Two others were killed in a landslide in a nearby quarry. Everyone else was worked to the brink of fatigue. But the work had progressed, and the preparations were nearly set for the assault on the fortifications.

"We can take the walls," Cazar and the lords said confidently.

The most worrisome aspect of the battle, however, would be what they found within the city. The best estimates of Jocum's rangers put the number of trolls as almost equal to the human attackers, but it was possible thousands more were hiding within the walls. They had no eyes within the city.

"We won't know for sure what we will find until we breach the defenses," Jocum said in an earlier meeting. "That's when the hard part will start."

"Aye," Cazar agreed. "It will be brutal hand-to-hand combat in the streets. And there will undoubtedly be traps around every turn. From what Eibbor told us, the city is a sprawling mess of cramped buildings and winding alleys." He showed them rough illustrations of the city layout pieced together from Eibbor's accounts of his imprisonment. "A single broad avenue runs through the heart of the city, straight from the gate to here." Cazar tapped a long finger on the dark shape at the center of the drawing.

Darvor's palace, Jonny shivered. "That's where we have to get," he told the other commanders.

The palace, if it could be called such, sat in the center of the city. It was an immense black pyramid raised from the same polished stone as the walls and towers. It rose five hundred feet above the surrounding city and was visible even from Jonny's seat in the command tent two leagues away. It was, he knew, where Darvor would be found. *That's where it will end.*

"We'll lose too many men trying to win the walls if we don't breach the gate," Lord Lethhull said, pulling Jonny's mind back to the present.

"I told you already," Rard growled. "I'll get us through the gate."

"But—"

The muscles in Rard's neck rippled. "No, little man. Leave the gate to me."

"Fine. Even if we assume Rard gets us through the gate," said a lordling to Jonny's left, "I still do not understand why the boy cannot use his magic. He can clear the wall of trolls in a moment with his fire."

Cazar raised a hand. "I understand your concern, but as I've said before, he cannot waste his strength before the right moment."

"But men will die if—"

Alyk snorted. "It's war. Men will die either way." He raised the plum to his mouth and sank his teeth into it.

"For the last time," Cazar sighed, "we must not expect Jonny's magic to help us with the trolls tomorrow. He will save his strength for the right moment." A few lords grumbled, but most nodded their understanding.

Cazar stood. "It will not be easy. Brutal, haunting, glorious, chaotic—but not easy. Few things that matter ever are. For centuries, men have fought to survive against the menace of the trolls, and tomorrow, we can end it. Forever." He scanned the room, looking each of the men in the eye. "We've planned and prepared. All that's left for tomorrow is to do." He shrugged. "That's it."

Klorvone stomped his foot on the ground in agreement. Rard pounded a fist to his broad chest. Several of the others shouted and clapped their hands. Their energy was palpable.

Jocum stood and, resting a hand on Cazar's shoulder, looked around the tent. "The Son of Aazar is right. You know your roles. Go pray, rest, eat . . . Tomorrow at first light, we assemble."

The men filed from the tent, leaving Jonny alone with Cazar.

"I hope this heat abates for tomorrow," Cazar said, running a hand along his brow.

"What will you do until the morning?" Jonny asked.

Cazar pressed his fingers to his eyelids as though trying to squeeze away the dark circles gathered there. Though he hid it well, Jonny could see the fatigue plaguing Cazar was enough to match his own.

"Sleep would be nice, but I think I'd be more likely to sprout wings and fly." He crossed to a table in the corner and poured some watered wine. "Delena," he said in a low tone as though speaking to himself. "I'll write a letter to my wife . . . take a walk, perhaps." He turned to Jonny, struck by a sudden thought. "Turion said something before he . . . well, it probably doesn't matter."

"What did he say?" Jonny asked.

Cazar paused, searching for the right words. "He said Darvor watches Delena at night, watches my son."

Jonny's chest tightened at the sound of Darvor's name. "Aye, and he knows where my family lives, even though they're not from . . . here. And then he left that burnt carcass in my tent—"

"What are we up against tomorrow?" Cazar asked. "Are you capable of defeating him?"

"I will be . . . I have to be." The words tasted hollow in his mouth.

Cazar studied Jonny for a long moment. Outside, the sun was setting, stretching the shadows in the tent. At last, Cazar nodded. "We'll get you to the pyramid. After that . . ."

Jonny offered a wan smile. "I know . . . thank you."

Cazar drained his glass, set it down, and crossed to exit the tent. He raised one of the flaps before pausing. "We're knocking on the devil's door. Do not be surprised when he answers."

He slipped out, letting the flap of the tent fall behind him. For an instant, Jonny caught a glimpse of the city in the distance, a black silhouette against the blood-red sky of the setting sun.

Memories of the eve of his last great battle washed unbidden into his mind. He had been a scared boy thrust unwillingly onto the stage of the grandest of battles. Now, he had chosen his role and walked on stage all on his own. *But has the rest changed at all? Am I still just a scared boy?* Hoping a walk would shake the dark thoughts loose, he slipped from the tent.

He turned his back on the city and the pyramid and headed for the edge of camp. The guards on the perimeter eyed him but said nothing. He was recognized everywhere he went in camp. Most of the soldiers treated him with respect bordering on reverence—behavior Jonny still struggled to handle. He offered a casual salute and carried on.

On a small hill just outside the camp, Jonny finally came to a stop. The sky to the west was purple, and flickers of orange fled to the horizon with the retreating sun. The heat had mellowed, leaving a pleasantly warm evening. He sank into the thick, soft grass, and the smell of wildflowers wafted up to greet him. The serenity of the place reminded him of the backyard of his home. At home, summer nights like this were warm and sweet. *But at home, there would be . . .*

As if on cue, a twinkle of light flashed near Jonny's elbow, then another twenty yards away. *Fireflies.* Jonny smiled. A moment later, dozens of them dotted the night air, bobbing and spiraling.

It's been a year, he realized with a pang. He had no calendar to mark the days and had not kept track of their passing, so he could not be sure of the exact anniversary of his crossing. *But it's close enough.* It had been the end of summer when he left home, and leaving for college was near at hand. The nights were warm, and fireflies lit up the backyard. *Why couldn't that life have been enough? Why did I have to go looking for trouble?* He looked to the sky and blinked back tears. There was no turning back now, he knew. There was no use dwelling on it. *If I defeat him, I can go back . . . I can finally have peace.*

"You're a hard one to find sometimes," Alyk said in a voice not weighed by any of the heaviness of the night. The archer strode from camp, coming up behind Jonny. The wild grass swirled around his ankles and engulfed him as he sat.

Jonny gestured to the wilderness stretched out around them. "I was enjoying the peacefulness out here."

"Well, don't worry, I won't bother you too long. I told myself I would get back before long anyway; someone must make sure Rard doesn't drink too much tonight . . . need him in good fightin' shape for tomorrow."

"Oh, it's no bother . . . I like your company. How's your arm?"

The archer no longer wore his sling, having abandoned it earlier in the day. He stretched his right arm over his head. "Not quite right, but not quite wrong."

"Have you tried drawing your bow?"

"No, what good would that do now?"

Jonny fixed him with a curious expression. "To make sure you're ready for tomorrow. We can certainly use your skill."

Alyk shrugged. "Don't worry. I'll be ready."

They sat for a moment in silence, watching the bursts of light.

"You know, when I was a child," Alyk started, "I thought they were magic . . . the fireflies. Thought it was real magic." He laughed. "Then, when I lived under Lord Groy's roof, one of his scholars told me they weren't. He said they contained a natural substance that caused them to light up, the same way a *tentali* lights up when it comes out of the water. After that, I didn't think I'd ever see real magic. Thought it just belonged in stories. That was, until I met you. Now everything has changed."

Jonny laughed. "I know the feeling. I was the same way once." He rolled his hand over and pulled a flame into his palm. "I wish it could go back to the way it was before. It was simpler then."

Alyk fixed Jonny with his fiery green eyes. "Are you scared?"

Jonny let the fire die in his hand. "Yes."

"Of dying?"

"No. Of being wrong."

Alyk blinked.

"What if I can't stop Darvor?"

"The rest of us are here to help. Rard, Klorvone, Cazar—"

"I know, but—"

"And remember, I've never missed." He stretched his arms as though shooting an imaginary bow. "I'll not start tomorrow." He winked.

Jonny reached out and gently curled his fingers around a burst of light. Pulling back his hand, he rolled open his fingers. The lightning bug shook its wings and crawled toward his wrist. It paused and emitted a soft glow.

"I want to say thank you," Jonny said.

"For what?"

"You're the only one who . . ." He paused as the firefly fluttered off his wrist, disappearing into the night sky. "Everyone else has always looked at me like I'm broken. After my adventure with the Cup, my parents always treated me like I needed fixing. Swarlar . . . Cazar too. They look at me like I'm damaged goods. But not you. You never make me feel like I'm broken."

"You're not. You carry the scars of what you've been through, aye, but who doesn't."

Jonny smiled. "You're a good friend, Alyk. My best, to be honest."

Alyk waved the words away. "Don't hold it against the rest of them. Your parents especially. They're just trying to help. You tell someone you're hungry and they know to bring you food. Say you're thirsty and they bring you water. People like to help—they want to. But when you hurt in places they can't see, that's harder. They will try, but they just don't always know how."

The words of a half-remembered poem sprung to Jonny's mind. "*We do not know what wars go on down there, where the spirit meets the bone.*"

"Aye," Alyk nodded. "Something like that." He rested a warm hand on Jonny's shoulder. "It's going to be all right . . . in time."

Jonny stretched his legs out, falling back on his elbows. "It's getting late," he said through a yawn.

"Speaking of best friends," Alyk said. "I actually came out here for a reason." He fidgeted and picked at a proud blade of grass. "I asked Siley to marry me."

Jonny bolted up with a smile. "And she said yes?"

"Of course she did!" Alyk smirked. "Look at me, I'm a treasure."

Laughing, Jonny threw a playful punch at the other's shoulder, aiming for the uninjured arm. "That's great!"

"Aye, I couldn't be happier." His smile stretched ear to ear. "I've known for some time I would ask."

"When did you pop the question?"

"Just now, after that last council meeting. When Cazar said the battle was to be tomorrow, I knew I had to ask her. Anything could happen tomorrow, and she should know how I feel. And I wanted to know I have her to look forward to when all this excitement is over."

"Oh, I'm so happy for you two!" Jonny's melancholy had lifted, if only for the moment.

"I . . ." Alyk shook his head. "You should have seen her face light up!"

Even in the dim light of the fireflies, Jonny could see his friend was blushing.

"We certainly need news like this to brighten nights like tonight," Jonny added. "Well, congratulations again." He traded a firm handshake. "You said you had a question?"

"Indeed," Alyk replied. "It won't be tonight, of course. The wedding, that is. But when it is . . . in the lakelands, there is a custom. Both the bride and groom have someone at their side for the rite, as a sacred witness—"

"You want me to be your best man?"

"I'm not familiar with the term, but if that's what you call it."

"I'd be honored." Jonny pushed to his feet. He offered a hand to Alyk and pulled the archer up. "Come on, let's get back to camp. I need to congratulate Siley myself."

"We'll save a celebratory drink for another night," Alyk chided. "Don't forget, we have a big day tomorrow.

With Alyk's words, Jonny's eyes fell on the city and the great black pyramid. The momentary brevity was gone. A chill ran down his spine. Somewhere within that hulking structure was Darvor. Somewhere within was the end.

To The End

"Never fight on an empty stomach. Whenever possible, eat breakfast on the morning of a battle." The words of one of Cazar's old instructors echoed in his head. The instructor, a former swordsman at the Academy, had hammered the lesson into generations of Guards. Cazar could still hear the man's gravelly voice barking orders in the training yard. *Terrible advice,* he mused. Most of what men put in their stomachs on the morning of a battle would come back up when the fighting started.

Today will be no different. He looked around at the rows of troops. *How many of you ate breakfast this morning?* And then a bleaker thought followed. *How many of you will live to eat breakfast tomorrow?*

"They await your command," Jocum said in a crisp, military tone.

Cazar spotted Jonny at his side. The boy was pale and haggard, his hair an unkempt mess, and dark lines hung from his eyes. But despite his fatigue, his jaw clenched in determination, and his eyes burned with steely ferocity. *He'll be ready.*

He looked back at Jocum. "All forward."

Jocum nodded and lifted a great, curled ram's horn to his lips. The note was long and low and roared across the moors all the way to the base of the Goulmcarns. When the last of the blast died away, the battle began.

Scores of trebuchets and catapults from both sides hurled massive stones and incendiaries, trading volleys and lives. The archers quickly closed the distance to the walls, and a torrent of arrows blew back and forth to the sounds of screams and death. All the while, foot soldiers raced to position bridges across the moat and drive the hulking siege towers forward.

Cazar remained with Jonny, Klorvone, Rard, and some of the other commanders on a low ridge less than a mile from the city, surveying the initial stages of the assault. Far enough to be out of range of the troll's ballistae, they could still shout orders to lieutenants nearer to the fight.

The morning had been gray and wet, and a thick haze hung low over the moorlands around the city. But the sun was rising, and with it, the temperature. *It will be another hot day . . .*

"When do we join the fight?" Lord Brenton squeaked. He stood on the ridge with a small circle of household guards. Still little more than a toddler, he had donned his finest battle armor, including a feathered helm that continually slid over his face and required frequent adjustments.

Jonny said nothing, his mind focused on the looming black pyramid.

Cazar raised a hand. "You are commanding the reserves. With the reserves, you are to remain back with the camp. Should the tide of battle turn poorly for us, and a retreat be needed, your job will be to shelter our retreat."

"Is that an important job?"

Cazar smiled despite himself. The boy's youthfulness was charming. "Oh yes, the commander of the reserves is always mentioned in the songs."

The boy glowed and puffed out his chest. "In that case, I'll stay here." His helmet slid down, and he adjusted it. "When will you join the fray?"

"Soon," Cazar replied.

"When the moment is right," Jonny added, the first words he had said all morning.

The haze had settled into a blanket of fog that clung to the lowlands between the city and the ridge on which they stood. The turrets and towers of the city wall rose above, appearing to float on a cloud. Beneath the shroud of fog, twenty thousand soldiers fought to gain the battlements. *Even if they can take the walls,* Cazar mulled, *none of this will matter if Jonny cannot defeat Darvor.*

"Here he comes," Rard said, pointing with a thick arm.

Alyk emerged from the fog, running toward them, bow in hand. "Arrows! I need more arrows!" He shouted to a nearby squire.

Drawing upon their position, he came to a stop. His brow was slick with sweat, and the sleeve of his tunic was torn where an arrow had grazed him. He greeted them with a swaggering smile. "Fifty arrows, fifty trolls. And my arm . . . I barely feel it. This is fun!"

Klorvone clicked his lips and gestured.

"Don't worry, I left you plenty." A loud crash made the archer glance back at the battle. A catapult had struck one of the towers, causing the top to calve away and shower the assailants with debris. Alyk continued, "My archers have thinned out the trolls by the gatehouse. And Lord Rosmar's men got a siege tower to the walls, so we've cleared the way all we can. You are up, big guy."

Rard gave out a hoot and cracked his knuckles. "It's 'bout time. See you fools on the other side!" He hoisted a huge barrier of wicker and hide and, holding it overhead, bounded forward into the fog.

So far, things had gone according to plan. How long that would last remained to be seen. The crux of the plan rested on getting through the gate quickly. And for that, Rard's brute strength was indispensable. And as with any well-laid plan, it was sure to go awry at some point.

They were greeted with loud booms and shearing metal. Frenzied war horns sounded from the trolls on the walls. The thunder of the battle rose to a roar. *He said he could do it,* Cazar repeated. *But that gate is huge.*

As if on cue, a flag appeared above the fog, hoisted on a tall pole.

Cazar turned to Jonny. "It's time." His throat tightened. "We're with you until the end."

— • ———— • —

Jonny saw the flag waving frantically above the fog, and swallowed hard, letting out a long exhale as he started forward. *It's all going to happen very fast now,* he thought. There would be no more time for thinking.

Cazar led the way while Alyk and Klorvone fell into place beside him. A dozen other soldiers circled them, raising their shields overhead for protection. They penetrated the fog, building speed as they went.

Within two hundred paces of the gate, they broke into a run. Stooped under the shell of shields, Jonny sprinted. He rested one hand on Cazar's back, following the warrior into the fray. Rocks and arrows bounced off the shields overhead. At one point, Jonny nearly tripped over the body of a slain soldier, but Alyk caught his elbow and shoved him forward. A moment later, an arrow found its way through a gap in the shields, and one of the soldiers fell with a scream. Klorvone snatched up the shield and closed the opening.

Nearly there . . . The sounds of battle drowned out the pounding of his heart.

They passed under the shadow of the gatehouse. Somewhere nearby, a man screamed as burning pitch splattered from above. Alyk bobbed out of the testudo to launch a barb at the defenders. In response, a troll fell from the battlements, bouncing off Klorvone's shield.

"Fifty-one!" Alyk quipped.

"Forward!" Cazar shouted. "Everyone forward! Through the gate! Into the city!"

The shields dropped, and Jonny could see Rard ahead. The giant man stood among the mangled ruins of the gate doors, holding up the iron portcullis like a colossus of Olympus.

"Go! Everyone in!" the man-giant bellowed. Blood stained his shirt, and deep wounds marred his chest and shoulders.

The flood of soldiers swept Jonny into the city. The battle was now on all sides of him. Trolls and soldiers collided with the crash of steel and broken limbs. *Save my magic, save my strength,* he repeated. He burned to help tilt the melee but knew he could not.

We're through the gate—ahead should be the way to the pyramid. Eibbor had described a broad avenue that ran straight to the base of the pyramid. It would be, they hoped, an easy path for Jonny to reach Darvor.

Klorvone, standing head and shoulders above the fray, let out a tongueless moan.

"What is it?!" Jonny cried.

Klorvone wrapped an arm around Jonny and hoisted him for a better view.

"That's no good." His heart seized at the sight. The avenue stretched before them, and a half-mile ahead, the massive pyramid rose toward the clouds. But between, a vast column of trolls barred the way. They stood shoulder to shoulder, forty across and two hundred deep. Even if Jonny were to use all his magic, he was not sure he could burn his way through all of them. And that would leave him with nothing to face Darvor.

In a panic, Jonny looked around. "There's too many—they're blocking the way!"

"What do we do?" Alyk was at his side, troll blood splattered across his face.

"There!" Jonny pointed. "Down the side streets. We go around."

Cazar was a step ahead, disappearing down a side street as Klorvone set Jonny down.

"Go!" Alyk shouted, pushing nearby soldiers toward the alley. "Follow the Son of Aazar. We must get the Cupbreaker to the pyramid."

Jonny paused to look back at Rard. The brute still held the portcullis high as a wash of soldiers flooded into the city around him. An arrow had planted itself in his arm and another in his thigh. They locked eyes, and, for a moment, Jonny was reminded of their first meeting when Rard had thrown himself into a pack of *grevices*. The man grimaced as another arrow lodged in his chest. "Good luck!" he said with blood in his teeth.

Without another word, Jonny was pulled into the alley. The streets were a winding maze, a web of dead-stops and circles without end. The buildings were a mash of two- and three-level hovels, built of hearkstone, blackwood, and hide. The stench of meat halls and rot pits stung Jonny's nose, and the forge smoke blinded his eyes. He coughed against the fumes and pressed forward.

Two trolls leapt from rooftops above, cutting down the soldier in front of Jonny and turning themselves on him with rusted dirks. Jonny stumbled back as Klorvone lunged to his rescue. With a swing of his poleaxe, the man slayed the beasts and jaunted forward.

"Watch above! They're on the roofs," Cazar barked. He drove Filwain through a troll's snarl as it stepped out of a doorway.

"I can't see the pyramid," Jonny cried. *The buildings are blocking it.*

"Aye," Alyk agreed. "Klorvone, give me a boost." He pointed up.

The mute nodded and bent over for Alyk to climb on his back. With agile movements, the archer sprung from his back to a balcony and, from there, to a narrow lip of stone. Hand over hand, he pulled himself up until he disappeared over the rooftop.

A moment later, the body of a troll fell beside them with an arrow between its ribs. Alyk's head appeared, staring down from above. "It's this way, not far. Turn at that next fork."

Cazar drove them forward, following Alyk's directions from on high. "Don't stop!" He pulled Jonny close. "You saw the pyramid. There are stairs up the front. Whatever happens, get up those stairs. That's where you'll find him. I'm certain of it!"

Jonny's head spun with the heat and the noise.

"Turn right!" Alyk shouted. Ahead of them, two more trolls fell dead from the rooftops.

Suddenly, a column of trolls emerged from a side alley. The nearest soldier caught a spear thrust in the gut, another an axe blow to his helm. The trolls drove the men back before Cazar and Klorvone could throw themselves into the fray. With sword swings and axe thrusts, the pair held the trolls briefly, but more foes kept coming.

"Go, Jonny!" Cazar shouted.

Jonny hesitated. He did not want to leave them. With a single blast of magic, he could drive the trolls back down the alley. But that would be a waste of precious strength for what lie ahead.

"Jonny!" Cazar drove a high kick into the chest of an oncoming troll, sending the creature into the flashing arc of Klorvone's poleaxe. With Ethwayl in one hand, he slid Filwain from the second scabbard at his hip. "You have to go. We will hold them." The two swords whistled through the air as he dove back into the fray. "Now, go!"

"That way!" Alyk echoed from above.

The old Guard was right, and Jonny could delay no longer. He squeezed past Cazar and darted down a narrow passage. It was dark, but a sliver of daylight gleamed ahead.

Alyk's voice carried from the rooftops. "It's just ahead—you're almost there."

At the cusp of the passage, a grip snared his ankle, and he tumbled, crashing into the cobblestones. A troll emerged from the shadows, brandishing a frightful mace. Jonny reached inside to pull flames to his hands, but even as he did, a shape dropped from the sky.

Alyk collided with the troll, driving the beast to the ground. On his feet in a heartbeat, Alyk was already reaching for his quiver. *He's only got two left,* Jonny realized, counting the arrows. The troll disentangled himself from Alyk and looked up. An arrow planted in the creature's eye, and it slumped to the ground.

"Go, I'll hold them." He slid his last arrow onto the bowstring. "For Siley." His green eyes flashed, and he was gone.

THE NAME OF EVIL

The pyramid stretched toward the sky, a looming black monolith reeking of doom and desolation. A single staircase was cut into its face while the rest was polished to a shine. *That's a lot of steps . . .* Jonny looked over his shoulder. Behind him, the broad avenue rolled straight to the gate. Man and troll collided in the boulevard, a maelstrom of violence. Pillars of smoke rose from the city and screams cut the heavy air.

Jonny had emerged from the cramped side alley where Cazar and others had battled to clear a path around the central avenue.

The only way is forward. He set a tired foot to the first step and started the climb. Step over step, he climbed. Higher, until his legs burned and chest heaved. Uncertainty swirled over what awaited him at the top. But the time for pondering the unknown had passed. All he could do was take the next step. *One foot at a time . . .*

At last, he neared the peak. The top came into view as he mounted the final steps. It was empty—*no Darvor.* The summit was a large, flat platform twenty yards to a side. Near the far side, an imposing throne sat on a low dais cut from the same black stone as all the rest. It was simple and unadorned, with a high back and sharp angles.

Jonny blinked. *Where is he?* He was so certain this was where Darvor would be. He spun, scanning the surroundings. From the summit, he could see ten leagues in any direction. Near the city walls, his army's camp was a small speckling of tents and wagons. Further afield, miles of moorland and untamed wilderness stretched. To the north, the brooding mountains scraped the clouds. The sky above was heavy and gray.

It made no sense. *He should be here.*

"I should think"—a voice split the air, cold and sharp as ice—"that you are looking for me."

Jonny wheeled around.

Darvor emerged from the shadows behind the throne. "Why do you look so surprised?" The man, if he could be called such, had not aged a day. His black hair was trimmed short and swept back, outlining his porcelain features and haunting eyes. Loose dark robes floated in the whispers of wind.

Jonny squared himself and fought to not melt under the man's piercing gaze. "I've come to call you to stand trial for your crimes. Or kill you if you won't."

A thin smile slipped across his face. "You won't kill me."

"I will if I must." Jonny's fingers curled into fists.

"Try." He spread his arms wide, inviting an attack.

"You must die."

Darvor floated around the chair and took a seat, pulling his robes around him. "You still think I am the villain." His smile returned. "I was not bothering anyone—in fact, I was reading in my library until that brute of yours started banging on the gates. And now you come into my home threatening to kill me. Why should anyone believe you are the hero?"

Jonny took a step forward. "You must pay for your crimes."

"And what crimes are those?" Darvor leaned forward.

"How about all those people on Guard Tower Island you killed, just for starters?"

"The trolls killed them. Not me."

"You command the trolls."

Darvor slammed a fist on the arm of the throne, anger bursting forth. "Then what of the thousands that have died at your command! And the thousands more that will die before the day is done! Will you stand trial beside me?"

Jonny flinched but did not step back. "That's different!"

"Only in the way of a mirror's reflection. Evil has many names, and mine is not one of them." A measured calm returned to him. "Go home, Jonny. I am no murderer, and I have no interest in killing you today." The melody of his voice danced unpredictably. "I have let you play out your fantasy as the gallant conqueror. Yes, hide your surprise. I let you march your little army here, let you knock down my door and fight my finest trolls, because it was harmless. I could have stopped you at any moment had I chosen to. But enough is enough. Return home, return to your family. I will not tolerate you trying to ruin everything I have built."

Jonny showed his teeth. "That's why I must stop you now. Before you can develop your next plot."

"My next plot?" He laughed. "It is all the same plot. From the beginning of time to the world's undoing. Nothing has not gone according to plan, and today will not be the start."

"The fountain in the Vale of Joy . . . that was your work. Another piece in this plot of yours?"

"Of course." His long fingers curled around the armrest of his throne. "And one of the last. There is nothing you can do to stop me now."

"What about killing you?" Jonny growled.

"Har!" Darvor flashed an unsettling smile. "I suppose that would, yes."

"Enough talk . . . I've come for a reason. Get up and fight!" His breath was hot in his throat.

"So soon . . . are you sure? You don't want to talk any longer? I could bring you some tea or food, perhaps; you do look like you have not been eating well." His frighteningly casual tone was unbearable.

"Ahh!" Jonny snapped a fireball into his hand and whipped it toward his enemy.

Darvor returned a lazy flick of the wrist, and the fireball wilted in the air. He feigned a yawn. "Very well. Let us dance." He was on his feet and already launching a series of flames.

Jonny waved away the first and second and spun from the third. He countered with a jet of fire that raced across the platform.

Darvor caught the jet in his left hand and returned it with his right. Jonny rolled under the spell and, landing on one knee, sent a series of fireballs cracking through the air. The first several were blocked, but the last one seared Darvor's boot and drove him back a step.

"Well, look at that." Darvor smirked and swept a lock of hair back into place. "You've improved. Not enough." He shrugged. "But some."

Jonny threw up a shield as a pillar of fire arced down on him. Through gritted teeth, he strained to hold the spell. Darvor's magic was powerful, and Jonny's strength waned with every spell. His legs grew heavy, and his breath caught in his lungs. *I must stop him!*

A second pillar of fire slammed into Jonny from the side, throwing him across the polished black stone. He slid to a stop with bruised ribs and a ringing head. The fire had charred away the cloth of his right sleeve, leaving the skin of his arm red and burnt. He raised his eyes, bracing for the next blow, but Darvor had lowered his hands.

"Are we done? Can we cease the charade? Go home. Live out the days that remain. Accept that this is a fight you will not win."

With feeble knees, Jonny pushed to his feet. "How did you know my address? How do you know where my family lives?"

Darvor squinted. "You don't think—"

"How?!"

"You don't think you are the only one to walk other worlds? Do not be so vain. I have journeyed through your land with its towering skyscrapers and metal birds. I have seen the sprawl of your cities, the weakness of your weapons." He waved a hand. "I have walked all the worlds. Worlds where winters last a generation, others where deserts consume planets. Lands where the sun rises in the west and sets in the east, where kingdoms sit underwater, where men fly ships between the stars. Places beyond your imagination. I have walked them all and learned their secrets. I know what your father does for work, what Delena had yesterday for dinner, what you do at night when the nightmares won't let you sleep. There is very little that I do not see . . . even less that I do not know."

Jonny straightened. *Can it be true? How can I stop someone like that?* He set his jaw and squared himself to Darvor. Once, years before, he had been so scared he could barely breathe. But in that darkest of moments, he had accepted his fear—let it wash through him, fill his soul, and strengthen him. Now this was every bit as dark, darker even. Years of worry and pain. Days of dread and nights without end. All the friends that had fought for him—bled for him. *Hold onto a little, let the rest go . . .* Alyk's words echoed in his mind. He closed his eyes and breathed deeply. *I am not afraid . . . let the rest go.*

With a shout, he lunged forward, blasting an explosive wall of fire at Darvor. The dark lord blocked it and returned a stronger spell. The flames collided with raw, unbridled fury, splitting the air with deafening thunder. They traded blow after blow, hurling flames of rage and power, each spell countered with something more.

But it was useless; Darvor showed no signs of slowing. His robes fluttered unburnt; his expressions unstrained. Jonny, however, was fading. His legs wobbled and his lungs ached. His vision narrowed, but still, he willed another spell from tired arms. And another.

"I am impressed," Darvor shouted over the crack and thunder of their spells. "You are stronger than I had expected. But it is not enough. Your strength fails you, and you have but scratched the surface of all I am capable of!"

He raised his arms over his head and an immense serpent of fire rose from behind the pyramid. The fire snake arced high into the sky, a thousand feet long. It was bathed in flames of bright red and orange, and lightning cracked in its belly. It rolled on itself and hurled back down, slamming toward the pyramid.

Jonny called upon his failing strength and threw up a flickering shield as the spell descended. It crashed into him with the force of an avalanche, bathing the top of the pyramid in light and heat. The shield shattered and the spell drove Jonny to the ground, searing his skin and stealing his breath.

The spell died and a quiet settled over the pyramid. Jonny lay trembling on the hot stone. His clothes were charred tatters, and his skin red and blistered. He stifled a whimper and pushed himself to his knees.

Darvor stood in front of the throne. His eyes were hollow and his voice empty. "Goodbye, Jonny." In his palm, a fireball swirled. More and more energy arced down his arm into the sphere, turning it bright red, then purple, then black.

There was nothing to be done. Jonny's strength had failed him; he was wrong. *It's over* . . . The despair swelled. He had failed everyone.

Darvor raised his hand, pulled back, and launched the fireball.

And then, unbidden and unexpected, a flash from the corner of Jonny's eye. It was the shape of someone running, jumping. The form cast itself into the path of the spell. Only then did Jonny realize it was Alyk. The archer hung in the air for a single heartbeat. His bow was out, loaded with his last remaining arrow. Nimble fingers were drawn back, stretching the bowstring.

The sharp *twang* of a bow, the whistle of an arrow, a flash.

The hot light blinded Jonny. He threw up his hand to shield himself and blinked against the heat.

When he opened his eyes, the archer was gone. A trail of ash swirled out across the smooth black stone. Jonny's throat tightened, and his soul caved under the blow. *No . . .*

He looked at Darvor.

"I . . . how?" The villain gasped and staggered, looking down to his chest. An arrow protruded from his right breast. He stumbled to one knee as the last color fled from his face. "I feel . . ." A ring of blood swelled around the arrow shaft, darkening his robes. He touched his chest and stared at the red stain of his fingers.

Then, with a muted grunt, he collapsed. He took a final, rasping breath and exhaled. As a last whisper parted his lips, he burst into a swirl of smoke. Black and turbid, it whirled in the dying wind and withered. In an instant, there was nothing. And Jonny was alone on the pyramid.

He rose to his feet. Approaching the spot where Darvor had been, he could only stare. The great villain was dead. *No trace but a memory of his evil.*

He turned. There was little more left of Alyk. The ash swirled this way and that, ebbed by the soft breeze.

Falling to his knees, Jonny hung his head. And then he cried.

WHAT REMAINS

With a heavy heart, Jonny descended the pyramid. His steps were slow and tired. Cupped in his burnt hands, his friend's ashes were still warm. The sounds of the battle had withered away, and the banners of the conquerors were being raised from the city's towers. Celebratory cheers drifted through the air. *Who knew victory could taste so hollow?*

At the base of the pyramid, Jonny found a small empty pot and poured the ashes into it. The simple white urn would not do as a final resting place but would serve for now. *He had no family,* Jonny thought numbly. *The ashes should go to Siley . . .*

He stood and cast his eyes down the long boulevard to the city gate. The way was riddled with the bodies of trolls, the cobblestones slick with blood. He did not relish finding out the number of human dead. *We won, but at what cost?*

Cradling the small urn, he started toward the gate. He made slow progress, stepping through the bodies. His legs were tired, and his shoulders ached to the bone. The wind stung the burnt skin of his arms. Halfway down the boulevard, he came upon Cazar.

Painted in the gore of battle, Cazar rose to greet his friend. He nodded and rested a hand on Jonny's shoulder but said nothing.

After a long moment, Jonny spoke. "It's done." He blinked back tears. "Darvor is dead."

"And we won," Cazar said, squeezing Jonny's shoulder. His expression was soft and gentle. "One moment, the trolls were giving us hell. Fighting over every inch of this damn place. The next moment, they fell apart. Their spirit, their discipline, their will . . . it all broke like a dam. When you defeated Darvor, whatever hold he had over them was gone. They scattered like leaves in the wind."

"Alyk is—" Jonny's voice cracked.

"I know." Cazar swallowed hard. "The trolls were on us, him and me. We were fighting, and we could see the flashes of fire from the top of the pyramid. He said he had to help. Then he was gone. Up the stairs and . . . gone."

Jonny shifted the urn in his arms. "I need to find Siley." With a stiff nod, he left Cazar and continued toward the gate.

Under the shadow of the walls, he stopped again. The body was lying facedown amid the destroyed remains of the gate. From the size, there was no mistaking it. A dozen arrows and two broken lances protruded from the hulk of muscle. Men were gathering, staring in stunned silence.

Klorvone knelt beside the body, one broad hand resting on the bloodied flesh. When Jonny approached, the axman looked up. Wet, red eyes brimmed with pain. He clicked a few quick notes and pulled a fist to his chest.

Swallowing back more tears, Jonny replied. "He was my friend too." *What else was there to say?* Alyk would not be the only friend he said goodbye to.

Outside the city, Jonny's feet carried him with slow strides back to the camp. Men and women had already begun carting the wounded to tents where healers worked to bind wounds and stanch bleeding.

He found Siley in a tent caring for the wounded. He tried to carry a brave countenance, but it was pointless. As soon as they met eyes, her face went pale. He pulled her outside and said what meager words of comfort he could muster. She cried as he knew she would, but she vowed to return the urn to her village. "He can rest on the shores of the Great Lake, as any true son of Lanak should." Even in sorrow, she spoke with grace. "We were to marry, you know."

Jonny nodded, but no words came to his lips.

She pulled him in for an embrace and held him tight. For a long moment, they stayed like that, supporting each other in their mutual grief, like two waystones listing against each other, both of which would fall without the other pushing back.

Afterward, she thanked him, and that only hurt even more. *If not for me, he would still be alive. If I had been stronger or quicker . . .*

Parting with her, Jonny left the camp and found a soft patch of heather in the sweeping moorlands. There, too far to hear the sounds of camp or smell the burning city, he lay down. His burnt skin stung at the coolness of the heather and grass. He rested on his back, watching the thick blanket of clouds float gray and formless above. His heart was a strange mix and resisted being framed by his thoughts. There was pain and deep sorrow, but buried beneath lurked relief and—although he struggled to believe it—hope. And so, with a tired body and tired mind, Jonny soon fell asleep. He slept long and deep, and, for the first time in years, no nightmares followed him.

After the battle, the days passed quickly. The wounded were mended, the dead buried. On the third day, a victory feast was celebrated. The remaining ale flowed freely, and dozens of hogs were roasted over roaring fires. Songs carried late into the night, though Jonny did not join. By the fifth day, the camp had disassembled, and the army started west, leaving behind the smoldering remnants of the troll city.

The trolls, they knew, were not yet gone from the earth. There were still scattered tribes in the mountains, and a few had fled the city at the end. But they would never threaten the world again. They would be left to lurk in the wilderness, haunting the remote corners of the world, to be hunted by adventure seekers, until one day, they would quietly fade into history—becoming another monster of legend.

The weather remained favorable as the army started west. With no threat from the trolls, they made good time, slowed only by the wounded they carried. After the long campaign, the army was well disciplined, and Jonny left the leadership to the lords and officers.

With Alyk and Rard gone and the threat of Darvor a memory, Jonny's band of friends was no more. Siley hid her grief in the business of caring for the wounded. Klorvone was solemn and distant. Cazar was cordial, but without the others' playful banter, the warrior seemed cool and stiff. Jonny found some company with various lords and lordlings, but often he rode alone. He reflected on all that had been or might have been.

Thoughts of home drifted in his head. He had been eager to leave and return to this wild land, but now, victorious, with the threat of Darvor gone, he yearned to see his family. Over a year had passed for Jonny, and he prayed the same was not true for his parents and brothers.

As the first autumn moon climbed the sky, they reached the Tannery Ford. By the waters of the East River, Jonny bid farewell to Jocum and the cohorts from Guard Tower Island. The Lord-regent had proven an indispensable aid in the war, and his soldiers were decisive in conquering the city. Jonny expressed his thanks to not just Jocum but to as many of the common soldiers as he could. They would return home as victors, and without the ever-present threat of the trolls on their border, the future looked bright for the people of Guard Tower Island.

A day later, Lord Brenton and his Forest Folk parted, turning south to their homelands. Jonny watched the young boy go. *His mother will be happy to have him come home a hero.* Over the following days, as the rest of the army continued west across the Plains of Lydie, others left too. First Klorvone and the highlanders; later the Lanaki and others from the south. When at last Jonny reached Gluton, little remained of the once grand army.

Word of the great victory and the end of the trolls had gone ahead, and when Jonny rode under the arch of Gluton's towering gate at the head of the remaining army, he was greeted with a grand celebration. Crowds lined the narrow streets, showering flower petals and ribbons. Cheers and songs filled the air. Mugs of ale were passed around. Tears of joy ran down cheeks as returning soldiers swept wives and children into their arms.

But, despite the celebrations, Jonny felt little joy. He won the victory he sought, but he could not feel it. Darvor was dead, the threat of the trolls forever gone. But it had come at such a cost . . . *Eibbor, Rard, Alyk* . . . For every two soldiers that returned to their families, one was left in a shallow grave outside the city of the trolls. Looking around, he knew that not all the tear-streaked cheeks were shining with joy. Thousands of families would be left with an empty seat at their tables. *And it is my fault.*

Reaching the palace gates, Jonny and Cazar dismounted.

Cazar wrapped the reins in his hand. "It is here I leave you, Cupbreaker."

Jonny stuck a thumb over his shoulder. "You won't come inside? Swarlar would love to have you stay for the night."

Cazar offered a tired smile. "No, thank you. I have been gone a long time; I need to return to my farm. I wish to see Delena."

"Fair enough." Jonny bit his lip. "I'm not quite sure what to say . . ."

"Will I see you again?"

"I don't think so." The words fell flat from his mouth. "I've done what I came for."

"That you did." Cazar ran a hand through his long hair. More grays flecked his dark locks than had when they set forth from Gluton months ago.

Jonny had known Cazar since the first day he had come into this world. Together, they had endured more than anyone could relate to. Jonny did not feel that any goodbye could be fitting after so much. A silence drifted between them, but only for a moment.

"How do you feel?" Jonny asked.

A twinkle danced in Cazar's eye. "My knee hurts worse than ever, and I've got a few new scars, but I'm sleeping better. I think everything will be all right, Jonny." He pulled the boy in for a tight hug. "I hope you feel the same."

Jonny held the old Guard tight for a long moment. "I'm not there yet, but I will be."

Cazar released the boy. "You will be." There was an admirable certainty to his voice. He swung a leg over his horse and looked down. "Practice," he added with a wink before riding away.

Jonny watched him until he disappeared into the crowd of King's Square. *Practice,* he repeated. *Practice and patience.* He turned and slipped through the palace gates. Across the courtyard, at the top of the stairs, King Swarlar was waiting. His white robes and whiter beard were bathed in the morning sun. "What a day this is!" His smile was warm.

Jonny passed the reins to a stableboy but said nothing.

Swarlar paused and raised his chin. "I see." He turned and gestured for Jonny to follow. "I think we'd best talk in the study."

In the palace, little had changed. They navigated the familiar passages and were soon alone in the king's study. More scrolls had been added to the desk, and the bookshelf sagged under the weight of new books, but the rest looked the same. Even the air had the same thick smell of old parchment.

Swarlar snapped his fingers, and a fire sprung to life in the hearth—a rare show of magic from the wizened king.

"Am I to understand," Swarlar started, sweeping open the curtains to fill the room with light, "that you are still mad at me?"

"You left me alone to face him."

"I have explained this to you before. My power is that of a shield. To a point, I can protect the world from his magic. I can shroud the palace from his eyes and, to a limited extent, shroud some few other things. Even that has grown harder in recent years. But for me to attack him . . ." He shook his head. "I would have been powerless."

"Why didn't you stop me? You knew how powerful he was. You knew I didn't stand a chance. You did nothing!"

"But you did stand a chance—after all, you are standing here now. And I did tell you that I didn't think you were ready. You didn't want to hear it."

"You should have stopped me if you knew what would happen!" Jonny shouted. His fingernails bit into his palms.

"Do not get angry at me." The king did not raise his voice, but his tone snapped like a whip. "You asked to be treated as an adult. I told you this would come at a cost and that if you could bear it, I would not stop you. Your friends have died for you, and the knowledge of that will burden you the rest of your days. That is the cost of your victory."

Jonny scowled. "If this is victory, where is my happy ending? This does not feel like the ending of a story should."

From beneath his white beard, Swarlar studied him. "Darvor is defeated, the threat of the trolls is no more—that is a happy ending. Only in stories is the triumph pure or the defeat absolute. In life, joy and pain cannot be so easily separated. To expect otherwise is greedy or foolish."

A wave of sadness and guilt swept over Jonny, and he sank into a chair. "I'm sorry." He hung his head in his hands. "Alyk died saving me. Rard, Eibbor, thousands of men—dead. Gone. It hurts. It hurts all the time . . . and it won't go away." When he looked up, tears clouded his vision.

Swarlar took the chair opposite him, resting an elbow on the stack of books beside it. "Aye, losing someone we care about always does. And I won't tell you it will go away tomorrow, or even next year. You'll carry a part of this hurt with you always." He leaned forward. "But you fought for something you believed in, and you made the world a better place for it. Alyk believed in the cause all the same. And could you ask him now, I'm sure he would choose to change nothing."

"Where do I go from here?"

"Go and live that life you've been missing—that life with all its beauty and laughter and pain and love."

"I feel so lost." Jonny ran a hand across his wet cheeks. "Darvor always believed this world was bad—that it was more hurt than joy. With all this pain, I feel like he's right."

Swarlar reached forward and set a comforting hand on Jonny's. "Prove him wrong. Let that be your compass. If you have defeated him in this world, set yourself to defeating him in your heart. Live each day with the goal of proving that this world is worth fighting for. Search out the good. Warm summer nights, laughter, games with friends, a tasty meal, the softness of a newborn's cheeks—find it and hold it. That is how you will beat him in your heart."

Jonny pulled his eyes off the king and let his focus fall on the gardens visible beyond the window. "Alyk would always say, 'Hold on to just enough and let the rest go.' But, for the life of me, I can't do it. There's too much."

Swarlar's voice was soft. "Hold on to hope, love, the memory of good times. The rest . . ." He waved a hand, his fingers tracing gentle arcs like grass blowing in the wind. "Do that, and tomorrow will be a little easier, and the next day easier still."

Jonny nodded and swallowed back more tears. "Darvor said he was planning something. He said the fountain in the Vale of Joy was one of the last pieces—what could he have meant? Do you know what he was planning?"

Swarlar sat back and stroked his beard. After a moment, he said, "Part of growing up, like learning to carry the cost of your decisions, is accepting that you can't have the answer for everything." A sly twinkle danced in his blue eyes. "Let that be another lesson you take from this ordeal."

Jonny rose to his feet. "I guess it doesn't matter. He's gone now."

"Indeed." Swarlar nodded.

"I think in the morning I will set off for home." He tapped the golden dragon pendant at his neck. "I think there is just enough magic in this thing for one more crossing."

"Is that your way of saying goodbye?"

A smile came unbidden to Jonny's face. "I'll save goodbye for the morning. But yes, this time, I don't think you'll be seeing me again."

Swarlar returned a warm smile. "Very well. I'll be sure to have the chef prepare some water carrots with dinner tonight. I do know how you like them." He gestured to the door and Jonny turned to leave.

"Oh, and Jonny," Swarlar added from his seat. "What did you do with the body?"

"The what?" Jonny stopped.

"Darvor's body. You said you would bring back his body."

"There was no body."

"I see . . ." Swarlar's voice trailed away.

"Oh, Your Majesty," Jonny added. "One other thing."

Swarlar looked up.

"Are we okay—you and me? I know I've been difficult."

The king smiled. "Yes, Jonny. We are okay."

Hearing the words brought a sense of relief. Despite their disagreements, Jonny still carried great respect for the king. He did not like the thought of parting on poor terms.

Another warm and rowdy feast filled Jonny's night as local lords and noblemen filled Swarlar's hall to celebrate the defeat of the trolls. The food was plentiful and the wine endless, and this time, Jonny joined in the songs.

Although the feast carried well past midnight, the sunrise found Jonny riding out the gates of Gluton and into the countryside. *It's time I got home,* he thought, passing beyond the city gates. *I've been gone too long.* He made good time, passing familiar farms and villages. The fields were rich in bounty, and everywhere, men and women worked to bring in the autumn harvest. It had been a good season, and wagons and barns would be filled to bursting by the start of winter.

As he had planned, he soon found the hamlet where he had first arrived, naked and seemingly lost. With coin Swarlar had given him, he repaid the surprised woman for the clothes he borrowed the year before.

Doubtless, she had shared the story with all the neighboring farms in the year since. She took the coin with a laugh and waved as Jonny rode on.

Soon after, he found the tree where he had stashed his modern clothes. The clothes smelled of mildew and old leaves, but he brushed them off and slipped them on. *A little dirtier and smellier, but they still fit.*

A little further and he came to the hollow in the forest. He paused, taking in the dusty hole and looming trees. Once before, he had stood in this spot, about to return to an uncertain home. He had been a small boy then, at the conclusion of a grand adventure. *Seven years and what has really changed?* He took his necklace in his hand. It rested cool on his skin, with only the slightest hint of life within. *Enough spark for one last trip?* He breathed deeply, filling his lungs with a final breath of this world.

Stepping forward, he stooped and crossed into the hollow. Just as before, the world swirled, and the floor swept up to meet him. Cold . . . darkness . . .

He pushed himself to his elbows. The air was cool and damp. He swallowed back the wave of nausea and climbed to his feet. The cave was dark, but a glimmer of light reached him from the entrance. He blinked and took a slow step forward.

It was morning, and the rising sun was waking the surrounding forest. Birds were chirping, and in the distance, the trickling babble of the creek was audible.

"Mom . . . Dad?" His voice was dry in his throat.

Wrapped in each other's arms, his parents sat on a rock by the cave's entrance. Startled, they stood and spun to face him. Their faces were a muddied mix of emotion. His mother's eyes, he noted with a pang of guilt, were red with tears.

"You're back?" Her voice was flecked with surprise.

"I'm sorry." Jonny swallowed. Again, he found himself unsure what to say. He started toward them and, by the second step, was running. "I'm so sorry . . ."

"We waited all night for you," his father said as he threw open his arms. There was no anger in his voice, only concern.

"All night . . . but it felt like so much longer," said his mother.

It was over a year for me, but only hours for them.

Jonny fell into his parents' arms. "I had to go. I'm sorry, but I had to." He gulped in the love of their tight hold.

"Did you do what you needed?" his mother asked softly.

"It's over," he sobbed. "I'm free of him now."

He burrowed his head into their embrace. His heart was still heavy with loss, but finally, the weight of dread lifted from his shoulders. The golden morning air was filled with the hope of an unbridled future and brimmed with possibility. The birds sang a melody of promise, and the air smelled alive. His parents' warm hold steadied and strengthened his tired soul.

He smiled through the tears. Once again, he was home.

Appendix C

The Decree of the Seven Lords and Damon's Precedent

King Swarlar of the Second Throne reigns as king during Jonny's time in the world beyond the cave. His authority arises from the agreement known as the Decree. An understanding of the Decree allows insight into the political landscape of the realm. The following excerpt was taken from *A History of House Voramandier*, written by the Honorable Jaysen, scholar to Lord Gavin Voramandier III, three hundred years before Jonny's arrival. Although not the most thorough account, Jaysen's version is often cited as one of the truest histories of the founding of the first throne.

Out of the darkness of the Broken Ages rose one of the great figures of the mythic past, Lord Gordon Voramandier. During his eighteenth year of reign, while campaigning in the moorlands west of Hedgewood, his host arrived at a village razed during the previous year's wars. Not a soul remained in the village, nor did a building still stand. Their horses trod heavy on the bones of the dead, and the fields had been charred and salted. Men wailed at the desolation of the place, and priests shouted prayers and curses in equal number. At the sight, Lord Voramandier turned to his master at arms [here some accounts say it was his brother] *and said, "These are dark times indeed. Wars without end. All my life, I have known nothing but war. Lord against lord, friend against friend, father against son, brother against brother. One year, this village is destroyed; next year, it will be another. Farmland is burned and the peasants die beyond counting. Famine and disease soon follow, and thus, in hunger and illness, more wars are born. The cycle must be broken."*

"Yes, my lord, but how?" the master-at-arms replied. Lord Voramandier was left to ponder this question for a full three years before arriving at an answer. In the spring of his twenty-second year as lord, he gathered seven riders and sent them forth with thrice-sealed letters. The recipients were the lords of each of the other great houses of the day: Groy, Hillan, Arthrin, Trelon, Craith, Brey, and Lyonis. [House Berlion had not yet ascended, and House Craith ruled in Burma. Similarly, Guard Tower Island was not yet founded; as such, House Leyne was not among the Great Houses. House Lyonis, as we know, was later destroyed during the fall of the city now known as the Old Ruins.] *The wording of the letters has not survived, but the message has. Lord Voramandier bid each of the high lords to meet on the summer solstice on the plains of Lydie at a well-known confluence of fae stones. They were to come alone, save for a single attendant or guard. There, they would discuss a new order with the goal of lasting peace.*

Though there was undoubtedly skepticism at the prospect, Lord Voramandier's call was answered. The leaders of seven of those eight great houses arrived at the solstice to find a pavilion erected over the fae stones [The Forest Folk, always an independent people, did not wish to become embroiled in the affairs of the world, and thus Lord Arthrin was not in attendance]. *Though boisterous, proud, and suspicious to a man, the lords consented to turning over their weapons to a priest and entered the pavilion. Inside, they were seated at a round table so that no one could claim a higher position than the next. "Thank you," Lord Voramandier, dressed in unassuming robes, began, "for answering my call. As you know, these broken centuries have seen nothing but bloodshed. Though each of us holds dear the glory of battle, these wars have left our realms depleted, hungry, and weak. We must lay the foundation for a lasting peace; if we fail here, we may never have another chance."*

Over the following days, the gathered lords, the Seven, as they came to be known, discussed, often heatedly, how to achieve unification. Though not always peaceful—it is said Lord Craith knocked out two of Lord Trelon's teeth, and Lord Lyonis stabbed Lord Brey's aide with a fork—the talks were productive. After a week of debate, a loose framework of governance had taken shape. The Decree of the Seven Lords, it was called, and though imperfect, it was a crucial step toward ending the Broken Ages.

The Decree detailed a hierarchy to the world, commoners serving their local lords, who in turn served the lords of the Great Houses. But just as commoners set their disputes at the feet of their local lesser lords, and lesser lords took their disputes to their liege lord, there was no arbiter of the disputes between high lords. That is, no arbiter but war. And so, as the Decree proclaimed, a new arbiter was to be appointed. To be called king, this person was to be a judge over the Great Houses. The king was to be chosen by way of a vote at a sacred ceremony, the Kingsmoot.

To this extent, it is said, the lords were quick to agree. The other stipulations had garnered far more debate. The king would serve for life but could be ousted from his rule if six of the seven lords agreed. To ensure that no Great House was put above the others—a great fear of the Seven—the king could not be chosen from a member of the Great Houses, nor could they be related by blood to a member of a Great House to the second degree. Other stipulations were included, too, and some have been added or removed in the intervening centuries, but the basic framework has lasted, an almost sacred and inviolable constitution, viewed by some to be as holy as the Seven Scrolls.

The Decree of the Seven Lords was written with the hope of bringing peace to the realm, but Lord Voramandier would die with his dream unrealized. As would his son. And his son's son. For although the kings managed to arbitrate peaceful solutions to the realm's conflicts during their lifetime, upon the death of each king, a succession crisis plunged the realm into fresh war. The Seven had refused to make the crown a hereditary title, so each Kingsmoot saw more bloodshed and conflict.

This problem would last until the reign of King Damon, remembered by history as one of the wisest and most effective rulers of the First Throne. Through artful leadership, King Damon was able to amass considerable power—a power which he translated into a solution to the ongoing issue of succession. In the middle decade of his long rule, King Damon identified a young scholar named Aythen, who he deigned to be his successor. Described by contemporaries as "tall, able-bodied, fair, and well-learned," Aythen was liked by all at court and respected by nobleman and commoner alike. With an eye to the future, King Damon bid each of the seven [current] high lords to swear that, upon his death, they would elect Aythen to be king. Damon ruled another fifteen years, during which time he meticulously groomed Aythen as *his successor. Upon Damon's death, as sworn, the high lords elected Aythen as king and Damon's Precedent was born.*

Thus, with few exceptions, for hundreds of years, each successive king has chosen his own replacement, like King Damon. Kingsmoots still occur but have largely become a formality. The system has not been perfect, and Jaysen's history and others like it provide a lengthy list of conflicts and intrigues. But by and large, the Decree and the Precedent have kept the realm stable through many struggles, from the fall of the Keepers of the Cup, to the many wars with the trolls, and countless other minor threats through the centuries.

Acknowledgments

As always, there are those without whom this book would never have come into existence. To Rose, to Donna, to Robert, Tim, and Steff, thank you and thank you again. An immense thank you to the team at Sunbury Press, including Sarah Peachey and Lawrence Knorr, for giving this book your time and energy. Without your dedication to books, this would still be a file on my computer. Finally, to you the reader—thank you for not only reading but sharing this story with those you know. It is always you, the reader, to whom a story truly belongs.

About the Author

R. KANE MAURER lives in Hershey with his wife and daughter. The Forbidden Powers is his first series. When he isn't writing, he devotes himself to reading, traveling, and spending time with his family. He enjoys skiing, surfing, and wakeboarding, but his enthusiasm far outdistances his aptitude.

www.rkanemaurer.com